It had been easier to get to this place than I ever could have known. It had been much easier to give in and admit I was fascinated by this platform and what it felt like to stand on it than it had been to fight the invitation to climb up here. I understood more than I ever had before—about myself, about sex, about what Jacques had wanted from me.

I was standing naked in the arena, and I was terrified of what was going to come, of what was going to happen to me. What was unexpected was my response to the terror. I was mesmerized by it. I loved it. It was making me feel more alive than I'd felt in years.

Other Books by John Preston

FICTION

Franny, the Queen of Provincetown, 1983.
Mr. Benson, 1983, 1992.
I Once Had a Master and Other Tales of Erotic Love, 1984.
"The Mission of Alex Kane."
    Volume I: *Sweet Dreams*, 1984, 1992.
    Volume II: *Golden Years*, 1984, 1992.
    Volume III: *Deadly Lies*, 1985, 1992.
    Volume IV: *Stolen Moments*, 1986, 1993.
    Volume V: *Secret Dangers*, 1986, 1993.
    Volume VI: *Lethal Silence*, 1987, 1993.
Entertainment for a Master, 1986.
Love of a Master, 1987.
The Heir, 1988, 1992.
In Search of a Master, 1989.
The King, 1992.
Tales from the Dark Lord, 1992. (Short Stories)

Edited:
    Hot Living: Erotic Stories about Safer Sex, 1985.
    Flesh and the Word: An Erotic Anthology, 1992.

NONFICTION

The Big Gay Book: A Man's Survival Guide for the Nineties, 1991.

With Frederick Brandt:
    Classified Affairs: The Gay Men's Guide to the Personals, 1984.
With Glenn Swann:
    Safe Sex: The Ultimate Erotic Guide, 1987.

Edited:
    Personal Dispatches: Writers Confront AIDS, 1989.
    Hometowns: Gay Men Write about Where They Belong, 1991.
    A Member of the Family: Gay Men Write about Their Families, 1992.

THE ARENA

JOHN PRESTON

BADBOY

The Arena
Copyright © 1993 by John Preston.
All Rights Reserved

No part of this book may be reproduced, stored in a retrieval system, or transmitted in any form, by any means, including mechanical, electronic, photocopying, recording or otherwise, without prior written permission of the publishers.

First BADBOY Edition 1993

First printing February 1993

ISBN 1-56333-083-0

Cover Design by Juli Getler

Cover Photograph © 1993 Susan McNamara

Manufactured in the United States of America
Published by Masquerade Books, Inc.
801 Second Avenue
New York, N.Y. 10017

The only way to get rid of a temptation is to yield to it.

—Oscar Wilde

For Mike and Owen
For Patrick
For Charles
For Kevin and Jon Carl
For Michael
For Tom
For Tony
For Wolf
and all the other young men
who are my inspirations

I arranged to have dinner with Jacques the night of my triumph. As I sat waiting for my old friend in the restaurant, I studied the smooth curves of the waiter's ass. He was wearing a pair of slacks without rear pockets, which gave me an unobstructed look at the round halves of his butt. I felt myself getting hard as I studied him, especially when he bent over a table to deliver a customer's order and his ass was displayed even more prominently.

It reminded me of Jacques and the years he'd spent examining my own body, unknown and silent. I remembered when the truth of his interest finally came out, and that was enough to make my dick even harder.

It was the day I graduated from college. I was

dressed in my scholar's robes when I'd gone to Jacques's office immediately after the ceremony. My parents were waiting to take us out to lunch—the honors graduate and his adviser. I'd wanted to say some last thing to Jacques in private before we went. He was, after all, the man who'd guided me through four years of undergraduate study.

I'd knocked on his door, and the familiar booming voice told me to enter. When I did, I found him sitting with his feet on top of his huge mahogany desk, a piece of substantial furniture of which he'd always been very proud. His chair was tilted backwards, and he was smoking one of the Havana cigars that were his trademark.

"Ah, Kevin," he said, exhaling a cloud of smoke, "you're a man now, I hear."

I blushed a little and nodded, my self-congratulatory smile bursting with my happiness.

"Good," Jacques said. He took his feet off the desk and sat up straight, looking me right in the eye. "Then I think it's about time I got my due.

"Kevin, I have tolerated your playing cocktease for four years now. I've sat still while you've pranced that pretty body of yours all around the campus, and I've pretended to not notice all the times you gave it away.

"I have an unfortunate scruple, you see; I have never fucked any of my students, no matter how appealing. You, Kevin, have been very appealing—and very trying. I've kept my hands off you in respect to our positions here at the university.

"Now you've graduated and, by God, I intend to make up for lost time."

I had never dreamed that Jacques knew about my escapades with other students. I didn't think anyone but my partners knew about those extracurricular

THE ARENA

activities. I felt exposed and vulnerable that my secrets had been spread around so easily.

"Come on, boy, get out of those clothes."

And now my favorite professor knew, and he wanted part of the prize. I stood there, frozen, and stared at him. Jacques got up and came around to where I stood at the front of the desk. He reached over and opened the cloak I was wearing, lifting it up off my shoulders so that it fell to the ground.

Jacques was an extraordinary-looking man. He was in his late thirties then, and his face went perfectly with the role of the distinguished scholar he'd become. He was black, with prematurely graying hair that made the chocolate color of his skin seem even darker. His lips were wide and sensuous. He was a large man, taller than my 5'10"; he was broad shouldered and, when he'd worn casual summer clothing, I'd seen the brawn of his arms and the width of his strong shoulders.

His fingers were working on my shirt buttons after having removed my tie. They were slowly moving down the front and, after each button had been undone, he pulled my shirt open as far as he could, exposing my bare chest more with each move. I could smell his breath, strongly masculine from the cigar.

"I don't know what you mean," I finally blurted out. Just as I did, he pulled my shirttails out from my belt and pulled the shirt off, leaving me stripped to the waist.

"I think you do," he said quietly. "You've been looking at me since the first day you walked into Freshman Economics. Your eyes have never left me. You've come after me for approval whenever you've had a chance. Even today, minutes after your graduation, you came right to my office. Those aren't mistakes, Kevin. Those aren't coincidental." His hands moved over my naked skin, carefully and gently feeling the expanse of my chest and the tightness of my stomach.

"But I never meant——"

"Yes, you did, Kevin. You most certainly did. And I intend to prove it to you."

He kissed me. His lips covered mine with their erotic expanse, and his tongue pried mine open. I couldn't handle my confusion or think about what was going on. I was taken up with the feel of him. My arms reached around his back, and I met his embrace. My own tongue finally responded to his probing and fought back, trying to do its own exploration of his mouth.

He broke away as soon as I'd surrendered that bit of hesitation. He smiled, looking at me while he still had his arms around my waist, more loosely now. "Get out of the rest of those clothes, Kevin. I'm going to fuck the bejesus out of you."

He locked his office door, and then he went back and picked up his cigar. He leaned against his desk and smiled as he watched me. Even as I was stepping out of my shoes and unbuckling my belt, I was holding on to some denial.

"Professor, I really haven't ever meant to lead you on. I mean, I wasn't aware I was doing those things to you."

He only studied me more carefully; the smirk never left his face. When I was down to my briefs, I stood there, as though I hoped this would be enough. Instead, he studied my groin as openly as anyone had ever dared to do. My erection was poking at the waistband of my undershorts, and there was already a wet stain where the head of my cock pressed against the constricting fabric.

"Naked, Kevin, I want to see you naked."

THE ARENA

I pulled at the elastic band, freeing my cock. When that last piece of clothing was pushed down to the floor, I stood up, my erection standing at nude attention, just as I was.

"Very nice. I've seen you, you know. I've watched you in the locker room at the gymnasium. But I wasn't able to take advantage of the situation to really study what a fine young specimen you are. Yes, indeed, a fine specimen."

He moved back over to me. I was ready for him to kiss me again. I wasn't thinking clearly—I honestly hadn't really imagined Jacques and myself as lovers—but something inside me was ready for his affection and for a replay of the responses I'd felt when he'd taken me in his arms only a few minutes earlier.

Jacques wasn't interested in sentiment. He had more basic things in mind. He pulled me out into the middle of the room, away from the wall. I found some kind of pride or modesty and tried to cover my engorged cock and my balls with my hands. He ignored that. He walked around me slowly, his hands trailing over the surfaces of my body, appreciatively exploring my ass, my back, my arms.

"As nice as I remembered, and so much more accessible than in a public place," he said—to himself, it seemed—not to me. He took me over to the sofa in the corner of his office.

"Here, put one leg up on that, I want you opened up; I want your butt spread apart."

I followed his order vacantly. I put one foot up on the sofa. The stance forced my ass open and left my balls hanging loose and free away from my thighs. The posture was obscene, both in the way I must have looked and in the way it left me feeling. Jacques's hand reached in between the halves of my ass and his fingers ran up and down the crack between them, their exploration made easier by the gathering sweat. One of them tentatively entered into the ring of my anus and then pushed hard to drive itself farther inside me.

I gasped with the intrusion and stiffened up. Jacques used his other hand to carefully, soothingly brush my shoulder. "Don't tighten up on me, Kevin. This is mine. You've been offering it to me for years, and now I'm going to take it."

There was an element of myself which was obviously responding to my professor's attention. My cock wasn't just erect, there was a string of thick liquid spilling out of its tip. Another part of me thought this was all too much, that I shouldn't be doing this with a faculty member—or that I shouldn't be doing this with Jacques. Something in me registered fear and that part of me knew that there was more going on than a simple postgraduation seduction.

"Stay just like that," Jacques said in his low voice. He moved away, his finger popping out of my anus with a sudden and unexpected pain. I didn't change my posture—for whatever reason, I was willing to keep my body in this lewd position for him, no matter how anxious I was about his plans. But I did look behind me to see what he was doing.

His own penis was sticking out of the fly of his pants. I had never seen it. I was mesmerized by the size of it and by the dark color of the shaft. What was even more amazing to me was the shocking pink color of the head where the foreskin had been pulled back.

Jacques was reaching into a drawer of his desk. He brought out a familiar packaged condom and a tube of lubricant. He moved towards me, his thick cock spearing the air in front of him.

When he got to me, he smiled at my frightened and questioning expression. "Come, now, Kevin, you know all about these things. You're experienced in the ways of men. I know you are."

He unrolled the latex over his dick. The translucent whitish cover took away some of the appeal of his color, but it didn't hide how hungrily hard his cock was. Then he smeared some of the grease over the plastic.

"This is going to be a great fuck, Kevin," he said softly, but with the same authority he always had in the classroom. "This is going to be a fuck you remember."

Then he pushed hard, and the whole length of his erection shoved its way into my ass. I howled with the shock of the invasion and with the pain. He ignored my protests. His arms grasped my waist and he held me firmly in place while he began to thrust his pelvis, driving himself in and out of my ass with pulsing lunges. My balls were hanging low, swinging back and forth from the pressure of the assault, slapping against my thighs.

He kept it up for some minutes before my body could adjust. Then, unwillingly, unconsciously, I began to move with him. I may not have dreamt of his dick up me before, but I certainly wanted it inside me now. It seemed as though all of my body wanted to take in his cock and squeeze it. My sphincter kept on opening and then shutting down on his erection.

He pulled out—I thought he was done. I collapsed gratefully onto the couch, hoping I could catch my breath and recover from the onslaught. Jacques wasn't having any of that. He only wanted to change positions.

He roughly turned me over onto my back. He lifted up my legs, exposing my sore anus once again. He put both my calves on his shoulders. I could see the smile on his face again. He was consumed with this lust he was acting out. I understood then that there wasn't any reason to resist at all. I was going to get fucked again, and it was going to be at least as aggressive this time as it had been before.

He had never taken off his clothing, none of it. His coat and tie were still on, and his shirt covered his chest. I suddenly wanted to feel that part of him, to have him as naked as I was. He knelt on the couch then, and his cock dove back inside me.

He leaned down, and at last he kissed me. My arms went around his shoulders again and I tried to lose myself into that kiss, tried to make this into a romantic encounter between us, but the thrusting of his cock didn't let me have that escape. He kept at my ass for minutes more.

I had lost my erection at some point, but now it came back. Once again, I could feel the ooze of pre-come escape from the slit and turn any attempt to make-believe I didn't want this into a lie. I knew I couldn't fight off a response to the friction of his suit pants against my hard dick as he moved in and out of me. I had no way to pull back from my building response. I could feel my cock swell even more, and I could sense the liquids getting ready to pour out of me. I started to scream again, but not in agony. This time my shouts were released by a primal urge, they were cries of ecstasy and they weren't held back by any attempt to be polite or circumspect.

My orgasm drove Jacques even further. Now I was sure I couldn't tolerate his assault anymore. I tried to ask him to stop. He wouldn't let words come out of my mouth, but covered it with his thick lips. I didn't think I could endure even a second more of it, but he kept on going. At some point I felt as though I surrendered. I remember forcing the sensation of being fucked out of my mind and, instead, I went back to grasping his shoulders and holding on to him. His tongue became even more insistent and more intrusive. I let it. I welcomed it in and began to suck on it desperately.

Finally, after I'd taken more than I ever thought possible, he did come. His whole torso shuddered from the force of his orgasm. He didn't pull away from me, but seemed to push in even farther, if that could have been possible. His entire body pressed against mine; the rough fabric of his suit seemed to make every inch of me aware of him, every part of me alive with him.

When he composed himself, Jacques pulled his cock out, being much more careful to hold the condom at the base of his cock to keep it on than he worried about how I felt. If the exit of his finger had seemed painful and had left me feeling empty before, the sudden expulsion of his big dick left a virtual void in my gut.

Jacques stood up, obviously very pleased with himself, and held his latex-covered dick in his hand. "Yes, yes, that was just as fine a fuck as I had expected." He unrolled the safe off his deflating dick and disposed of the slimy evidence in his trash can. He put his cock back in his pants and then zipped up. He went to a mirror on the wall and stood there, rearranging himself to cover up any sign that he was anything but the distinguished professor of economics at a major university.

"Come on, Kevin, get up and get dressed. We have a luncheon with your parents to attend."

The waiter came to the table and offered me a cocktail. He looked Latin, I assumed Italian. I saw how tightly curled his black hair was. I asked for some wine.

After he left, I thought about Jacques's hair, even more wiry than the waiter's. I spent many hours getting used to the feel of his kinky hair after that first afternoon in his office.

Jacques was my mentor after graduation, just as he'd been my senior adviser during my days as a student. He'd been the one who'd gotten me my first job, who counseled me on how to navigate the strange ways of a corporate bureaucracy. He taught me everything. There was a tuition to be paid for that education, and it wasn't to be delivered in currency.

I'd call and ask him for guidance on some personal issue, or else seek his opinion on an investment, and he'd tell me precisely what the cost would be. "Get fucked tonight and I'll tell you." Or "I want my dick sucked this afternoon. Come by and we can talk afterwards."

There was something utterly liberating in the brazen way he bartered with me. I responded immediately to his challenges. I ended up with my face buried in the forest of his bristly pubic hair, his cock down my throat. Or else I'd strip naked and lean over his desk and spread my ass for him.

The excitement had its limits, though, and Jacques took me to the wall much too soon. The first incident had been with a visiting dignitary from Nigeria, someone he'd met at a conference on African-American trade.

"Let Mohammed fuck you," he said on the phone one day. "I told him you were good, and he wants to have a go at a white boy."

I rebelled. I told him I wasn't someone he could just give away like that. I wasn't a concubine that he could share.

"Think carefully before you tell me what you are and what you aren't," Jacques had cautioned. "Think about it very cautiously." I ended up in Mohammed's hotel room later in the afternoon, feeling humiliated and angry about the manipulations I'd bought into, but also feeling strangely and wonderfully exotic as the noble African examined my naked body—as though I were a potential investment, not a possible lover—and then used me with consummate skill.

Not long after, Jacques started to expand the repertory of the acts he himself wanted to commit on my body. "I bought a paddle at a sex store when I was in San Francisco," he announced. "I intend to use it on that nice pale butt of yours."

I wasn't going to be hurt, I insisted. I wasn't going to enter into those kinds of self-destructive activities.

"It's really a question of what's destructive and what isn't," he said quietly. "I'm not sure you're experienced enough to make the distinction yourself."

That time I convinced myself that it was only a game and there was nothing to lose in playing it out. If Jacques wanted to believe I was some naughty schoolboy who needed discipline, I could indulge him. I wasn't able to go to the gym for a week afterwards; it took that long for the bruises to heal.

All of it began to escalate, and I wanted out. I was frightened by the demands Jacques was making and by my response to them. I told him I wasn't going to do any more of the strange new things he wanted. I was available for sucking and fucking, but that was it. Just straight stuff from then on, I insisted.

Jacques looked at me coldly after I'd made my declaration. "You're young. You need time." And that was the end of the conversation. It was also the sudden end of sex between us. After that, there came a long string of other young men whom I would meet occasionally as we passed in the doorway to Jacques's apartment, or perhaps in a bar where we'd arranged to meet. They'd always go on their way quietly, almost meekly, and I was never invited to have any kind of real conversation with them.

Who Jacques was sexually and what he did with his lovers wasn't something that was mentioned ever again. We continued our friendship. In fact, it became even more of an intimate working relationship, as though the times he'd demanded my ass had never occurred.

Our partnership expanded, and he provided the capital investment I needed when I wanted to start my own company. He'd advised me well as the concern expanded and prospered. Now, today, I'd sold it. That's why I was sitting there waiting for him. We were going to celebrate my great coup. I had built up my own firm and guided it to the point where it provided me with a handsome profit. Jacques had shared in the revenue as well. But it was *my* accomplishment. No matter how much support he had given me, I was the one who carried off the implementation of the plan. I was the success.

"You're looking good, as well you should." Jacques was smiling when he sat down at the table. "This is quite the day for you."

The waiter came over to us. "A scotch, Marcel; you know the brand." So they already knew one another. I shouldn't have been surprised.

The waiter bowed a little bit and smiled. I felt a hot flush move through my body when I saw that little gesture. It was the kind of thing that Jacques had always tried to get me to do when we were together, when he was trying to mold me into the kind of young man he liked to have around for sex ... and for service. I shook the thought from my mind. After all, Marcel was probably only going after a good tip.

Jacques and I made small talk until his drink arrived. He paid no attention to the obsequious waiter, who had made a grand presentation, and waved away the offer of menus. When Marcel left, Jacques took a sip of his scotch and beamed. "This is quite the day. You're only thirty and you already have made a sizable fortune."

"Perhaps not a fortune," I said, trying to be unassuming.

"Your modesty is misplaced. You have enough money now that you'll never have to worry about working again. You have a security that most men only dream of—financially, at least. Of course, you've never been as secure as you should be in other areas.

"Now that you've taken your time to prove yourself on the battlefield of business, I expect you'll be able to give up some of the defenses you've gathered around yourself in such an adolescent fashion."

"I don't understand what you mean." I did know that he was baiting me, and it angered me that he was succeeding.

"You've been given opportunities to explore yourself and your sexuality that others can't even imagine. You were on the right track, at least for a while there. You withdrew, becoming a spiteful little snot while you redirected your energy into your business life. Well, you've proven yourself.

"Business is the battlefield of modern times, after all. It is the place where contemporary soldier proves his manhood. Your achievement is as significant as any warrior's in another age. Now that you have the badge of your manhood, it's time for you to pick up the exploration that I know is so important for you."

I was angry at his pretension. I *was* a success. I had accomplished what I'd set out to do in the business world. I was thirty. I wanted him to give up his mentor role and accept me as an equal.

My silence didn't mean a thing to him. He kept on going. "You have an phenomenal sexual appetite and a marvelous sexual ability. It's wasted on the kind of life that you've been living. You have occasional tricks, a few lovers who last a month or two, and that's it. I would have known if you'd been doing anything interesting with your sex life in this city." It suddenly dawned on me that he would have. He knew an amazing number of people. Of course they would have told him if I had been up to anything.

"You do make the intermittent foray into leather bars, especially those with backrooms." He even knew about that. "I've been particularly disappointed that you seemed to find it necessary to get drunk to do what you obviously want to do."

He sipped some more of his drink and seemed to wait for me to respond. I wouldn't do it. I don't think I could have. I could only remember, with some guilt and more excitement, the nights I had gone to clubs like the Nighthawk and wandered into the dark corners where the men dressed in full leather and played the roughest games. My cock was extending again. I could feel the dampness that was being soaked up in my briefs.

"I've invested a great deal of time in you, and effort. I was obstructed when you became so obdurate a few years ago and began to refuse my instructions, but I was willing to wait. I knew that you had the possibility of a certain genius in you, and I was amenable to biding my time until you were ready. You may have been an advanced student of finance, but you were not as clever as I hoped about the more important things in life."

"'The more important things?'" I asked. "That's a strange way for a professor of economics to put it. After all, that's your life."

"No, you're wrong." Jacques lifted his now empty scotch glass in the air and silently commanded Marcel's attention. The waiter came over quickly and fetched it, taking it to the bar for a refill. "Teaching economics is simply a way to pay some bills. I understand perfectly well what are the most important things in my life, and what they could be in yours. They have little to do with double-entry bookkeeping."

The scotch glass appeared. Marcel seemed to linger a bit, as though he hoped for some other command. I wanted him to stay even longer, just to avoid this conversation, but he did leave.

"I think you've done enough to expand my horizons," I said, trying to lighten up the discussion. "I remember more than a few instances when you were able to broaden my experiences quite a bit."

"Yes, and the way you took to them proves my point, that you have a genius for sex. It frightened you. You withdrew. But those kinds of decisions don't have to be set in concrete. You have the necessary maturity for another step. I think we should take it."

"Jacques, this is ridiculous. I'm a self-made man. I don't have to take this kind of lecture from you."

"You don't *have* to, but I suspect you will." Jacques smiled again.

He flicked a hand and a menu appeared. The waiter stood by the table, expectantly. Jacques had trained the staff of all his favorite restaurants to ignore his guests when it came time to order. Jacques always insisted on choosing our meals, forcing me into a passivity that I had to admit I'd grown accustomed to.

"The main courses here are quite good," Jacques said while he still had the menu open. "But the appetizers can be even better."

I stared at him for a moment. Then he looked up at the waiter who instantly blushed. Marcel's crotch was right at our eye level. I hadn't noticed quite how large the bulge in his pants was—I had been paying more attention to his ass—but now I could see that the mound of flesh was growing, just from Jacques's statement. My own groin was feeling warm again, and even wetter.

"Why don't you both go to the men's room," Jacques said in a light conversational tone. "Start your celebration, Kevin. Begin your meal without me. I'll make some other decisions while you're gone."

Marcel didn't say a word. He simply disappeared. I tried to say something to Jacques about the insult of all this, the way he was treating me as though I were a college student again, someone who he could just direct to act out his sexual fantasies and forget. I wanted to rebel. Instead, I stood up and walked towards the back of the restaurant, where the waiter had disappeared.

I knew the door would be unlocked. I pushed it open and found Marcel there waiting for me. His pants were off, carefully folded and put on a shelf. He had on only his shirt. His dick was half-hard, sweeping out in an arc away from the remarkably hairy balls that hung low between his legs.

"Please hurry," he said almost desperately. "If the manager knows I left the floor, I'll get in trouble." He moved toward me and groped for my fly. He yanked it down and reached in to pull out my cock.

He had a condom already for me in his hand. "What do you want?" he asked. "I've been told you can have anything."

I wanted to see his chest. With the heavy covering of hair on the part of his body I could see, I imagined that his chest was handsomely cloaked. I wanted to feel it. I wanted to imagine whether I could see his tits as they stuck out through the heavy pelt. He obviously wasn't in the mood for something even that sophisticated. His hands were moving on my now-fully-erect cock, anxiously trying to elicit a quick response. He ripped open the condom and quickly and efficiently moved to wrap it over my dick. The sensation of his handling my cock was wonderful, his fingers moved so swiftly and so carefully over my tender flesh.

His odor was magical. There was that muskiness that comes with a hirsute body, but there was a cleanliness about it as well. "Please, tell me what you want," he pleaded.

"Blow me," I said. I wasn't pleased by the rush. I would have liked to have done so much more. Still, my dick was anxious. I had been watching this man's butt and thinking about sex for nearly an hour. I needed some satisfaction.

He dropped to his knees and sucked in my hard cock. I have never had an experience so wonderful as the first moment a man's mouth embraces my prick. No layer of latex was capable of diminishing that pleasure. That wet warmth is the finest sensation I know. I threw my head back against the wall and let him work at it.

I could have let it go on, just like that, but I had to explore his ass. I reached down over him, letting the back-and-forth motions of his head brush against me, and grabbed hold of one of the solid globes of his butt. As hairy as the rest of him was, his ass was smooth. I pushed my hand into his crack and discovered the rich pelt there, but the fleshy knolls themselves were hairless. I thought the contrast was especially erotic.

The waiter was frenzied as he continued to suck me. He was good at it, I had to admit that. There were a few choking noises, but there was no resistance when I moved my hips forward and shoved my dick farther into his mouth. He used his tongue to good advantage, wrapping it around my shaft while he continued to tease me towards my orgasm.

It broke through in a short time. I stood up, releasing my hold on his ass, and grabbed hold of his long hair with both my hands. I forced his face farther down on my shaft, just as I exploded my load into the scumbag. He had to resist then; there was no way he could take that assault of my expanding dick without some difficulty. Still, I was impressed by how hard he tried to surrender to my aggression.

As soon as the last drop of come had splashed out of me, he jumped up and put his pants back on. "I apologize for the hurry," he said. I actually believed that he meant it. As soon as he could, he pushed past me and back into the restaurant. I took a little while to get rid of the condom and compose myself, then zipped up and went back to the table.

"You must feel much better," Jacques said as I sat down.

Actually, I was furious with him. I was also furious with myself. As soon as he'd flashed a piece of ass, I'd gone for it.

There were salads at each of our places. A bottle of white wine had been opened and was chilling beside the table. As soon as I sat down, Marcel came over and poured a glass for Jacques and then one for me. He didn't acknowledge me at all, he just resumed his servile manner.

"What is it you expect me to do?" I asked, refusing to look Jacques in the eye.

"Kevin, I expect you to realize your potential. I expect you to take advantage of some unique opportunities I can offer you."

I finished the salad without saying a word to him. When I put down my fork, I said, "I suppose this has to do with nocturnal visits to your friends' hotel rooms. Do you really think I have much to learn from being a small-time whore? I would think that even you would realize that I'm not cut out to be a boy toy to visiting dignitaries."

Jacques seemed to be amused by my little flare of insurrection. "I have something much more complicated and much more interesting set up for you," he said. "I told you, I want to give you something from which you can learn. You already have had those other lessons, haven't you? And, no matter how much you want to complain, you did learn from them.

"It's time to move on. You've graduated from boot camp, and you've gotten your stripes out in the field. It's time for you to take advantage of your freedom. Come now, Kevin. You haven't even asked me what this is about. You haven't even asked me for details. I'm a bit disappointed in you. After all, no matter how defiant you'd like to make yourself out to be, you *did* go with the waiter when I told you to, didn't you? You were intrigued enough to explore that possibility, yet it was so mundane. Why don't you trust me now? This is something much more eventful."

The building was near the waterfront. When I got out

of our cab, I couldn't see anything that was open in the neighborhood at this time of night. The few street lamps that were on only seemed to create more shadows and a sense of uncertainty of what could be hidden within their darkness.

I followed Jacques when he walked towards a row of small warehouses. He knocked on a door. It opened a bit and I could see a part of a man's face peering out, checking up on us. "Professor," the voice said, "welcome."

The door wasn't opened fully, just enough for the two of us to slip inside. There wasn't much more light in the entry and what there was had a heavy red tint to it. There was music playing in the background. It seemed to be a chant of some sort, though the heavy synthesizer told me it wasn't Gregorian or, if it were, it had been modernized drastically.

The man who'd opened the door was rough looking, but handsome in that way. He was wearing well-worn leather pants and a leather vest without a shirt underneath. His chest was smooth. He had extravagant tattoos. They were an oriental design that didn't seem to portray any obvious image.

"Is it a good night, Duane?" Jacques asked.

"Aren't they all, professor?"

The doorman opened the second door only when the first had been securely shut. The music was a bit louder when we walked through it. The heat was high; the room seemed almost too warm for clothing. There was a definite moisture in the air, as well. The lighting was the same.

It all combined to create an atmosphere of anticipation. I still smelt the odor of leather and flesh. I thought it was coming from Duane, but he had gone back to his original post. Leather and flesh wasn't something exclusive to him. They were part of this place.

THE ARENA

I followed Jacques to one of the many tables that lined the walls of the expansive inner room. As my eyes adjusted to the light, I could make out other men sitting at their own tables or standing at a small bar at the opposite corner of the room. The customers were dressed in a variety of outfits, from dramatic heavy leather to sophisticated business suits to simple slacks and shirts.

I could also see that there were platforms placed at irregular intervals against the walls. They were deep, covered with carpet. Obviously they'd be comfortable to sit on—or lie on, for that matter.

As soon as we sat down, one of the men who had been wandering the floor came over to us. He wore nothing but a leather pouch over his genitals and a pair of boots. The pouch could barely contain his cock and balls, which were clearly apparent through their thin covering. This must have been the most delicate leather made. I could actually see the outline of the head of the man's cock through the hide. A bandanna was wrapped around his neck.

Both his nipples and both his ears were pierced with large gold rings. The two pairs of piercings were incredibly erotic. A single pierced tit might have been attractive, but the two together were fascinating. The addition of the earrings gave the man the appearance of a pirate from some long-past period. I had to wonder what I would feel like if I had gold rings attached to my body that way.

"Professor, a drink?" He seemed to be on very friendly terms with Jacques, who reached up and cupped one of the waiter's naked asscheeks with his palm.

"Something light, Paul, and the same for my friend." Jacques slapped the waiter's ass playfully.

The man had a very good body. His legs were

sharply etched with the outline of sinew and muscle. Yet his butt was soft-looking and quivered with a particularly sensual suppleness when Jacques hit it. I found my mouth watering at the sight. I tried to put that thought out of my mind.

"This is it?" I said sarcastically. "You want me to be a waiter in a nude bar?"

Jacques scoffed at me. "You know I have more in mind than anything as simple as that."

Some of the lights came up just then. They still had a reddish hue, but the center of the room was illuminated more brightly. The music didn't change. The same kind of haunting melody played over the hidden loudspeakers. Without any fanfare, a naked man stepped into the circle of light.

It was Marcel, the waiter from the restaurant. His head was bent respectfully to the audience. He spread his legs far apart and then lifted his arms so they stood out from his body, parallel to the floor. As soon as he had taken that position, a large metal device began to lower from the ceiling.

It appeared to be an enormous gyroscope made out of brightly polished stainless steel. It attracted and magnified all the scarlet illumination in the room. When it had reached the floor, Marcel simply stood there. Two men appeared on either side of him. They each took one of his arms and led him backwards into the gyroscope's space. They moved quickly and with great assuredness as they attached restraints to his wrists and ankles and then other supports to his waist and chest. Then they stood back.

Marcel was bound to an inner circle of metal. It, in turn, seemed to be attached to another metal circle that was anchored in a square. The machine was lifted up again, the waiter caught in its mechanical embrace.

When the device was off the ground, Marcel's

body began to spin slowly. It was no simple spin, but a multidimensional movement. There seemed to be nothing directing the course his body would follow. At first he was parallel to the floor, his legs spread wide open by the restraints so that we were looking directly at his balls as they hung down over his ass. Then he was moving horizontally, and we were looking at the smooth lines of his side. The thick hair on his chest appeared to be an aura over the light skin of his torso, highlighted by the redness that permeated the room.

As soon as I was used to that sight, the apparatus shifted again, turning Marcel upside-down with his back to us, his perfect and hairless ass right in front of us.

The low hush of conversation continued without any noticeable change. Paul went back to his work, delivering our drinks, then taking other orders.

Only a few hours earlier, this man had been sucking me off in a john. I had accepted his hurried blowjob and been satisfied with it, even as I wanted to see what his body had looked like and had wanted to feel it. Now it was on exhibition for me. It kept on its languid movements, giving me a constantly changing but always intimate view of every part of him. His head would fall back and forth slowly as he moved, as though he wanted to give in to the flow of it all, as though he didn't want to resist any of it in any way.

The sight was hypnotic, especially with the heavy music in the background. Jacques and I sat silently and studied the offered torso with minute concentration. We weren't the only ones. Some of the other men in the room stood up and casually walked toward the man trapped in the machine. They stood, some of them alone, others in pairs, and studied the entertainment.

If I had more sense about me, I would have joined them. I found myself wondering just what those balls looked like close-up. I wanted to see if his ass was as flawless to the eye as it had been to my touch. I wanted to watch his muscles strain as he was put in one position after another; each one had to put different stress on his body. But I sat there silently with Jacques. This time it wasn't just my crotch that was wet from the excitement. My shirt at my armpits was soaked with sweat. My palms were clammy. I was watching an aberration—I was convinced of that—but it was one that sent messages of electric excitement through my whole being.

One of the men who stood close to Marcel reached out and took hold of his nipples. Marcel had maintained a rapturous appearance, but the stimulation must have included some pain; his face began to contort. Another man took hold of Marcel's balls and seemed to heft them, as though he were studying some fruit in a market. The two men managed to manipulate the frame so that Marcel was perpendicular to the floor. A third man stepped behind him and slapped Marcel's ass hard; a sharp *crack* sounded through the room.

The trio stood back then, and I could hear a low laugh. One of them sent the frame moving quickly, racing inside the metal structure. Marcel must have been horribly disoriented by it all. It must have been jarring when the men suddenly stopped the movement.

They'd decided to go further. Their pants were undone and their cocks were hanging out; not quite hard yet, but all of them clearly intent on satisfaction. The men began what looked like an innocent circle jerk, stroking their own dicks to erection. Paul appeared with condoms and knelt in front of each man, encasing each one's already drooling cock in latex. The men maneuvered the steel frame so that Marcel's mouth was positioned the way they wanted it. Then the first one stepped forward and shoved his cock in Marcel's face.

Marcel's long hair was hanging downwards, toward the floor. He was desperately trying to accommodate the large cock that was pressing between his lips.

"He's come a long way," Jacques said. "He used to be so inhibited."

While Marcel was sucking that cock, one of the other men moved behind him and began to ease his fingers, one by one, into Marcel's asshole. Someone brought over some thick white grease. The man used it to lubricate his whole fist.

The entire audience watched the scene with anticipation. This show was finally capturing their attention. Slowly the man's fingers had all disappeared into Marcel's body. The man had collapsed his hand and the greatest width was pushing into Marcel, who couldn't accept the intrusion without trying to put up some resistance. I could see his face twist in agony; but his bondage was so complete, the vulnerability so total, that there was no way for Marcel to avoid the fist-fucking.

I heard a couple men sigh with pleasure when the fist moved beyond Marcel's sphincter and the fucker's whole hand disappeared into Marcel's ass.

"Another drink?" Jacques asked, "Or would you prefer a change of scenery?"

I hadn't been able to see them from our seats, but there were openings all along the walls of the front room. They were covered with large leather curtains. I followed Jacques through one of them. We stepped into a smaller chamber.

It had the same reddish lighting. There was another servant dressed in a leather jock pouch, but he wasn't the main attraction.

In the center of the room was a slightly elevated stage, about the size of a boxing ring. "We call this the arena," Jacques said in a low voice. "That's also the name of the entire establishment."

Six men stood on the platform. They were all naked. Around each of their necks hung a small key on a silver chain. I assumed that the key went with the handcuffs that securely fastened each one's hands behind his neck. Each man also had a leather band wrapped around the base of his balls. There was a small D-ring on the band.

Most of the men stood there passively, with their heads down, looking submissively towards the floor. But one of them was staring at us defiantly. He seemed to attract Jacques, who walked up to him and ran a hand along the outside of the man's muscular flanks.

"This is Franco," Jacques said. "He used to be known as one of the most vicious and popular tops in the city. He would go to many of those same leather bars that you like so much and stand there, waiting for his subjects to come and worship him. They did, too. They adored him."

I knew all about Franco. I was embarrassed to have him see me here. I used to see him in the bars all the time. He wore leather chaps, boots, jacket, and cap—the complete uniform. He had the whole thing down perfectly. He could stand in the shadows of a room and make me feel weak with passion. His presence could provoke an disconcerting desire to submit. I had spent many nights longing for him, wondering what it would be like to be in his control.

He was certainly handsome, in a rough manner.

He had dark eyes and he used to have a heavy beard, though he was clean shaven now. Franco was also well built. His chest was covered with thick dark hair. His arms were substantial, and each of his biceps was covered with a tattoo. One was a black panther, the other a serpent that wrapped around the whole upper half of Franco's arm. I had seen those tattoos on summer nights when he used to strip off his jacket and shirt in the bar and stand there, a god of flesh waiting for the rest of us to glorify him. I had hated him as much as I had wanted him, and now he was in the arena, naked.

Franco stood there with his feet firmly planted on the bare wood floor and accepted Jacques's impersonal caresses without ever lowering his eyes or shying away from Jacques's hand.

"Franco met his match though. Always so rough on the outside, he finally found someone to love, such a tedious goal for such a fine specimen. It would be his luck that his new friend was also a top, and one of the most adamant. They had a test of wills. Franco lost. In order to have his relationship, he had to agree to sexual servitude."

Jacques's hands had continued exploring Franco's body while he talked. One of them finally cupped the naked man's cock. At the tip of it was a large golden ring. I was both excited and repelled by the thought of a needle spearing through Franco's cock and piercing him.

"You can imagine that, with his background, Franco has a strong defiant streak in him. It's a hindrance to his new master. One of the ways that man has to keep Franco in his place and to remind of his agreement is to bring Franco here, to the arena, on a regular basis."

Jacques stood back. He seemed to be displeased

by something. He gestured to the attendant who had stood in the background. "Get him hard. I want to examine him with an erection."

The man moved forward and knelt in front of Franco. He had a rubber that looked foolish when it first went on Franco's near-flaccid penis. Then the attendant took the big man's dick in his mouth and began to suck on it. Franco seemed to try to fight off the sensation, but he wouldn't be able to do it for long. I could see his flat, hard abdomen begin to contract as the other man's ministrations began to take effect.

"Any of the men who walk onto this platform are here for the enjoyment of any of our members." Jacques was enjoying this chance to deliver a lecture. "There's no sadism too harsh, no humiliation too deep. There are no negotiations. There is only submission. Franco knows that, and his regular visits here do wonders for his attitude."

The attendant moved back and away from Franco, then stood up and returned to his corner. The latex covering on Franco's now-erect dick glistened with the sheen of spit the man had left on it. His raised hard-on seemed to be crowned by the golden circle of metal that was trapped inside the translucent latex covering.

"Yes, he is a handsome man. And he attracts many of our members. Some of them remember times when he turned them down in a bar or made comments about them in a group. They find a special satisfaction in making him beg for their attentions now.

"Others find it appealing to have a man who they know was once dominant himself. It satisfies some need in them. I, myself, prefer someone more completely submissive, someone whom I don't have to fight into his place."

Jacques flicked a hand and dismissed Franco, who glowered even as he followed the unspoken order and moved backwards into the arena. Jacques looked over the rest of the field and his attention fell on a young blond man. He moved to one of the attendants again. "Put a cock in his mouth. I can never really tell how handsome a man is unless he's got dick down his throat."

The attendant smiled. He moved onto the platform and undid his leather jock, letting it fall to the floor. He had a solid thick uncut cock that quickly grew to an unexpectedly large size when he played with it. It was the kind of dick that makes your mouth water as you contemplate the taste of it. Circumcised cock can sometimes be so clean, so lacking in real tang, but a meaty uncut one like this always had some special flavor that you could savor. The idea of it didn't diminish when the cock was sheathed in a condom.

The blond man seemed frightened by the attention he was receiving. While Franco had been defiant, this man was scared. His eyes darted between Jacques and me and the attendant, as though he were looking for a definitive order, afraid that he might displease one or all of us.

"Kneel," the attendant said. The young man obliged immediately. I loved watching the way his muscles moved as he managed to get on his knees gracefully. He didn't have the bulk that Franco had. This man's muscles were sleek. There were lines through his flesh at his belly, on his thighs, around his back. He was certainly solidly built, but it was a build that promised something smooth and even slippery to the touch. There was hardly any hair on him; only a few wisps on his legs and small patches above his cock and under his arms.

The blond instinctively moved forward towards the attendant's cock and sucked it. Jacques was right; having dick in his mouth changed the way the man looked. He seemed slightly angelic now, with his cheeks caved in over the thick meat. He kept his eyes open and he was looking up towards the attendant with an expression that was utterly worshipful.

"Yes, he's quite good, isn't he?" Jacques said. He knelt and ran a hand over the blond's butt. The man intuitively spread his knees farther apart to give Jacques even easier access.

"What's his name?" Jacques asked the attendant.

"Chris."

"What's his background?"

"He's an apprentice. He hasn't been here often. He's fresh." The attendant was having a difficult time talking. He was obviously enjoying the blowjob that was taking him close to his orgasm. Yet he managed to go on. "He tends to shy away from the heavy stuff, but he shows potential."

Jacques nodded and then moved away. As I followed him, I could see that the attendant was very disappointed. He evidently needed the presence of one of the members to continue working on the young man and, when Jacques left the arena, his permission was removed. He took his cock out of Chris's mouth and leaned over to pick up his jock.

Jacques led me through another leather curtain and into a long hallway. It seemed even warmer here. I took off my shirt and hung it from my belt. The air moving over my naked chest felt unexpectedly erotic. I couldn't help but think of hands moving across it and grabbing my nipples, which were hardening with the idea.

Jacques remained composed as he slowly looked into the spaces off the corridor. Each one looked like a cell. There was a wooden platform in the center of each one. It was obviously made to allow a man to be spread on it. At each corner there were leather restraints attached to firmly grounded chains. Along the walls, each room had a slightly different set of implements. There were almost always paddles and riding crops; occasionally there would be a brutal-looking whip. There were sometimes dildos, a few or a whole selection of them.

There were people in the third cell that we came to. A naked man was sprawled out over the rack. A rubber ball was forced into his mouth and kept in place by straps that wove around his skull. The gag was obviously very effective; he was trying to scream, but couldn't.

He was trying to scream because another man stood leaning over him applying absolutely brutal clamps to each of his nipples. My own seemed to react to the sight, becoming even more erect as I watched the jagged teeth bite into the bound man's tits.

The tormentor was deceptively dressed in plain chino pants and a polo shirt that set off his own well-developed chest and arms. He didn't look like a fierce S&M master, but he clearly was. Once the clamps were firmly attached, he began to play with them, making them press down even harder on his victim's defenseless flesh. His quarry was writhing in suffering, twisting his body in a valiant but vain attempt to escape the anguish.

The torturer stood back and seemed to study his handiwork. Then he took more clamps from the wall and began to apply them to the captive's balls.

I was sweating with excitement over the scene. My interest only increased when the tormentor brought out a bag of wooden clothespins and began to apply them to the prisoner's inner thighs. The added clips created an image of almost-unending agony. There were so many of them, and there were so many exposed pieces of skin where they could be attached.

Jacques didn't say anything, but moved away from the scene. I didn't dare exhibit the extent of my interest. I knew that Jacques had led me into very dangerous ground. It was so perilous. I knew I was in greater danger than I could fathom.

There were similar scenes in a few of the other cells, but Jacques didn't appear interested in them. He walked through still another curtain at the end of the hallway. When I followed him through the leather flaps, I found that we'd entered into a much more elaborate and well-equipped chamber than the semiprivate ones we'd passed.

This room was in use. There was a man secured in old-fashioned stocks in the middle of the space. He looked beautiful. His ankles were trapped in boards near the floor. His head and wrists were locked in by another board that was placed in such a position that he was forced to bend over.

His ass looked startlingly white in contrast to the rest of him. He'd obviously been on the beach a lot, and had a deep, dark tan that made his butt all the more appealing. I didn't wait for any leads from Jacques this time. I moved forward to get a better look. I was surprised by how excited I became when I saw that the man's ass and balls had been shaved cleaned. The small asshole seemed so pristine. I moved around to the side and realized that his crotch had been shaved as well, leaving his ample dick and balls looking even larger.

But when I stood in front of him, I saw something else. I recognized him. This was Barry Strum. He'd been one of the star football players when I'd been at the university, famous for his willingness to struggle against all odds on the gridiron. Barry had been one of the men who we'd all looked up to at school, one of the students who had defined masculinity for us.

We used to be in classes together. I remembered the arrogant way he would sit in a chair with his legs sprawled open, as though he were daring someone to notice. He had been a celebrated athlete, and so much more. Now he was naked, trapped in the embrace of wooden planks, waiting for his master to begin his assault.

A man in leather pants and nothing else stood behind the stocks. He had a wide leather paddle in his hands. I could tell from Barry's unflawed pale butt that the other man hadn't had a chance to use his implement before we interrupted.

Not that the man seemed to be upset by the intrusion. On the contrary, he smiled a greeting to Jacques before he stepped back and lifted the paddle. He seemed to appreciate the chance to show off to an audience. Barry stretched to try to see who was there, but I didn't think he could make us out. We were too far back for him to see us. In any event, he wasn't going to be able to worry about such a small thing as who was observing his humiliation. He obviously was going to have to deal with some pain, and that was going to be more than enough to take up all his concentration.

The leather slammed against the prisoner's ass. Barry convulsed with the sudden excruciating shock. There was no escape, of course; there was no way for him to avoid the punishment he was going to receive. The leather was raised again and then fell once more on his butt. Just those two blows were enough to raise a pair of violent red streaks on Barry's ass.

The beating continued, the captive desperately but

unsuccessfully tried to find a position that would make the blows less painful. It was an astonishing sight. The mass of Barry's muscles quivered with every blow. His ass seemed so soft compared to the hardness of the rest of him, but it didn't make any difference; the leather forced all of him to quiver when it fell.

Barry should be used to this mistreatment, I thought. After all, he would come to class every Monday after a game with a mass of black-and-blue marks. He might even enjoy it, I thought, with a slight snigger. This must remind him of his glory days on the football field.

I was so aroused that I lost any hope of being in control of my emotions. I couldn't help feeling the hard bulge in my pants as I watched the handsomely beefy ass being worked over, changing color. Barry's butt shuddered with each blow. It was exciting to watch, to think of this man so desperate for mercy. Spit was building up in my mouth. I wanted to lick his hot skin and handle it. That I knew Barry from another time in our lives only made the whole thing more erotic.

"Don't," Jacques said. He took my hand away from my crotch. I felt disgraced, as though I were a little boy who'd been caught doing something naughty and had to be reprimanded. "Don't waste it all yet," Jacques explained. "There's so much more to see. There's so much more that goes on in here."

The next chamber was a total change from the previous rooms. It was lushly carpeted. There didn't seem to be any implements of torture here; no rough wooden racks, no threatening stocks. Instead there were large pillows strewn around in piles. On them sat a few men, obviously members, dressed in the same range of leather and cloth that I'd seen before.

They were carrying on quiet conversations. There were three naked men with telltale leather ball-straps. They were also sprawled on the pillows, but they seemed to move with elegance to meet the mainly unspoken commands of their masters. Hands would reach out, and nipples and asses would move to accommodate them. One of the slaves was thrashing with passion as a single finger was exploring his asshole. The manipulator ignored all that motion and carried on his conversation with another of the masters.

"This is the members' room," Jacques said. "Quiet is respected here. While sex dominates the other spaces, this one is devoted primarily to conversation and other more subtle pleasures." There was a library of books, I saw. I walked up to one of the bookcases and saw that the titles were all the classics: *The Claiming of Sleeping Beauty, Justine,* untold numbers of volumes authored by "Anonymous."

"There's no pleasure that we deny our members," Jacques explained. "The kitchen is especially unique. You'll have to come some evening for dinner. It will amuse you."

There was something about this "quiet" room that bothered me even more than the others. The lighting was much brighter and had none of the red hue that I'd become accustomed to. There weren't any instruments to keep the servants in bondage. There was nothing that implied force or subjugation. There was only the naked reality of the slaves' servitude. I found that deeply alarming. I declined Jacques's offer to continue the tour. Even while I wondered what more could possibly exist here, I had seen more than enough.

I was relieved to get back. I welcomed the familiar odor of sweat and leather that infused the front room. No matter how extreme this place was, the front room had at least some resemblance to things with which I was familiar. It wasn't as foreign to me—nor as threatening—as the members' room. Marcel had disappeared, along with his metal frame. We took our table again. There were more people in the place now than there had been. There was much more action as well.

At the bar across the room three men were fondling a fourth, a naked man I had seen in the arena. He had a very impressive build, not so much because of any bulk, but because of the sharp definition of his lithe muscles. The men were obviously exciting him even as they tormented him. His cock—nicely sized and nearly perfect in form—stood at a right angle to his hard belly. It was obvious that he couldn't keep track of what hands were doing what to him. Some fingers were pushed into his asshole. Others were playing with his nipples, while still others grabbed and twisted his balls. He tried to move away from each assault, but every movement only delivered him more firmly into the grip of another attack. The trio of aggressors was amused with all his maneuvering, and whatever protests or attempts to escape the man made, they only increased their efforts.

Everyone acted as though this were perfectly normal behavior. While others, like me, were obviously watching the small show, more of the customers continued their own conversations. I could see that at least one man had someone naked kneeling between his legs. The body was under the table and was hardly visible to the rest of us. It wasn't even moving, as far as I could see. I imagined that the mouth was

THE ARENA

holding the other's cock, just allowing the man's shaft to rest between his lips.

"I told you it was a remarkable place," Jacques said nonchalantly.

"How can it exist?" That's what I really wanted to know. I'd never heard of this place, this arena. I knew enough people that I should have at least gotten a hint that someplace like this was in the city.

"This is a very private club, and it is able to provide all the interests for its members. I doubt that you see many of these men in the places you frequent."

He was right. I could only recognize a few of them, and none of those seemed to be men that I'd run across any time recently.

"It wouldn't do for the arena to turn into just another backroom bar," Jacques said. "That would defeat its purpose."

"What is its purpose, then?"

Jacques paused and took out a new cigar. He went through his ritual of clipping its end and then lighting it. Only when he had finished would he continue.

"Many of us have become distressed by the way the scene has been developing recently. It's not just that there are so many tourists in the bars and clubs that we used to frequent—though they are annoying, the ones who only come to look and not to become part of the action.

"What really concerned us was the way that so many people were moving away from the essence of the experience. They talked about it too much and did it too little. They worried about relationships between people, as though a torture chamber were a place for a sensitivity group.

"We worried about disease, as well, as everyone must these days. There were too many instances when men were involved in sex and recreation where they were too drugged or too drunk and were doing too many things they shouldn't do.

"Some stimulants are fine, but they all need to be handled responsibly.

"A few of us who had been talking about the situation got together and tried to come up with a solution. The arena was the answer. This is the one place in the world—at least the only place we know of—where the sexuality of the place is paramount. We don't care how much alcohol we sell, and we don't care about any recent trends. Our membership is very limited. You'd be impressed by the interrogation that applicants have to go through before they're allowed in here. It's much more stringent than any of the civic organizations I've joined." He seemed to find this funny and laughed out loud at the idea.

"You must all be rich to afford this. The equipment and the salaries must be huge."

"Much of this is accomplished by volunteer labor. You should realize that there is such a wide spectrum of fetish and fantasy in the world, and that there are many people who will gladly go through anything to experience them.

"The attendants, for instance—" he gestured towards the barely clothed men who were delivering drinks and having their bodies felt by the members—"are very often volunteers who find an evening at this work one of the most exciting things that could happen to them.

"There are coordinators who make sure that all the shifts are covered and who step in when their own services are needed. One does have to have that much organization."

"But the slaves——"

"Yes, them." Jacques was very pleased with the topic. "There are luckily so many men who are so obsessed with submissive sex that it hasn't been difficult to find many of them to offer their services. We have been known to employ some of the men, especially if they have a aptitude for the work, especially if they need a small stipend to allow them to devote themselves to it full time."

One of the attendants came over to the table to see if Jacques wanted anything. "Yes, actually. There's one named Chris back in the arena. Bring him out, will you?"

"It's that simple?" I asked

"That's the whole point."

The attendant brought Chris almost immediately. Now I saw the reason for the D-ring on the leather ball-strap. It was attached to a long leash. Chris still had his hands cuffed behind his back. The leash led him to our table. The display had one of the most remarkable effects I could imagine. The leather band around his balls was so effective that the man had no opportunity to resist being led on the leash. It made him appear so much more honestly vulnerable than he would have been if they'd used a more theatrical neck-collar.

When they were in front of us, the attendant undid the lead and handed Jacques the leash. Chris was obviously his now. Jacques dismissed the attendant and then nodded gently to Chris. The blond man understood the command and fell to his knees. He buried his head in Jacques's lap.

"You should take advantage of this evening," Jacques said as he petted Chris's head. "There are limits to how often a guest can be brought into the arena. Tonight you have all privileges. Everything—and everyone—is at your disposal. Why don't you wander back through the maze and see if there isn't something that you could find to entertain yourself?"

It was obvious that Jacques intended to divert himself with Chris. I was in the way. I stood up and walked away from the table, but didn't leave the front room. I went and sat on one of the platforms. An attendant came over immediately and asked if there was anything I wanted. I asked for a soft drink, wanting to keep my head clear. He brought it right over. "Perhaps you'd like someone from the arena?" he asked as I took the glass from him.

"No."

He didn't press the point, but moved away to one of the tables where other members were sitting.

The truth was that I was most interested in those members. There were four men at the table. Two of them appeared to be together, a couple. They were both had large bodies, but they appeared to be firmly built. They wore long beards and both had on flannel shirts and jeans along with roughly worn black leather boots. I could imagine their hairy bodies pressing me between them. They were laughing and smiling, obviously having a good time with one another and with their friends at the table. I wondered how they would like to have another join them, one who would be interested in more than conversation.

I studied the other two men at the table. One of them I thought I recognized from the leather bars. He was wearing only a vest and jeans. I could see his prominent chest. I wished he'd move just enough so I could also see his nipples. I remembered them as being very well developed, large nubs of hard flesh that had made me salivate when I'd thought about sucking on them.

The other man was dressed in a suit, as though he

had come here directly from an office. He had a thick mustache, and his eyes were sparkling from the humor in the conversation. When the attendant came by their table again, this man reached out and grabbed hold of his leather pouch, using his hold to draw the nearly naked servant over to him. He didn't look at the man, but continued his conversation with the others while he moved his hand over the servant's naked ass.

Eventually he leaned over and ran his mouth over the leather triangle that encased the attendant's genitals. I could see that the servant's cock was getting hard. The man eventually unbuckled the pouch and let the waiter's cock swing freely. His friends kept on talking as though nothing out of the ordinary were happening while he expertly put on a condom and then took the waiter's now hard prick into his mouth and began to suck on it.

A slight bit of cocksucking wasn't anything extraordinary in this place. No one paid attention to it. Except for me. My own dick was revolting against the confines of my underwear. I still hadn't put my shirt back on, and now the odor from my armpits seemed to be rising up, joining the smell of leather and flesh, mingling with it, making me all the more aware of the carnal realities of this place. I was part of it. Just as my odors were mixing with the fragrance of sex and bodies, so were my fantasies merging with those that were the currency here.

I suddenly worried about the other men in the room seeing my nipples. They were too honest. They were hard, erect with desire, obvious markers that could let any other man know that I was desperate for sex now. Every little breath of air that moved across them seemed to send shivers through my body. I sat there and imagined one of the men at the table coming over and clamping his teeth on my tits The very thought was enough to make my cock rock-hard.

I felt a need to escape, even as my desire to join that table full of friends was building. I was in danger in this place. I knew that's why Jacques had brought me here, but knowledge didn't change anything. Peril was omnipresent; passion was its ally; rationality couldn't defy it. Being here was being in the grip of a seduction far more powerful than any simple sex act. This was a fantasy that had become a reality, and it was one that could suck me in the moment I let down my guard.

Action seemed necessary. I knew I should leave. That would have been the smartest thing to do. But I also found another compulsion building within me. There was something else I wanted to do here. I could move away from these men and whatever it was that made them so menacing. I could take a different path than the smart one, the one that led me back out onto the street.

I saw Jacques and Chris as I moved across the room. Jacques's familiar black dick was out of his pants. It was hard, with that amazing pink knob at the head of it spearing the air. Chris was on his knees, his long tongue lapping away at Jacques's ebony balls.

I went through the curtains and into the room with the arena. Franco was still there. I stood by the stage and studied him some more. He was defiant in the same way I had noticed before, refusing to look down, forbidding himself the simple escape of averting his eyes from the others that were studying him.

I went over to the attendant. "I'm a guest. I want that one. I want to take him to the large chamber at the end of the hall."

"Of course," he replied. He handed me a long

leash. "All you have to do is attach this to his strap, and he'll follow you and all your orders. You won't have any trouble with that one." He smiled. "He'd like to give you a hard time, but there are repercussions that he won't want to face if he presents any problems."

I took the leash and went to the edge of the stage. I reached up and grabbed hold of Franco's dense balls. He seemed to stiffen, as though he expected some attack. I only used my grip to get hold of his strap and then to attach it to the leash. I tugged.

Franco seemed honestly surprised to find himself in my power. I wonder what he used to think of me in the bars, what had gone through his mind when he'd turned me away so ruthlessly. Had he ever conceived that he'd end up in a place like this, or that I would be someone to whom he'd have to submit?

The thoughts were a jolting aphrodisiac. I was the one that had the power now. I was the one who would decide what we were going to do. This evening was going to make up for a lot of history between us.

I dragged Franco's leash through the corridor. There were more scenes being played out in the cells along the way, but I didn't linger this time to see what they were or who was involved. Franco tried to. He kept attempting to look at each of the displays as we passed the cell doors. He must have been in each of them often. He could vividly imagine what tools were being put to what use in each one.

I think he was surprised when we entered the last chamber—surprised that we hadn't stopped in one of the cells, that is. There were other people here already. This larger room wasn't designed for private use; there were so many devices here that a dozen actions could be going on at once. There was one naked man who was chained with his back to a wall, spread-eagled. In front of him stood another man who was chewing on his nipples. He must have been gnawing hard; his captive was twisting violently against his bonds and was protesting loudly.

I ignored them. I was happy to see that the stocks were free. I led Franco up to them. He seemed unsure how to act until I bent over and directed first one, then the other ankle into the holes between the two planks on the floor. I shoved the boards together and latched them securely.

I took the key from around his neck and undid his handcuffs. There were red marks around his wrists where the metal had dug into his flesh. He quickly rubbed the sore areas, taking advantage of his moment of freedom. I wasn't going to give him that much comfort, though.

I put a hand on the back of his neck and pushed him down into the wooden embrace of the stocks. I placed his bruised wrists in their holes. Then I put the second board in place, tightly securing him.

Franco was as defenseless as Barry had been. Franco's ass wasn't as beefy as Barry's; it was more lean, more muscular. I ran a hand over it. He didn't have the same sharp tan line that Barry had either. Obviously, he hadn't spent as much time outdoors.

Franco started at the touch of my palm on his butt. "You don't have any marks here," I said. It was a simple statement of fact. "Why?"

"I don't know what you mean, sir."

"Why hasn't anyone beaten your ass lately, Franco? Have you been such a good boy that your master hasn't had to discipline you?"

Franco seemed to hate the teasing tone more than he minded his confinement. He didn't answer at first. I slapped him hard across the ass, enough to get him to flinch. "Answer my question, Franco."

THE ARENA

"I—I've been well trained, sir. I haven't done anything to get my master angry."

"But he brought you here."

"Because he thinks it's good for me, sir."

"I can't believe he doesn't get some pleasure just from the sight of beating your ass, Franco."

He hesitated again. I slapped him even harder this time. "I think he does, sir—sometimes, at least. But there are other things he likes to do even more."

"I bet there are, Franco." I reached beneath his spread thighs and grabbed hold of Franco's balls. Even while I squeezed them, making Franco writhe from the pressure, I was amazed by how wonderfully satin the ball-sac felt.

I began to jerk the handful of testicles back and forth. "Move your butt for me, Franco. Let me see how nice you can make your butt look."

Franco was a big man, and he carried himself with a firmly masculine air. It was hard for him to swivel his ass the way I wanted him to, the way a cheap slut would do it. I had to yank hard at his balls to get the movements just right, to have his behind circling in the air. His muscles swelled and contracted with the shameful motion. After a while, though, he seemed to get into it. My dark lord Franco began to turn his butt as if he were selling it on a street corner.

I let go of his balls and shoved a finger up his ass. It went right in, no resistance. I used my finger as a new kind of hold to direct Franco's body. He was moving in larger circles now, twisting and turning his butt as far as he could in the enclosure of the stocks.

It was wildly obscene to have control of his body with just my one finger. I could direct him in any way I wanted to. I couldn't linger on and enjoy the sensation, though. My cock was too hungry; it needed attention, and it needed it now.

I pulled my finger out of Franco's ass. I walked around to the front of him and put it between his lips. "Clean it off, Franco. I think I have some of your shit on it."

Franco sucked in my finger. He tried to look up at me, but he couldn't move his head because of the stocks. He moved his eyes up to try to see me. It made his expression look singularly pleading. I liked that look on his face. I also like the way his tongue was moving around my finger while he sucked it.

I stood back and undid my pants. I took a rubber out of my pocket. Then I pulled my slacks and my underwear down to the floor. I unrolled the cool latex over the heated surface of my prick, then shoved it between his lips, right where my finger had just been.

Franco was a better cocksucker than I expected. I didn't suppose he'd had much practice at it in the old days. His new master must have been giving him some good lessons. Someone had undeniably taught him the tricks that were making my cock jump with pleasure.

"I should beat your ass, Franco," I said in a low voice, as harsh sounding as I could make it.

He seemed to speed up his actions when he heard the threat. My cock slipped farther back in his mouth.

"I should leave you with welts all over your butt."

Franco's tongue darted out of his mouth and tried to lick at my balls. It was a good move. It felt magnificent to have this onetime master so desperately trying to please me. I loved the way the threat inspired him.

"I'll send you home tonight with marks on you that won't go away for weeks. Your master will be proud to send you back to the arena after I'm done, Franco. Everyone will think that he's the one who did it. I'm

THE ARENA

going to hurt you so bad you'll be happy to crawl, Franco. You'll be damned happy to be able to crawl."

I kept up the talk while I shoved my cock in and out of his mouth. He continued to try desperately to satisfy me. Even as I spoke, I began to reconsider: maybe I should whip him. Maybe that would give me enough pleasure that I wouldn't worry about the other opportunities here in the arena.

It was the very thought of the options that took me over the line. As soon as those fantasies entered into my mind, I lost the ability to control the vehemence of my sexual desire. I began to shove my cock into Franco even harder, deeper. He choked and made strangling noise as my dick filled up his gullet.

"Take it, Franco, take my load and remember every time you told me I couldn't have yours!"

I shot, every muscle in my body contracting to force the liquid through my cock. I collapsed against the stocks, my dick still in his mouth. I hadn't even noticed doing it, but I'd been playing with my nipples. I stood there with my cock in Franco, my own hands on my chest. I was satisfied—that was for sure—but I was also strangely empty.

I didn't say anything more to him. I got dressed again. I opened the stocks, cuffed his hands back behind him, and picked up the leash. I led him back through the corridors past the cells. They were much busier now that it was later in the evening. I didn't pay any more attention to them this time than I had when I was leading Franco in the other direction only a while earlier.

When we got to the room with the arena in it, I handed the leash to the attendant. I didn't say anything to him or to Franco. I just left, pushing my way through the leather curtains into the front room.

Jacques was still going at it with Chris. My professor was naked this time. I could see the powerful muscles of his arms while he lifted Chris's head up and down on his ebony cock.

They didn't notice me. They were much too involved in their own entertainment. I willed myself to ignore the rest of the men in the room. I walked past them all and into the antechamber that led to the street.

I wanted to get out of that place as much as I wanted to stay. I couldn't deal with the complex emotions it evoked. I just knew that, at that moment, I hated Jacques for having introduced me to it. I also hated him because I was sure he was just as aware of my struggles about it. Jacques could trap me in something much more restraining than a set of wooden stocks. I knew it now.

The next week was hell. I had looked forward to leaving my business and having spare time—something that had been in short supply while I was the head of my own company. Now I hated the lack of daily tasks. I wanted them back. I wanted to have an office to go to, a job to perform, people counting on me. I wanted anything that would stop my daydreams.

They were always about the arena. While I was in conscious control of the images, I would remember only leading Franco into the back rooms of the club. I would just recall putting him into the stocks and standing back to admire my handiwork. When my mind drifted, though, the roles would be changed. I wouldn't be the master holding another man by his cockleash. I would be the naked man who was standing in the arena, anxiously waiting to see who would choose him, and what would happen after the choice had been made.

It didn't help that my cock would become rigid and seep ooze with desire when those images came to my mind. I was upset by them. More than upset, I was terrified of them. There was an allure to the thought of myself as one of the toys of the arena that I hadn't ever thought was inside me.

I cursed Jacques daily, twice daily, three times daily. I was sure my old professor wanted me to react this way. He was manipulating me, playing with my emotions, trying to assert his control over me. I waited for him to call. I wanted to confront him; I wanted him to confront me. If I could only yell at him and tell him to go to hell, to forget his sex games and his mind domination, then perhaps I could exorcise these demons from my head.

I didn't dare call him myself. I went to the phone a few times and once actually dialed his number, but the sound of the ring on the other end of the line was too much for me.

The worst was at night. If my self-image wandered into submission when I daydreamed, it took on diabolical forms when I slept. I would see Jacques as a Santeria priest. I would be bound to his altar. I wasn't unwilling. I wasn't pulling away from him. Instead my cock was hard and erect, standing straight up as though it were longing to merge with him. He was offering his black cock with that violently pink head on it. A long string of come was seeping from its slit, forming a small pool of wetness on my bare belly.

I woke up screaming the first time I had that dream. I was soaked in sweat. I couldn't go back to sleep for hours, frightened that Jacques would conquer my unconscious once more. If I had been rebelling in the dream, I could have taken some solace. If I had been struggling against my bondage, I could have found some strength in myself. None of that happened in that dream, though—not a bit of it. Instead, I stayed there on the stone altar with my erection begging to be taken by Jacques, taken in whatever form he wanted it.

The vision reappeared every night, as soon as I would drift off to sleep. I tried everything to overcome it. I only wanted it to go away. Most important, I wanted to defeat it. My body defeated me instead. Every time I had the dream, I would wake up in wet sheets with my hard cock demanding that I pay attention to what was going on.

But I didn't even know what was going on. I had to do something, though, to regain some perspective on my life.

I finally did make a phone call, but not to Jacques. I called Barry Strum at work. I gave my name to the receptionist and waited while she put me through to his office. I had prepared a whole line for him. I wasn't even sure that he knew who I was. Our relationship in college had never been close. But when he came on the line, he said immediately, "So, Kevin, that was you the other night!"

"Yes." That's all I could get out.

Obviously, Barry didn't find the situation difficult. He laughed out loud, his deep baritone reverberating over the wires. "Jesus, I thought so. I didn't even know.... Hell, let's get together. Come on, let's get together and we'll talk about—" he laughed again—"We'll talk about *things,* Kevin. Let's have a talk about things."

Everyone with a subscription to the college alumni magazine would have known how to get a hold of Barry Strum; we all knew his life story. Damn near everyone in the city knew the whole story. He'd gone from being a star player at school into the professionals. He'd had two glorious seasons, then wrecked his knees in a freak accident. He recovered, but it was the end of his gridiron career.

He didn't walk off the field a defeated man. He'd married the head cheerleader of the college squad, whose father happened to have major bucks. Even if Barry hadn't gotten a signing bonus from the pros that was big enough to secure a decent income for the rest of his life—and he had—he was never going to worry about money.

I doubted he ever needed his father-in-law's help. Barry was big-time in our city. He moved right into a job managing an auto agency. There were lots of people who would buy their cars from him just so they could shake Barry's hand and tell their children about the time he'd won the game against Penn State or scored the last-minute touchdown against the Chicago Bears.

I was surprised that he was able to come over that night. "I get out of here early today, then go to the gym. I can come by, say, at six. How'd that be?"

He showed up right on time, his hair still wet from his shower. I had thought that I'd exaggerated his size in my memory. I hadn't. He was a giant. He stood well over 6'5" and he still carried over three hundred pounds of muscle on his heavy frame. Barry wore a pair of tight stone-washed jeans that showed off his ample butt. He had on a shirt open nearly to his waist that let me see the expanse of his chest and stomach. He had on a set of gold chains, at least four of them. He wore a stylish leather jacket over that, and a pair of aviator sunglasses. He looked just like what he was: the still-in-shape athlete on the make. I could have found a dozen clones of him in every sports bar in the city.

I offered him a beer after he sat down in the living room. "Love one," he said as he took off his jacket

JOHN PRESTON

and his glasses. By the time I'd returned from the kitchen with our drinks, he already had his cock out of his pants. He was sprawled over the black leather couch in front of the picture window overlooking the city, lewdly stroking his hard dick. Barry decided not to wait for preliminaries.

I wasn't sure what to say. I just put down the cans and stood there looking at him. His stomach was clenching while he masturbated, his chest was beginning to heave with his deep breaths. "Working out always leaves me horny, you know? There's the physical turn-on of just doing the stuff yourself, but you also get to look at all the other guys in there, sweating away. It makes me hot."

For me, Barry had always been unattainable in college. He was the one others dreamed of, not the one who sat in your living room whacking his meat. Some long-ago fantasy about the big football player drew me closer to him. I reached over and pushed aside his open shirt and took hold of one of his nipples. It was surprisingly large; well developed wouldn't begin to describe it. The hard flesh protruded from his smooth, beefy chest. I flicked his tit between my fingers, getting a loud gasp of breath in response.

It was only the slightest hint, but I knew what it meant. I took his nipple between my fingers again and began to squeeze. Barry hissed in reaction and lifted his torso up off the leather pillows, asking for more.

I took both tits and began to twist them between my fingernails. I waited for some indication that I was going too far, but there was never any implication that I was doing anything more than Barry wanted—in fact, he wanted it very badly.

The big man got up, moving carefully so my hands

didn't lose contact with his nipples, and slipped onto his knees in front of me. He let go of his dick and tore off his jacket and then his shirt. He unbuckled his pants and pushed them down to the floor. The whole time I kept up the work on his tits—twisting, turning, hurting them. Barry let his cock stick out hard from his groin. He communicated just what he wanted by leaving his dick alone and putting his hands behind his back, offering himself as a supplicant to the tension I was creating on his body.

I was rock-hard from the sight of the jock kneeling before me. I hadn't really understood something the night I'd seen him at the arena. It wasn't just that his cock, balls, and ass were shaved, his whole body was. The skin on his pectorals was as smooth as possible; his legs were as unflawed as fine silk.

Barry leaned forward and pressed his face against my crotch. "Let me have it, Kevin. Let me suck it."

I hadn't even thought this was a possibility when I'd called him, but I couldn't deny my interest as his mouth grabbed hold of my erection and blew hot air on it through the cloth. I thrust my pelvis forward. Barry took that as assent. He brought his hands forward and began to fumble with my belt and zipper. He pulled down my clothes, and my dick sprang to freedom. He moaned at the simple sight of it, then began to lap frantically at my balls.

I rewarded him with renewed pressure on his tits. It wasn't just that I was turned on—I was amazed by how much mistreatment the two lumps of prominent flesh could take. It became a contest. I wanted him to say no. I wanted him to ask me to stop. I pulled at them, dug my nails into them even harder, but all I got were more hisses of sexual delight and his continued shoving his pecs towards me.

The only way I could disappoint this man was to

let go of his nipples. When I did just that, he groaned with frustration. He leaned back away from my balls, leaving a thick coating of saliva all over them. He was back on his haunches, his hands behind himself once more.

"Please, Kevin, please ..."

I kicked off my shoes and stepped out of my pants. I reached over to the table and took out a condom. He seemed disconsolate while he watched me unravel the rubber over my dick, like a small boy whose parent has taken away his favorite toy. But when my cock was well wrapped and I leaned forward, obviously giving him permission to take the length of latex-covered flesh in his mouth, he dove for it.

My body shuddered from the sensation of that so-sensitive part of myself that Barry was consuming. The wet warmth seemed to envelop all of me, not just those inches of blood-filled dick that were packaged by the athlete's mouth.

I was so swept up in the ecstasy of it that I had to reward him. My fingers went back over the slippery surface of his massive chest and found his nipples once more. I began to play with them again. Barry gulped deeper, taking in all of my shaft in his own private delight when he felt my nails once again working him over.

He was a remarkable sight. The gold chains were all that covered the upper half of his body. They had looked foolish before, the ostentation of a too-wealthy young man, but now they had the appearance of necklaces of some slave who had been well trained in some long-past time.

He was enormous, of course, from his athletics. All his beefy muscles were pumped up from the workout he'd just had. His arms were particularly impressive. Thick veins were visible underneath the tight-stretched skin. His belly was surprisingly well muscled for someone who was so large. There were very attractive lines that came down from his broad chest to his narrow waist and then led even more distinctly towards an apex at his hairless crotch.

His thighs were the most developed part of his torso. They were slabs of muscle put together to produce a columnlike effect. All of him was covered with a slight gleam of sweat, just enough to make the surface of his body look even more statuesque.

He moved forward and his hard cock began to rub against my right leg, riding up and down on my shin. He forced his balls against my hard bone and pressed them hard, rubbing his dick against me with long, slow movements.

I wasn't ever in control of the situation, not really. I could feel Barry's cock swelling. I knew he was getting ready to come. I kept on playing with his chest, indulging myself now that I knew there was no limit to how much punishment I could give his nipples. My cock had a mind of its own. It was ballooning, matching the distension of Barry's as he ground it against me.

I felt Barry stiffen. Then the waves of hot come broke against my leg while he pumped away, a dog in heat, an animal in need. The come seemed to splash out from him, gushing from a well deep inside him.

My own orgasm broke at the same time. My body strained against the impending flood. I threw my head back, pulled once more on Barry's tits, then felt myself explode. Barry whined when he realized I was coming. He began to shove himself farther against my crotch, his throat muscles constricting on my suddenly-tender dick. I let my cock pump itself dry, then finally let go of Barry's nipples. I stood back, disengaging even though my dick was still nearly hard.

Barry stayed on his knees, looking up at the condom's reservoir with its cache of slime.

Then he bent over and licked his own come off my leg, catching the streams of the white stuff that were flowing down to my feet. He took the come with long strokes of his tongue. "At least I can still eat my own," he smiled when he was done. He wiped the back of his hand across his lips. "Thanks, Kevin, thanks a lot."

He stood up and stretched. I expected him to get dressed, but instead he untied his shoes and then pulled off his socks and the pants that had gathered around his calves. He gathered me in his tremendous arms and embraced me. "I needed that, Kevin, I really needed that."

Barry sat down on the couch, nude, and played lazily with his cock and balls.

"I didn't even know you were gay," I said. I sat down next to him on the sofa and let the side of his body press against mine. The warm feeling of intimacy made it easier for me to make my confession.

"I wondered about you," he admitted, "just because of you and that econ. prof. You two were always with one another. I figured something had to be going on."

"And you were at it all the time, yourself."

"Just a bit, just the usual stuff; a few blowjobs with a pal when you had too much to drink, a few jerk-off sessions with a guy on the team when you were alone in the shower. Just that, horseplay, nothing serious."

"You got married when you were still in school."

"Hey, still am! Kathy's a great girl, a great wife. She and I are doing just fine." He was bloated with pride.

"With all of this?" I could never understand how a man and a woman could have a relationship that allowed this kind of action. But wasn't that my problem? That I couldn't understand how any *life* could handle this kind of passion?

Barry smiled and put an arm around my shoulder. "I like this," he said simply. He pulled me closer and kissed me for the first time, his mouth sloppy with spit as his tongue explored mine. The other huge arm came around me and pulled me over towards him. I ended up with my back across his lap, his soft dick and balls pressing against me, my arms around his. My mouth moved down over the slick hairless body and found his nipples once again. I sucked them tenderly this time, getting a soft "Oh, yeah!" from him.

I let my embrace relax after a short while and lay back against his thighs. My hands wandered over his body, gliding over the hairlessness of it.

Barry anticipated my need to talk. "All this doesn't mean that I don't get it on with women, Kevin. I do. I had trouble with women when I was young. I used to really envy you, you know that? You were the slick fraternity boy with the right clothes and the right moves. I'd grown up always thinking about how big I was. Everyone was always yelling at me for being awkward, for bumping into things.

"I felt good on the field, but that was the only place. Take me off the field, and I was self-conscious and uncoordinated as you could imagine. Trying to date a girl was torture. I'd stand in front of one of them and ask them to dance, and I didn't know which would be worse, if they turned me down and humiliated me or said yes and then I'd have to go onto the dance floor and everyone could see that I had two left feet and no balance in that small space."

"But you were the big star, the one they all wanted ..."

"Yeah, but I didn't know what to do with it. There

were some women who just wanted to make it with that big star, you know the type. They were rough and they didn't care about how graceful I was; in fact, they wanted it rugged, in a way.

"You know, men were almost as bad. I admitted I jerked off with a couple of guys on the team and even sucked a couple of cocks, but it was only a little easier. At least some of them were as big as I was and I didn't have to feel self-conscious about my size.

"Kathy was the first one to make me feel a difference. Man, if I only understood back then what was happening!" Barry broke into another big laugh; this one shook his body so hard that my head bounced against his belly. "She had me *down*. But we didn't even know it.

"Suddenly there was this little, little person—she's only about five-three—and she was making all my decisions for me. I was so grateful that someone was telling me what to wear, how to act, all of that. I was putty, man, just putty in her hands.

"Sex was something wonderful. She was so small that I always approached her like she was a china doll. Can you imagine this gut on top of a little thing like her? I used to lie on my back and pick her up and gently, gently bring her down on my dick. I was so amazed that she could take it that I didn't dare move fast or anything. I'd just let her take the lead.

"The girl *loved* it that way. She never hesitated—either telling me what to do outside the bedroom or climbing on top of me when we were inside it.

"We didn't know what it was all about, but it worked for us. I was the big buffoon who was willing to do whatever my princess told me to.

"It finally changed when I got into the pros the first year. They've got some heavy hazing in the professionals, really heavy-duty stuff. They have all these young assholes like I was who'd been big deals in college and who were used to star treatment. We had to be put in our place, and there were a lot of the bruisers who were ready to do it, too.

"The first week of training camp was hell. Everything you ever heard of happening in boot camp and more. It was regular humiliation—physical and mental.

"I loved it. I ate it up. I hadn't had so much fun since the first time I had sex with Kathy. My big problem was keeping my dick down. I kept on coming close to throwing hard-ons when I thought about the team doing me, or making me do them.

"Only one guy noticed—Luc—or at least he's the only one I knew who noticed. He wasn't one of the big linemen. He was the smallest guy on the squad. He was the field-goal kicker. He was French; they brought him over from some soccer club in Europe.

"He saw something in all the hazing that interested him. I could tell almost immediately. I was scared shitless. I didn't want anyone to know the games my mind was playing during all of that stuff.

"It was all from having grown up so big, feeling so clumsy. One of the things about football had always been that guys on the field didn't worry about hurting you. They just came at you. They just treated you like a regular guy—less, they treated you like a thing that had to be knocked down and knocked out. It was one place where I didn't have to worry about hurting people, about doing anything that would cause them to get angry with me.

"I even liked it on the field when I got hit. It was like I didn't have to pay attention and could let myself go wild. I was so used to controlling my motions and how I touched people that I felt good when someone would just slam into me and let me have it, let me have it hard.

"Luc understood how all that had mixed in my head. He understood lots. When the guys started to lighten up on the hazing, he just increased it. There wasn't any official reason anymore why I had to take it, but I did. I took whatever he put out.

"It was easy stuff at first, a swipe at my ass with a wet towel when I was coming out of the shower, or else a sucker punch in my gut when I wasn't expecting it. But he kept pressing. He started to get into my room at the camp. He'd play like a drill sergeant, tell me I was slacking off with my exercises, make me do a whole other set of push-ups and sit-ups to make up for what he called my laziness in the gym.

"I didn't just not complain. Man, I fucking *loved* it. I'd wait every night for him to come into my room. I'd find excuses not to be dressed, or just to have on my jock. I got so far into it that I couldn't hide my hard-on.

"Luc just played with me more and more. He moved into sex real easily, without my paying any attention to it. He had a thick uncut cock, and I didn't even think in terms of safety back then. I just took what he offered and took it whenever I could.

"There was something special about how small he was; there was the same kind of special thing that I felt with Kathy, about her being so small but being in charge."

"When did she find out? Did she ever?"

Barry laughed again. "Did she! Let me tell you the whole story, Kevin. Let me tell you the whole thing.

"See, Luc wasn't just fooling around. He knew what was going on. He didn't just want a buddy-fuck on the side, he wanted a slave, the whole thing. He broke me into it slowly, at first, but his demands got bigger and bigger.

"By the time the season started, he'd arranged for us to be roommates; not because we were going to be friends, but because he wanted me there and ready for him whenever he wanted. I didn't have a chance. Everything he was doing to me was stuff so outrageous and so hot I hadn't even considered it before in my life. And that dick of his! Jesus, Kevin, I learned to worship the thing. He could make me cry real tears just begging to let me suck on it.

"I'd wait all day till we were alone so I could get my tongue under his foreskin. I used to plead with him not to wash under there, so I could get a real good taste. I was had, I was owned. Anything Luc wanted, I was going to give him.

"Shaving my body was just a regular hazing thing, at first; they made all the rookies do it. We had to line up in the shower and shave ourselves while the rest of the guys hooted at us. I don't think there's a pro athlete who hasn't gone through that.

"Luc decided that he liked it. He wanted me to stay that way. Kathy knew about the hazing, so she just laughed at me, made fun of my butt feeling like a baby's ass. She actually told me it made my cock look bigger.

"Sometime she must have realized that the other rookies had their hair back on their chests and on their forearms, but she never said anything about that.

"I wasn't even sure if she paid any attention to the bruises that Luc would give me. After all, whenever I was away from her, I was out on the field playing football. A guy gets pretty messed up on the field; just a good practice session can end up with a lot of marks.

"Luc was the one who queered it. He pushed too far, asked too much. He began to send notes to me at home, or leave strange messages on the machine that I could understand—like telling me what was going to happen when we went back on the road—but they made Kathy suspicious.

"I was a mess from it all. I was excited beyond belief by the sex that was happening with Luc, but it was just so far out I couldn't figure out how to handle it. It was like a compulsion, something that had to be done. I had no control whenever Luc would begin to give me orders, but it confused me.

"I was mainly terrified that Kathy would find out. The way I was acting just made her more leery. She began to pay more attention to things, ask more questions, be more distrustful. I picked up on that and became even more skittish around her.

"Finally she just confronted me. She knew something was going on, and she wanted to know what it was. We were at home when it happened, and I just sat down and started to cry—first time I cried that I can remember. I broke a leg in a game against Syracuse once and I never shed a tear, but this time I bawled like a baby. I told her the whole thing. I couldn't stand it anymore. I couldn't stand lying to her.

"I figured she'd toss me out—and when she found out that Luc and I had been having unprotected sex, she nearly did. She got furious. She slapped me across the face—hard, real hard for a little woman like that. She called me every name in the book. She hit me in the gut; she kicked me. I'd never seen her so mad.

"I just got a hard-on. I couldn't believe it, but my cock just sprang up and wouldn't go down. The little lady was throwing a fit, and I loved it.

"She loved it, too. Getting all that anger out just was the best thing she ever felt. She went back to slapping me and kept on going. I didn't do a thing to stop her. I was just as bad as she said I was. I deserved whatever punishment she gave me.

"Somehow we ended up naked on the floor, her on top of me, fucking like we hadn't fucked since we'd been in college.

"That was the last time I had sex without a rubber," he sighed, "and she makes me get tested all the time anyway. But that part turned out okay. Well," he smiled, "every part turned out okay.

"At first I broke off with Luc. I turned into a real wimp at home, doing whatever Kathy said I should do. One of the first things that happened was that I started to let my body hair grow back."

Barry ran a hand down his sleek belly. "The first time Kathy felt the stubble, she threw another fit. She'd be damned if I was going to scratch her. She sent me right into the bathroom to shave it off again. She followed me in and stood there and watched while I did it. She was fascinated, just so turned on she couldn't believe. it. 'Let me see you do your ass,' she whispered. I bent over and then put a leg up on the toilet so I could get everything. That was it for her, seeing me that way. We ended up fucking again.

"Then she started demanding that I confess more. She wanted to hear more details. They were humiliating. I tried to avoid telling her anything, but she insisted. She wanted to know all about my sucking cock, but she was even more interested in knowing about Luc giving me orders. She got real interested in that.

"She said she wanted to 'understand' more about what went on. All I was beginning to understand was that she was wet and ready after all these little disclosures of mine. It finally dawned on me that I was turning her on.

"Once I realized that, I began to play it up. There was nothing more I wanted to do than get her hot and horny. There was no one I wanted to please more. I had started out holding back the details, but I started to give them even more color.

"She began to want to 'see' some of the things I was talking about. I'll never forget the first time she took a belt to my ass. I felt like I was totally dominated, that I'd given up all control I ever had. There was that small woman standing over me with the belt while I was bent over the bed, my ass sticking up in the air, taking whatever she wanted to give me.

"We kept on going. It was slower than with Luc, and it was different, but it became more exciting."

"But the arena? How did you ever——"

Barry put his hand over my mouth. "Let me tell you the whole thing, like I said I would.

"Kathy finally got to admit that she liked these games; she liked them a whole lot. I finally admitted to her that I liked them with her—but I needed them with men, too. She wasn't upset any more. She was into it.

"I went back to Luc, but before Kathy was willing to let that happen, she made a deal. It was kinky enough that Luc went for it. The first part was that she got to watch. He came over to our house, and we drank a bottle of wine. Then he went to work on me right in my own bedroom, with Kathy standing in the corner, silent, watching every damn thing that happened.

"Luc put me through my paces. He tied my hands behind my back then tortured my balls like they've never been hurt before. He had me begging him to stop; tears were running down my face. I had been self-conscious before, about doing all this in front of my wife, but the agony he was causing did away with any little social concern like that. I was hurting, man, I was ready to do anything.

"He wanted to show Kathy just what I was like. He made me beg him to let me suck his dick. He was squeezing my balls like they were little sponges, rolling them hard against each other. I would have asked him for anything to get that pain to stop.

"But, of course, I also did want to suck his dick." Barry laughed at himself. "That's what so much of this is for, so far as I'm concerned. Giving me an excuse to beg for the things I really want. I always wanted Luc's cock. The only difference was, I was admitting it in front of my wife.

"She got to see me swallow the whole thing down. She got to see the way he would shove his cock so far down my throat that I'd gag. The stuff in my belly would come up my throat, and thick ropes of it would drool out of my mouth. She also got to see that I loved sucking dick so much that none of that made me stop. She got to see her big football hero begging for cock and not caring what anyone thought about it.

"Luc had a trick: he would walk around the room while his dick was in my mouth. If I wanted to serve him, I had to hurry along on my knees or else I'd lose it, I'd lose his cock. Once he had put it away when I'd let go, told me I didn't deserve it. The bastard kept his word, too; he put on his clothes, and I was left there with nothing in my mouth. He only had to pull that once to prove to me that he really meant it. I never let it happen again.

"That meant that I'd do anything to keep his cock inside me. I would move along the floor like I was some kind of puppy, some kind of needy animal that couldn't give up the bone it had just found. I didn't care, when I really got into it. I didn't care what I looked like, this big guy scampering all over the floor desperate to keep his French lover's dick in his mouth. I did it. I did anything I had to in order to keep that cock with me.

"Luc ran me ragged. I was sweating like a roast pig when he was done playing his game with me. I was whining, simpering, not even able to say words. I just knew I still had his dick. I had won something.

"He did lots of other things that night in front of Kathy. Lots of things. She got to see me getting fucked. She got to see me spread my ass apart to take his big French tool up my chute. Luc could make me so hot that I didn't even care what she thought when it was over. I barely even knew she was in the room when he was getting dressed, a big proud smirk on his face. He'd proven something to himself. He was happy.

"While he was dressing, I started to get concerned. I couldn't believe I'd let all that go on. I couldn't believe that I'd done it all in front of Kathy. I figured she'd walk on me. I was consumed with that fear, that I had lost my wife by going into that dark world with Luc, by letting her see that side of me.

"But when Luc left, she jumped on me, she was so hot. Afterwards she made me promise the second part: I had to tell her whenever it happened, and I had to tell her everything that happened. She wanted the details and she wanted lots of them."

"Does she know you're here?"

Barry laughed again. "Kevin, she's the one who *made* me come here. I told her I'd seen you at the arena, and we made a bet that you'd call. When you did, she said, I was supposed to come right over and then go home and tell her what happened."

I hated the idea that the picture-perfect Kathy knew about what we'd done, knew that I had been to the arena. But I couldn't let my discomfort get in the way of talking to Barry about the place. I pressed him to tell me how he got there.

"Luc knew some people. They invited us. I was worried—I was still worried in those days about what people thought of me. But the idea was too wonderful—I had to try it out. Kathy said it'd be okay. So I went.

"I walked in and I thought I had gone to heaven. The first night I wanted to climb into the arena. They won't let that happen, though. You have to go through evaluation and training first, to make sure you can be trusted——"

"Evaluation? Hell, I'd think it was enough that you were willing to put yourself through all of that."

"Nah, Kevin, no way. It's a hard row to get to the arena. They make it look easy, at first—inviting you in like it was just some bar down the street or something—but it's not. It's at least as hard as rookie year in football. I had to put out just as much to make the grade at the arena as I did in training camp. But it was worth it. I had a place to take all this stuff, and I could trust them. The only rules they have are for health—Kathy's made that a big deal; you can understand that. And, like I said, they're good about who they let in.

"Even before your friend took you, at least a couple other people had to approve of you. You can't just invite some stranger into the place."

"Jacques told other people he was going to take me there?" I was furious. I felt betrayed.

"You bet. He had to. And once you start going there, they start to monitor you. There are people watching out for you now, waiting to see if you'll go back, waiting to see what you'll do."

"I'm not at all sure I'm going back."

Barry reached down and tenderly cupped my balls in his huge paw. "Why not, Kevin? What happens there that you don't want to face? Seems like you enjoy the scene more than well enough. Wouldn't you like a chance to top other guys the way you did me, even harder? Or what?"

Yeah. *Or what.*

I made my own confessions to Barry. I told him that I was frightened, scared that I was going to be drawn into the place and never find my way out.

"That doesn't have to be a problem, you know." That's all he said while he continued to play with my balls.

The time with him had become tranquil; it seemed as though he was the special kind of fraternity brother I'd always wanted. We talked more about college and joked about what we'd missed out on. I'd played my few sex games only on campus, and Barry even fewer. We hadn't taken advantage of the situation at all.

"Kevin, if I had known what I wanted, I could have shot the moon. I mean, I could have had all of them. They were as stupid as I was; they didn't know what was going on. You, you were a great-looking guy. You would have cleaned up, too. Instead we just fooled around a bit and wasted years."

"Wasted years," was all I could say in response. It sounded like such a sad statement.

"You're happy with all this?" I asked him suddenly, shaking off the melancholy that seemed to be approaching.

"Kevin, I got it all. I got Kathy and all that happens between us. See these chains?" He still had his gold on. "They came after she found out about Luc and me and started to get into it herself. Those are my shackles, she says. One for every year she's in control. It's one of the rules. I can't take them off—only she can—and she only does that when she wants to wrap them around my balls.

"You see my tits? That's from her—from those long, mean fingernails of hers. She's been working on my nipples for years; they're just now getting to the size she likes them, she says.

"The rest of it.... When Luc got traded to another team, Kathy decided she didn't want to deal with any competition anymore. So that's one rule—I can't have any regulars like Luc was, no one who thinks he has a hold on me. Another is that I *have* to get it on with guys every once in a while, just to keep me fresh, she says." He laughed. "Sometimes I think she just likes to hear the dirty stories."

"How often do you go there?" I didn't want to know about any of his boyfriends. I only wanted to know about the place.

"Kathy makes me go pretty often. It helps me learn my lessons, she says, and it keeps me going, keeps me out of trouble looking for dick in other places. If she ever gets the idea that my mind is wandering, or she sees me looking over some guy for too long, she packs me off to the arena to get my butt beat and my cock off.

"Most of the guys go in twice a week, the ones who aren't married and who don't have to travel for work."

I was single. I didn't have a job. I didn't have any responsibilities. I could end up there that often.

"I know some of the guys even live there, full time. A lot of others go in nearly every night."

"Jesus."

I felt a weight falling on me. I had relaxed in the

embrace of this big jock, my newfound college friend, my fraternity brother. I had let a few minutes go by when I thought this was all just a prank that we were playing with one another. Now it was returning, the truth about the arena and what it might mean to me. The idea that there were men who lived there—that I might become one of them—hit me.

"I do know one thing, Kevin," Barry said. He'd turned serious, dropping the good-ol'-boy routine. "You can't stop this. You have to follow it through. Whatever's going on, it's important to you. Get rid of it, or else get into it. Just do something about it."

That sounded right. It was scary. But it sounded like the truth.

I finally called Jacques back again the next day. It seemed that spending the evening with Barry had been a bridge that helped me get over it. I tried to sound cool, distant, when Jacques answered the phone.

"What can I do for you, Kevin?" he asked as though we'd last seen each other at a business meeting.

I'd planned all kinds of declarations, but they escaped me. I just cut to the chase. "I want to go back again."

There was a slight hesitation on the other end of the phone. "We're happy you made that decision."

"All I said is that I want to go back, just once more."

"That would be fine. When?"

Duane answered the door again. He was in another outfit that displayed his pairs of rings. I was even more impressed by them. I tried to imagine what it would feel like to have those metal hoops in my ears and on my chest. Whatever pain the idea conjured up, there was plenty of excitement to balance it.

"Back for more, huh?" Duane smiled as he let me in. I couldn't answer him. It didn't matter that I'd thought about this for days, that I'd fantasized about walking back into the arena. There wasn't any amount of practice that I could have had that could have gotten me over the waves of anxiety that flooded my mind.

Duane smiled when he saw my discomfort. It was a mean smile, a sly one. It was that kind of look people give you when they're sure they know more about you than you know yourself. It was the kind of expression that made you feel like a fool when you realized they were probably right.

At least this time I was better dressed for the occasion. Duane might have been making his cunning judgments about me, but he was also taking in an image that was new to him. I had on my tightest jeans, so worn that the original blue color had almost disappeared. I wore an athletic T-shirt that was molded to my body, showing off my pecs and my overly sensitive nipples through the ribbed fabric. I was wearing engineer boots and my heavy leather jacket. I looked good. If I hadn't believed it, I only had to glance at the way that Duane was studying me to get my proof.

I walked through the second door and looked around the room, trying to find Jacques. As soon as I did, I understood at least one of the ways he'd learned so much about my sexual life. I nearly turned around and left—not the first time I had that desire—but I heard Barry's voice telling me to own up to my feelings. I walked over to the table.

Jacques was talking with a man I'd met at the Nighthawk. I knew him only as Guido. He was one of those who would stand in the darkest corner of the backroom and wait, the way a hunter lies in hiding for his prey. I walked into him a few times—more than a few times. I usually had to be drunk when it happened. Guido played rough, and you didn't offer yourself to the experience unless you had some preparation.

He'd tried to get me to go home with him, but, even drunk, I knew there were good reasons not to. I would put myself into his hands in the backroom only the few times I was ready for him. Every time I did, I knew that my body would be bruised the next day. I knew that I'd be hurt. I knew that I would have a time that was as exciting as I could find in the leather bars of the city. But I also always knew that I couldn't take too much of it. It wasn't just the physical pain that bothered me—in fact, there was something exhilarating about that.

I was worried about something just like this—something like standing in front of Guido and Jacques in a sex club that surpassed my imagination. The adventures I could conceive were extreme enough. My fear was that there were men like this who had envisioned something that went even further than my dreams.

"Have a seat, Kevin," Jacques said pleasantly.

Guido nodded to me. It was just a slight acknowledgment. I thought someone who'd fucked me more than once could have been more friendly.

"We're very happy you decided to return."

"I'm not making any commitments," I reminded him. "I had a good time. I just wanted to come here again."

"Of course." Jacques waved to a waiter who came over and took his order for a round of drinks.

I looked at the man who obviously was with Guido. He was a floor show of his own. He stood behind Guido's chair and stared right back at me, even though he was naked. He had a hard build, but he was actually slight. There seemed to be only sinew and bone about him.

That, and an enormous dick that was rampantly hard. He was that kind of thin man who seemed to have more weight in his cock than anywhere else. His hair was cut very short, almost shaved, and that made his image all the more severe, almost as if he were an inmate in a concentration camp. I couldn't help but eye the thick, long piece of flesh that stood up between his legs. It wasn't circumcised. The long foreskin was stretched over the head of his dick where it was gathered up by a ring that was held in place with a small padlock. His foreskin was pierced; he couldn't have moved it all the way up and down his shaft without removing the padlock, and I was sure that he, himself, didn't have the key. He would be able to move his foreskin a little bit, enough to begin the sensation of pleasure, but there was no way to pull it back from his glans. It was a exquisite kind of bondage, the reality of having someone else in control of one's body and sex.

His balls hung very low in a long elastic sac. His cock was so outsized that it didn't even seem attractive, and his balls were so exposed, they were suspended so far down, that they appeared to be a great vulnerability.

The naked man had his hands behind his back. I could see that they weren't bound there. He stood with his legs spread far apart, as though he were making a presentation of his cock and balls. He didn't convey any sense of embarrassment or awkwardness. He seemed to think this was the most normal thing in the world, to be obedient and nude in a place like this with his prick standing at attention.

Guido seemed to enjoy my interest in his companion. He nonchalantly reached back and grabbed hold of the other man's cock. He pulled the tight foreskin back and forth with casual motions. He man closed his eyes with a bit of gratitude and pleasure.

Guido apparently had made his point. He let go of the swelling tube. The man's face turned from delight to frustration.

"There are limits to the number of times someone can be a guest here. You do understand?"

"Of course I do, Jacques. Are you two the membership committee?"

"We are part of it," Jacques admitted. "But you don't have to go through anything formal this evening. You're here to enjoy yourself. That's just what you should do. Unless——"

"I should have realized there was an 'unless,'" I said suspiciously.

"Nothing needs to happen," Jacques continued. "But, of course, if you feel ready to make a greater dedication to what goes on here——"

"I'm doing as much as I feel comfortable doing," I answered. Our drinks arrived.

Finally Guido spoke. "I'm glad you've come back. I think there are some real possibilities here for you."

I couldn't think of an answer I was willing to articulate. "Let's go for a walk, Kevin, shall we?" Jacques asked.

Guido didn't seem to be very concerned about being left at the table. As soon as Jacques and I stood up, he moved his chair back a bit and his companion immediately fell to his knees between Guido's legs, his hands still behind him. I hadn't realized what Guido was wearing until then. He had on a pair of leather chaps, but without anything else underneath him. His naked crotch had been hidden by the table until he had moved his chair. The heavy dark cock that I'd played with in the shadows of the Nighthawk, but hadn't actually seen very well in that dim light, was naked. The other man began to lick at Guido's balls.

Electric charges seemed to go off in my brain. I remembered the taste and feel of Guido's dick. It hadn't been as huge as the bottom's, but it had been substantial, fleshy, a delight to have in my hand or my mouth. I suddenly felt as though I missed it, the way you remember missing a favorite toy from your youth.

Jacques and I moved through the room. It was more crowded tonight, though there seemed to be less overt action going on. This could have passed for a cocktail hour at a bar, or even a private party, except there were occasionally naked or near-naked men standing in the groups that were talking. I could see flashes of other dicks, the swing of other balls, the exposure of other asses.

The very fact that they were there and available made a difference, I realized. To see displays of sex like that made me want to join in, made me want to have sex in a way that I might have been able to deny in another time and place. It was a question of gradations. In the straight world—in college, for instance—male sex wasn't talked about and didn't seem to be possible. That's why Barry and I had gone so long with so little. Going to a gay bar or party had upped the ante, made sex more possible and, far from satiating the need for it, increased the desire. A bathhouse or a backroom like the Nighthawk's was a further step. Yes, you could get off quickly and efficiently, and that might have been more than enough for others; but it was never a sufficient act for someone who had the hunger that Barry experienced. The added drama and the costuming and posturing, the acts of offering and taking, all produced even greater needs.

I had a sinking sense of inevitability as those thoughts went through my mind. I had begun the trip that was ending here in the arena long ago. I was destined to be here, it seemed. Or, even more upsetting, perhaps there was going to be a place beyond this where I would have to go next.

Jacques led me into the next room and the sudden sight of the men who stood in the arena. They seemed different to me now, less like victims, more intriguing. They even seemed to have a pride about them. That was distressing. It was much more comfortable when I'd thought of them as casualties of some kind of sex game.

Franco was there again. I was relieved, as though his familiarity would make this all a great deal easier. Our eyes met quickly, but he moved his glance away from me, looking back down at the floor. Suddenly he seemed more handsome because of that gesture. I liked seeing him that way, and I liked having him see me while I was wearing my leather jacket. I looked at his cock and saw that it was reacting, arching a little away from his belly. I liked the idea that Franco had responded to me. I liked it a lot.

Jacques didn't even comment on him. Instead he was taken with another black man who stood on the stage, his hands cuffed behind him. There was a dangerous excitement about the picture. To see a naked black man like that was almost too real. It was easy to forget that this was the twentieth century and instead let your mind wander back to another time and place, one where a predicament like the arena would be much more real for a man of color.

The man's body was smooth and nearly hairless.

His legs were especially muscular and his thighs were thick with well-developed muscles. His nipples were flat, a dark burgundy color against the even darker ebony of his skin. I have always thought that the body hair of a black man was particularly attractive, and the kinky bush of hair that crowned his cock and balls was appealing. If Jacques hadn't acted so quickly and called for a leash for his new find, I might have been tempted myself. But when they moved on, into the passageways in the back, I didn't even look over the rest of the men. I just took Franco myself.

He seemed to be resigned to my choosing him. He didn't reveal any emotions as I took a leash and attached it to his ball-ring. He stepped down from the platform and followed me obediently into the back rooms without any comment and certainly without any resistance.

I took him into one of the empty cells. By the time I reached down and unhooked his leash, there certainly was an emotion that was affecting him—he was frightened. He was almost hyperventilating. His chest was expanding and contracting with his sharp breathing. There was a handsome gleam of sweat covering his body, even soaking his chest hair enough to plaster it against his skin.

I nodded toward the platform that stood in the center of the room, and Franco seemed to resign himself further. He moved to the table and sat on it, then sprawled out on his stomach, leaving his beautiful ass sticking up in the air, his hands still cuffed at the small of his back.

I ran a hand down the length of his spine. Starting with his neck, I let my fingers glide over the slick surface skin. The stress and the sweat were combining to produce a strong odor. It wafted up to my nostrils from his underarms and from his crotch. I had a rush of excitement when I realized that he was mine—to do with whatever I chose.

The pornographic fantasies that filled my head were inflaming, but they weren't the real reason I'd come back to this place, and they weren't even the main reason I had chosen Franco without even seriously considering most of the other men who had stood on the stage.

I didn't say anything to Franco. I reached down and took the key from his neck, then used it to unlatch his handcuffs. I used my hands to firmly direct him to turn over on to his back. When he had, I took up the shackles that were attached to each corner of the table and secured them to his wrists and his ankles. When I was done Franco was anchored to the table. I began to run my hands over him again, this time lingering over his hardened nipples, pinching them just enough to get a small hiss of pain from him.

I stood back and took off my leather jacket. I threw it into the corner. I pulled the T-shirt up over my head and then stood there, half-naked. I stared at Franco, letting the difference in our status sink in. I ran a hand over my belly and up over my chest. I could feel my cock filling up the cup of my jockstrap under my jeans. I knew Franco could see the swelling.

I wasn't just showing off, though. I was taking in the picture of Franco's captivity as well. His underarms, since they were forcibly exposed by his bound position, seemed a particularly handsome and accessible part of his body. The dark hair was massed against the pale skin.

The hair on the rest of Franco's body was also handsome. The expanse that covered his chest wasn't very thick, but it was spread nicely over the whole of his upper torso. It all seemed to gather at a point below his pectorals and became a small stream of darkness that fell over his tight stomach and past his navel to spread out again in a rich bush just over his cock and balls.

His balls were too easy a target. I picked them up in one hand and clasped them firmly. The unexpected move was obviously more painful, if no less sexually exciting, than what I'd done to his nipples. Franco nearly cried out, stopping himself just in time by biting hard on his lips.

I enjoyed his response and the way his stomach tensed, his abdominals clenching in sharp relief, but this wasn't my real purpose. I let go of his hair and instead stroked his cock, already half-hard, no matter what kind of ache I'd caused.

Franco finally relaxed. His cock began to swell even more, and soon it stiffened over his belly. A small drop of translucent fluid escaped from the slit at the head. This was how I really wanted him to be.

"How did you get here, Franco?" I asked finally. I kept my voice low, trying to sound calm, trying to remove any threat from the situation. I wanted to seduce him into honesty.

Franco looked at me silently for a moment, but then it seemed that I'd achieved my goal. He seemed willing to talk to me while I continued to caress his hard dick.

"What do you really want to know?" he asked.

"I used to see you at the Nighthawk and the other leather bars. You were the great top back then, Franco. You made me weak in the knees whenever I saw you. You had the heaviest leather, the meanest attitude, the most authentic scowl. You were it, man—you were just what you wanted to be.

"I saw you often enough that I know it wasn't an

act. I saw who you went home with. I saw how you treated them. What happened. That's what I really want to know—what happened to you? My friend said it was love—what does that mean?"

My fingertips were still gliding over his skin, making a few more stops on the harder flesh of his tits. The subtle massaging motions seemed to relax him. My enticement to confession seemed to be working. Other things were working as well: Franco's cock was dripping a string of thick liquid. Some men like talking about sex as much as they like doing it. Maybe Franco was one of them, or maybe just the things I was asking him about were enough to inflame him. Something was working; something was luring him into the open.

"Yeah. I remember you watching me," he admitted. He sighed, as though the memory was one he hadn't uncovered in a long time. "I saw lots of men looking at me. It was one of my kicks.

"I met ... him at the Nighthawk, too. He started to come in almost as regularly as I did. The first time I saw him, I knew he was something I wasn't. I knew he was real. That's the word for it; he was real. I was dressed up. I had the moves. I knew the walk. But he was real.

"He was older than I was. He was good-looking, but he wasn't good-looking the way I was. He had a decent body, but he didn't look as though he just walked out of the gym, the way I looked. He liked that body of his, too. You could tell. He was comfortable with it. It wasn't like the way I saw mine, something that should be shown off like an object. Some nights he'd come in with a leather jacket; some nights he'd arrive with a regular shirt on and a pair of chinos; some summer nights he'd even come in without any shirt on at all, his big chest and his hot tits there for every one to see. He knew he didn't have to show off anything but what he had. That was enough.

"He didn't take the place seriously, either. I thought it was a goddamn church. I went all the time, every night, because I thought it was the most intense place in the city. A bunch of the guys had gotten together and formed a leather group—a support group—we took it all so solemnly that we figured it needed to have a group. We thought we knew it all. We thought that we were the source, the place it all came from. We knew how it was done; we gave lessons; we even had a fucking newsletter to prove how serious we were. We were the ones who were making it all happen.

"He destroyed that illusion, he fucking nuked it. He walked in, and I knew he was real and the rest of us were playing games.

"You know, we had colors, insignia that we wore on our leather jackets. The colors were supposed to be the sign that we were really into it, that we were the real thing, the hot stuff. We said we were using them to identify ourselves to one another and the other men who were into the scene. The colors were supposed to be a badge of honor, something we could be proud of. He made me realize they had all the meaning of a Cub Scout uniform."

I wasn't sure if his cock was jerking because of the special attention I was giving his tits or because of the memory of those first times he saw his master, but I backed off, taking my hands off Franco's body for the first time since I'd bound him to the table. I didn't want s revelations to stop because he came. I wanted him to keep on going.

Franco didn't seem to even notice that I wasn't feeling him up anymore. He didn't seem to care that his wrists and ankles were secured by tight leather restraints. The memory of his man had begun to come to the front of his mind, and all he wanted to do was wallow in it.

"I came on to him. I tried every trick I knew to get his attention. He seemed to think it was cute—that's all, just cute. He would smile strangely when I'd come up and talk to him. He was interested, that's for sure, but I couldn't ever get a take on him.

"Finally I asked him to let me top him. He laughed right in my face.

"'That's what you want to do? Do they teach you that in one of those seminars your group gives? How to top someone?'

"I wasn't going to laugh at all our stuff. I answered him straightforwardly. I said it was just what we were doing. I proved it to him by saying I wanted to negotiate the scene first. He thought that was a joke. I told him I was serious. I'd respect his limits. He looked at me blankly. 'There are no limits, Franco. Just do what you want.'

"'I don't want to violate you,' I said. 'I want you to trust me and know that I respect you.' That was our line, of course; that it was all a mutual thing between consenting adults; no coercion, nothing that would really hurt the identity of the person who was on the bottom.

"'This I gotta see,' he said and he walked out of the door, expecting me to follow.

"Of course I did; that's what I was after. We went back to my place and he stripped as soon as he walked in the door. He refused to even discuss a contract or an agreement. He just wanted to *do it,* he said.

"His body was different from what I expected, what I was used to. It was more comfortable than the other young guys I went with, but solid—he was solid. His muscles looked like they had ripened; they had curves where a younger guy would have had hard edges, but those were real muscles, there was no doubt about it.

"His dick was beautiful—it was fat, not that long, but thick. It had burly blue veins running up and down it. It wasn't hard, but I couldn't wait to make it get that way.

"I went through the whole thing—I knew how to do it, remember? I was in the group. I had taken my lessons."

Franco snorted, as though he were disgusted by his own innocence. "I thought I knew so much.

"I had him tied up and I whipped his butt. I had him lick my boots. I yelled at him. I slapped his face. I spit on him. I did it all.

"He just went through the motions. He just did what I told him and acted as though the whole thing was a laboratory experiment or something, like it was something he wanted to study.

"He didn't get hard until I played with his dick, and then it took a lot to make him shoot.

"I'd been with lots of guys. I'd done that scene with most of them. I'd never been with someone who was so uninvolved with it all. A little bit of pain didn't hurt him very much. If I wanted him to lift up his ass to run my belt over it, he did it. When I said I was going to fuck him, he just pulled the cheeks of his ass apart for me. But he was never into it. Never. He was just walking through it all.

"He got up when we were finished and put on his clothes. 'Interesting.' That's all he said. Then, just as he was leaving, 'See you around, Franco.'

"I'd gotten off, but I stood in my apartment after he left, and I felt like I had missed the train. I had lost something. I hadn't even known what to look for.

My cock may have shot off, but I suddenly knew I had missed the real orgasm."

Franco stopped. He seemed to drift away. He stretched against the restraints, then relaxed again. I felt I was letting him drift too far away. I put my hands back on his warm flesh and began to massage his muscles once more. I was kneading his thighs, those remarkable ropes of muscle that felt so wonderful in my grip. It must have been enough, it must have been what he wanted, because he began to talk again.

"I knew the man had some secret that I didn't have a clue about. I kept on hitting on him at the Nighthawk whenever he showed up. He'd just smile and most often—not always, but most often—he'd let me take him home. He'd go through the motions again for me, but he'd never really react.

"Finally, one night when I came on to him, he just said, 'Aren't you tired of all that? Don't you really want me to do it? I mean, wouldn't you like to know what it's *really* all about?'

"I was fucking furious. *I* knew what it was all about. I was a charter member of the group that did it all. I was the one who was king of the walk at the Nighthawk. And I was the top. Not just with this guy, with *everyone*.

"I told him to fuck off. He just shrugged and walked away from me.

"It started to get to me, every time I'd see him after that. What did he really mean when he'd said he knew what it was really about?

"I swear to God, I never had thought of myself as a bottom before then. I swear to God, I never thought that I wanted anything out of the Nighthawk but a good time and maybe a lover—someone who'd be a partner, an equal partner, just like the romances say you should get.

"This guy ruined me. He had gotten into my head, and he'd messed it up something horrible. What was real, I started to wonder. What was really real?

"I drank more than usual one night at the Nighthawk, and then he walked in. I went up to him and asked him just that: 'What's real?'

"He looked at me and smiled again, but differently than he'd ever done before. 'Real is knowing you need it. Real is having to have to have it so bad you'd do anything to get it. Real is needing it so badly you'll give up everything else to kneel at my feet in front of all these people and beg me for it and be proud that you were doing it.'

"Just like that, he said it all.

"I couldn't even answer. I walked away. The next time I saw him, I was more together. I asked him to go home with me again. He said it would be too boring."

Just saying that word—boring—seemed to take Franco away from me again. I moved my hands up to his chest and pulled at his nipples. It didn't take much to bring him back. I wanted him to be even more engaged though; I wanted this disclosure to keep on going. It was important to me. I had to know what he had gone through.

I leaned forward until my own tits were right at Franco's mouth. He didn't need any encouragement. His thick lips parted, and his pink tongue flew out from between them and began to lick me. The wet touch sent both chills and waves of heat through my body. He sucked on my nearest tit, forcing its hard flesh between his teeth. He began to nibble at the sensitive nubs of my body.

I looked down and saw that not only was his dick hard again, it had sent a new, thicker ribbon of viscous liquid out from the piss slit. I had Franco back now. I pulled away, causing the grip of his teeth to hurt my nipples even more. I wasn't surprised that the sudden sharp feeling was pleasant. It felt so good, in fact, that I nearly bent over so he could chew on the other tit. But that could wait. I might need that to keep both of us going later on.

"So you gave in—so you wouldn't be boring."

"It took a while," he said. That was all. I lifted up his balls and squeezed them gently.

"How long did it take you, Franco?"

"It took a while," he repeated, as though he wouldn't—or couldn't—go on.

I put more pressure on his balls. It was enough to let him know that I wouldn't tolerate his shutting down on me. I wanted the whole story. He winced with pain and began to squirm on the table. "Okay, okay," he said. "I'll tell you about it."

I let go and he relaxed. He didn't take long to start up again.

"It was a showdown; there was no question in my mind about it. Whenever he walked into the Nighthawk after that I went on red alert. I was ready for him. I wasn't going to let a damn thing happen.

"He didn't even seem to notice. Here he was, the biggest thing in my life—sometimes I spent every waking hour wondering what he meant when he said 'real'—and he acted like I wasn't even there.

"It drove me nuts. It drove me nuts to think about what he'd said about me wanting his cock. It was always more than just wanting to suck on him—I understood that.

"He meant control. He meant giving it up to him. Giving it *all* up to him. I started to get hard whenever I saw him and realized that. I started to have strange dreams at night. It used to be that I had dreams about myself in full leather, some stud sucking at me or my dick in his ass, but those dreams all vanished.

"The new dreams were of me naked. Me not being able to move. Me being desperate to make him happy. Me being worried that my asshole wasn't tight enough or my tits weren't hard enough for him. I'd wake up in wet sheets, my prick hard and damp.

"I gave in. Yeah. That's what you can say. I gave in one night. I finally said, 'Let's go.' I meant it to be all there was. I thought that's what he wanted.

"'What?' he asked. 'What are you saying?'

"'I'm saying, let's go,' I repeated. 'I'm willing.'

"He smirked. 'You should never assume that *I'm* willing, Franco. You should always ask if I am. That's an important first step.'

"'Please, let's go,' I finally said.

"'*Beg,* Franco. You have to understand that you have to beg.' His eyes had gotten hard. He wasn't joking. He really expected me to beg for him. I finally did.

"'Please take me.'

"'Take you as what, Franco? A trick? A boyfriend? A pal?'

"I knew none of those were what he had in mind. I knew there what it was that he really wanted by then. I could barely get the words out. 'Take me as your slave,' I finally said.

"It was against all I believed in, because I wasn't saying that he should take me as a slave for the night, just for some playtime. I meant it the way he wanted me to mean it.

"He didn't even respond, he just walked out of the bar. He knew I'd be following.

"As soon as we got outside, he grabbed me and threw me up against the brick wall of the building. Before I even knew what he was doing, he had cuffs on my wrists. Then he tossed me around and reached up and ripped open the front of my T-shirt.

"I got ready for him to go to work on my tits; I figured that's what he was after. I didn't understand. That would have been so minor. What he wanted was for me to walk down the street in front of all the other guys who were going in and out of the bars near there. He wanted them to see me with the handcuffs on and with my shirt torn open. The display was just as important as anything else.

"We went to his place. He made me stand in the middle of the room while he undid the cuffs, took off my clothes, then put the cuffs back on me when I was naked.

"'Now, Franco, remember all the things you did to me and tell me what you thought they were about. Tell me what you thought you were accomplishing.'

"I went through them all. I talked about slapping his butt like it was something to increase his sensitivity.

"'No, Franco,' he said. 'That's not what it's for. I'm going to beat your ass, and I don't care what kind of sensitivity you have. I'm going to do it because it'll make you writhe all over the floor and I like to see that, and because it's going to make your skin red so it feels hot when I fuck it. I think it's more important that I feel good when I fuck you than it is to worry about how much you have to go through to make me feel that way. Don't you agree?'

"That was the start, man; that was the start. Making him feel good was the whole point. I was never going to be a partner or a buddy or any of that. I was his piece of meat. I was 'convenient,' he told me, because I had a couple of holes that came in handy when he wanted to stuff them with something.

"He didn't like my clothes—he didn't like any

clothes—so I had to strip naked whenever I went to my apartment or he came to mine. He could have cared less about the leather jacket with the club colors and everything like that. He just wanted my skin.

"He fucked me like no one else ever had. I realized, finally, that it was because he was just doing it for his own purposes. He wanted it to last a long time, not because he wanted me to get into it, but because it made him feel better. And if it hurt a little bit while he was going at it? Well, it made my ass tighten up—didn't it?—and that was good; it made it better for him.

"And I wanted him to want it. My ass began to feel differently after he'd had it a few times. It started to feel empty whenever there wasn't his dick up it. My tits felt funny if I couldn't feel a little leftover pain from when he used them.

"Things changed inside. He never really humiliated me—not the way some guys do when they're tripping on you, when they just want to create a scene, a little play they can walk through. You can do that easy because you know that's all it is. They call you names, they say you're a piece of shit; you ignore it. It's just something that's going to get them off. Later you can have a beer together and you can forget it all.

"He wasn't willing to take something as little as that. He even talked a bunch of things as though they were compliments—like he'd tell me that it was a good thing I had two holes—my ass and my mouth—so he could use them both. He was happy when I told him it was a gym day because, he said, it meant my pecs would be bigger when he wanted to chew on them.

"It was subtle, the way everything changed, how it was all for his pleasure, and it was even more subtle how I fell into it, how good it became when I realized I was sinking into something.

"That was about the time he really started in on me—slowly at first—but for real."

Franco stopped again. I ran my hands over his chest and slid them through the damp armpit hair. He was just getting ready to move into the most dangerous territory. Suddenly I wasn't sure I wanted him to go there.

"He started by making a few demands. He decided I should wear a collar to the Nighthawk one night, just so people would know I was getting fucked. 'Are you ashamed to have people know I'm dicking you?' he asked me.

"I couldn't stand that idea, because he was also letting me know that, if I was ashamed, we didn't have to do it anymore. Hell, we did too have to do it some more.

"It was the most humiliating thing I had done—up to that point—God, it's hard to believe I actually thought it was humiliating back then—but I did it. I wore a thick dog collar he picked up at a pet store.

"No one said anything. After all, it was supposed to be okay to be a bottom, right?

"He began to escalate everything after that. It was slow. Sometimes it was just his saying things that made me so sad, so sorry I had denied him something. I'd been proud of my tattoos, but when he looked at them he'd seem discouraged. He'd tell me it was a shame I'd gotten them, since it meant that I wasn't a perfectly blank canvas for him to work on. What if they kept him from seeing bruises he made on me? I felt terrible when he'd say something like that. Sometimes I barely understood what had happened. But sometimes it was so heavy I had to admit it.

"He decided once that he wanted to see me without hair on my body—any hair on any of my body. He had me shave off everything—every piece of hair I had. He made a whole scene out of it. First he used clippers and took off most of my hair; then he had me shave the stubble off while I stood in the bathtub and he sat on the toilet next to it and watched. When I was finished, just to make sure it was complete, he ran his hand over every inch of my body, even where my eyebrows had been, and, if he found a rough spot, he cleaned it right off with a razor himself. Then he rubbed me with oil, all over, hard, and often. He had me polished like I was a statue. Then he fucked me right on the bathroom floor.

"He told me it looked so hot I had to show it off. I didn't know just what he meant until he brought out a pair of boxer shorts, white ones, the thick cotton kind, almost gym shorts. He had me put them on. They were so tight it was difficult getting them over my hips. The fly gaped open, and you could see my bare skin where my pubic hair should have been. My cock was pressed against the shorts, and you could make out every single vein on my shaft.

"He put the collar back on and had me pull on my socks and boots. Then he handed me my jacket. Finally he decided that it would finish the whole thing off if I had my heavy black leather belt on. He cinched it across my belly, just leaving it there without any pants. That's what he meant by showing it off. That's how he wanted me to go to the bar that night.

"I begged him not to make me do it. I couldn't stop him though and, when he told me to follow him to his car, I did it. I cried when he pulled into a parking space on the street and I realized he was going to insist that I follow through.

"I was the prize stud. I was the hot one. I was the

guy you and the rest of them used to dream about. Now I was down to a pair of skimpy boxers and not a single hair on my body. He wasn't willing to just let it be. He wanted me to show it off and be proud of it.

"We went into the bar, and the guys who I knew so well were all pretty shocked. But no one said anything. We just stood there and had a couple beers and when the guys came over and talked to me, they looked at me—that was all. They all acted like there was nothing different.

"That didn't seem to make him happy. The next night we went back, but this time he had a new idea. When we got to the front door he said, 'If anyone speaks to you tonight, you just say your master has told you to be silent. That's all you say. Not another word of explanation, nothing.'

"I nearly broke. Somehow I had known there was a new step that was going to take place, I don't know how, but I knew there would be. I just didn't know what that step was going to be. I never expected it to be something like that.

"I complained again, but there was a hardness on him now. 'I told you what to do. If you don't want to do it, you can go home. Home to your own place, not mine, and you can stay there. I'm real; Franco, I never lied to you about that. You've known what I am all along.'

"Then he went inside. I followed him.

"The first guy who came up asked me if I was going to a club meeting the next day. I looked at him for a minute, knowing that he was looking at me, too, and I said what I was supposed to: 'My master has told me to be silent.'

"My friend looked at the two of us and shook his head. He walked away. The scene got repeated all night. Either people I knew would come up to me

THE ARENA

and I would put them off when they tried to talk, or else guys would try to pick me up.

"My man walked away from me in the bar once he knew that I was going to follow orders. He stood in a far corner and observed. There was plenty to see. Once they understood what was happening, a lot of the guys I'd given a hard time came over and tried to get me into trouble, or got me to make my statement just so they could enjoy the role reversal. They loved having me in a place where I had to embarrass myself over and over again. They played it for all it was worth.

"Toward the end of the night, by the time all my buddies understood that I was really into the deep shit with this guy, it was mainly strangers who were coming up to me. Somehow the word spread among them, and they started to make it all work big-time, I mean big-time.

"They'd come up to me and they'd pull at my hairless tits or reach under my shorts and finger my smooth ass, and they'd proposition me. I was into it by then. I was really into it. I wouldn't answer their questions or accept their offers, I'd just stand there and say, over and over again, 'My master has told me to be silent.'

"It made some of them real hot; some of them thought it was funny. They all just came on to me stronger and stronger, harder and harder. He didn't do a thing about it for a long time, he just stood there and watched while a group of them surrounded me and tormented me.

"Finally he did come over. He had a leash in his pocket, one I'd never seen. He attached it to my collar and jerked on it. 'Time to go home, boy,' is all he said. He'd waited till there was a maximum number of people standing around me before he did it. He wanted them all to know.

"I kept silent all the way home in the car. He still had the leash on my collar when we got to his house. I followed him inside obediently. I never thought it through, but I knew what I had to do. When the door closed, I got on my knees and I thanked him. Because I realized I *should* thank him. He had claimed me in front of the whole group, and that was the most important thing he could do for me; claim me as his own.

"I always used to think it would have taken torture to make me into a slave that way. I used to think that I would never give into anything but the worst agony. But that's not true. You give in when you find the right person at the right time. Then you don't even worry about it. You just do it.

"And being the stud? The top cock in a leather bar? That's what I had been, and now I knew it meant nothing. Lots of guys can buy a leather outfit, pick up some attitude, put in a few hours in a gym, and they can be that—it doesn't take much guts to do that. But this was different. I was proud of myself. I'd done things in public and in private that the rest of them wouldn't ever even admit they wanted to do. I had *done* them, and I was damn proud of it. It took a lot more to strip down to that outfit and show off my shaved body in that bar than anything I ever had done before.

"That was another reason to thank him, because he'd given me an opportunity that I wouldn't have known before. Once I got a taste of it, I liked it, I liked it enough that I wanted more. I decided that I wanted whatever it was that he would give me.

"I moved into his house. There was no need to pay rent on my own place. I had no reason for privacy anymore. I had only him.

"A couple of months later, a group of his friends

came over for drinks. He had me serve them naked, just wearing my collar. Even though most of my hair had grown back in, it still felt normal and ... *right* to be nude in front of his friends that way. It's a good thing I thought like that, because it was an ominous occasion.

"They were there to tell him about the arena, this place they were starting up. He thought it was a good idea—it would build my character, he said—and he volunteered me to be the first man they put up on the platform.

"That was how I started here. That's how I came to be here. I had decided that I would do whatever he wanted me to do, and this is what he decided I needed. I obeyed.

"It gives me perspective, he says. It gives me a sense of who I really am."

I was the one who was shaking now. There was a part of Franco's story that I never wanted to understand. I leaned over and put one of my nipples in his mouth. He chewed immediately. I felt the flash of turn-on surge through my body. I wanted to have that feeling, I wanted to have it take my mind out of the place where it was stuck.

I really wanted the old Franco back—that's the one I had always remembered, the one I had seen when I first walked into this place. He was right; it would be much easier to deal with the old Franco—the one with an indifferent posture and a cold bearing, than it was to deal with this new Franco, this man who was willing to turn his body over to his master for the sake of his pleasure. I didn't want to think about these strange men of the arena. I wanted to be back to a safe place, one like the backroom of the Nighthawk.

God! Only a little while earlier, I had thought the

Nighthawk was the most frightening and electrifying place in the world. I thought it was the edge of experience, the cutting edge of what was possible in the sex world. I hadn't been able to handle it unless I was desperately in need, and usually drunk. Now I discovered there was this other world, this arena, and it went beyond my wildest fantasies. Worst: I was tempted by it. The Nighthawk and all the other leather bars in the world were easy to take; they were easy to leave as well. They didn't even ask for your name—you could be there and be totally anonymous. You could be whoever you presented yourself as being. But the arena demanded more.

I stood back and left Franco's mouth empty. I was thankful to have the cool air drift over my wet tit. I started to undo the cuffs that held Franco down to the table. He didn't know what I was up to, but he didn't resist. He was stiff from the prolonged bondage, and it took him a while to get his arms and legs limber again, but he finally followed my lead and stood up.

I went over to the corner and picked up my leather jacket. I brought it over and put it on him. I leaned down and pulled off my boots and my socks. I had him sit on the edge of the platform while I put those on his feet. Then I had him stand up.

He was the image I had dreamed about. This was the safe vision I had of who Franco was. That black jacket against his muscular chest and those boots were the symbols of a leather bar that I needed to see once more. Franco, so recently a bound slave, was once again the black knight in leather that I had worshiped. Now I could go back to that time in our lives again. Now I could do what I was trying to convince myself I really wanted to do, that I could avoid this new temptation of the arena. I would put it out of my mind.

THE ARENA

I sank slowly down onto my knees. Franco's cock bobbed with anticipation as I approached it with my mouth open. I licked at his balls, those low-hanging orbs that fell so beautifully between his full thighs. I was losing myself in this. I had been so foolish when I had put him in the stocks the first time. I had been so wasteful. It was just this; a chance to put a man in a leather jacket in a place that was already infused with its own odors of leather and flesh and indulge myself in him. This was all there was. I began to wonder just where there would be a condom in the cell. I could slip it over the dark red head of Franco's cock and I could——

"Don't you think you should come with me, Kevin?"

Guido's voice broke through my fantasy and hurled me back into this reality, the reality of this place called the arena.

I stood up, a bit of drool running out of the side of my mouth and down over my chin. I looked at him. He was standing on the other side of the bars that encompassed the cell.

I knew instantly what he meant. Even when I was given the power to have a man like this, I expressed the deepest part of my own psyche. I knelt at his feet. I sucked at his balls. I turned him into my master. I looked over at Franco, who seemed to understand as well. He lowered his head; his cock began to shrink. He was waiting for Guido to come in and take him away. And he knew that Guido would take me as well.

And that, as simple as it was, was the first time I walked up onto the arena. It happened quickly, and it happened without another word being exchanged. I had been caught without my mental defenses. I had exposed my innermost self to Franco, and Guido had witnessed it.

It was, after all, why I had come back to the arena, wasn't it? If I hadn't really wanted to do this thing, I wouldn't have passed through the doors again. I would have stayed on the outside. If I hadn't wanted to be a part of this, I would have been happy to dismiss the men who came here as sick, or at least twisted or, perhaps, I could just have said that they were into something that I wasn't.

But I wasn't able to do any of that. I returned here because it enticed me. I came back to the arena because it put on exhibit things that I hadn't even allowed myself to imagine. Once I had been forced to witness them, then I had no choice but to understand that they were temptations that I wanted to taste. It had been foolish to avoid them, to try to deny them.

The temptations were cock. They were other men's desires. They were spiked sensations that didn't fit into the definitions of either pain or pleasure. They were the ordeal of having my facades torn away from me. They were the temptations of becoming something new and different for other men, of having my ass and mouth used at their will, of having my body aflame with feelings—good or bad—every night.

Those were the temptations to which I suddenly knew I had to surrender. Perhaps Jacques was right; perhaps I would have a genius for this. I didn't know. But I had to find out.

Guido had come into the cell and had undone my pants and pulled them and my jockstrap off me. I was naked. He ran a hand over my body and then he confided to me, "We knew." I understood. I finally abdicated. I didn't argue with him.

He put one of those horrible ball-straps on me. I

felt, for the first time, the grip of the leather as it tightened around my scrotum. There was another pair of handcuffs as well. My hands were secured behind my back, and one of the thin metal necklaces with the handcuff key went around my neck, just like the other men who stood in the arena.

Guido did his work quickly and efficiently. In no time, Franco and I were both being led down the corridors, past the other cells from which came a symphony of moans of distress and pleasure. We were lead into the room where the arena was. I stepped up, no longer questioning the rightness of all this. I stood beside Franco and I watched while Guido undid the leashes and then stepped back to look over his handiwork. He was pleased.

"We can touch each other," Franco whispered to me. "They like it, actually. And it makes things easier."

Easier.... What a word to use! It had been easier to get to this place than I ever could have known. It had been much easier to give in and admit I was fascinated by this platform and what it felt like to stand on it than it had been to fight the invitation to climb up here. I understood more than I ever had before—about myself, about sex, about what Jacques had wanted from me.

I was standing naked in the arena, and I was terrified of what was going to come, of what was going to happen to me. What was unexpected was my response to the terror. I was mesmerized by it. I loved it. It was making me feel more alive than I'd felt in years.

I hadn't spent much time in the room. I had only been through quickly. Before, I'd been here to pick up a man. I'd taken whom I'd wanted and gone on my way, to the back. I hadn't actually observed the way the arena worked. That ignorance threw a new layer of fright over me. I would have panicked, but Franco moved closer to me.

His lips grazed mine. He moved so that our chests rubbed against one another. The slight feel of his nipples barely moving against mine was charged with sexuality. His cock was getting hard again. Its knob moved against my thighs and I was humiliated to sense that my own dick was stiffening.

He took his lips away from mine and moved his face down to lick at my nipples. I pushed my chest out, making it easier for him to find the tit he was searching for. He sucked it in and played with it for a while. Then he stood up straight.

I was getting off on the idea that we could touch, but not with our hands. Both of us had our wrists fastened behind us. The usual way we could stroke one another was taken away. We had to improvise; we had to use all of our bodies to sense each other.

Our cocks extended to their full length. They stretched up, hard against each other's stomachs. Franco began to move his hips lewdly, just the way I'd made him do it when he'd been in the stocks, rotating his midsection so it pushed and pulled against my own.

We began to whisper again, "I told you, they like it. They like to see our dicks hard. They like us to be ready for them."

Before I could even think to answer, there were suddenly people in front of us. "Don't look at them," Franco whispered. "Don't even think about them. We're doing the right thing, getting hard, turning them on...."

He shoved his erection against me again, and I met his thrust. Vague thoughts were trying to escape from the back of my mind. Why was it so easy to do

THE ARENA

all this? Why wasn't I rebelling? What was it that made me like having those strange men watch while I exhibited myself this way?

Someone moved up onto the stage with us. At first I thought it must be someone who was coming to claim one of us. My balls shrunk; they tried to pull themselves up into my belly for protection. Then I looked over and realized it was Duane, the doorman.

He smiled at us paternally, like a coach happy that his team was doing a good job on the field. He reached down and took hold of both of our sets of balls, one in each palm. He pressed them, but not painfully, just firmly enough to let us feel his control. His smile widened.

Duane used his grip to pull us apart. He was also forcing us down. Franco and I both knew what he wanted. We knelt in front of him. He unzipped his leather pants and pulled out his cock and balls. There were even more piercings. A heavy gold ring was embedded in the head of his dick. Another dug into his flesh at the base of his cock, where the bottom of his shaft met his balls. When I followed the lead of his hand and began to lick his testicles, I discovered still another ring on the other side of his sac, just between it and the crack of his ass.

"Eat up, boys," Duane whispered. "Show the nice men how hungry you are."

And I *was* hungry. I slurped at Duane's metal rings and tasted the salt from the skin of his balls. I could smell the ripeness of his ass, and I felt deprived that I couldn't get my tongue to go in there to give me a taste of it.

"I can't see their assholes," a voice said from behind us. "Get their legs spread apart."

I didn't have to receive any special instructions. I was into this scene now. I moved my legs backwards and spread my knees as far apart as I could. As I was licking away at Duane's body, I pictured how my own asshole was exposed. All the men were looking at me. I remembered back to all the times I'd stood in the backrooms of leather bars and been groped in the dark. That had been so minor, so inconsequential. I was in the light now, my butt displayed for onlookers whom I couldn't even see.

I knew that their view was unhindered. They could see the wrinkled skin of my asshole. They could see the line of flesh that bisected my testicles and then moved past my balls and disappeared in my anus. My balls were hanging free. They could see that they were good sized, that they were desirable.

I felt a swell of pride. I was good looking when I was kneeling like this, wasn't I? And I was the center of attention. I reached down with my handcuffed hands and was able to get a grip on the two mounds of my asscheeks and pull them even farther apart. I was rewarded with a lecherous whistle from the audience. There was another one in a moment, and I realized that Franco must have done the same thing, or something similar.

We had the crowd even more interested now. I could sense bodies moving toward us, stepping up onto the arena platform. They surrounded us; I didn't know how many there were. I could feel denim- and leather-covered legs moving against my naked back. It was intoxicating. I was drunk like I'd never been before. There was something especially exciting about having my hands cuffed and being naked on my knees in front of these men whose faces I hadn't even seen.

A strange hand explored the crevice of my ass, one of its leather-gloved fingers pushing against my sphincter. Another reached over my shoulder and punished one of my tits. Someone was jealous of the attention my tongue was giving Duane; he roughly tore me away from the doorman's balls and confronted me with a commanding erection, covered with latex, insisting that I take care of it.

I dove on the fleshy length and tasted the antiseptic flavor of the condom, then was rewarded with the salty smell of his crotch as my nose pushed against his pubic hairs. He grabbed my hair and used it as a lead to abruptly pull me away from Duane and Franco. I was shoved up against the brick wall at the back of the arena. He began to fuck my mouth, slamming my head against the brick over and over again.

There wasn't any way to catch my breath or do anything but offer up myself for his assault. I felt my insides churn. A bitter batch of bile forced its way up my throat. I choked on it. He didn't slow his fucking movements. The viscous fluid only encouraged my aggressor, acting like a lubricant, making it easier for his cock to shove past my guarding throat muscles.

My guts went through agony, and more bile was pumped up from my belly. It filled my mouth, made me feel disgusting, ran down out of the corners of my mouth and onto my chest. The man liked that. He kept up the attack.

I could finally sense his cock beginning to swell even more inside its condom. Its head, with a big, fat knob, was beginning to inflate with his blood lust. One last shove, provoking one last wave of bile, and he was pulsing his come into the reservoir at the end of the rubber. Only when the last of his contractions was done did he pull out.

I wanted to look at him, to see what this top man who had so easily and thoughtlessly abused me looked like. But I didn't have time. There was another condom-wrapped dick pressing between my lips before I could calm the heaving of my chest. Even while I was sucking at the new—and thankfully smaller—dick, I could feel other hands once again roaming over my body. But I realized that this time these weren't aimless investigations. The hands were seeking out my balls. Even as I began to choke on the new cock, someone was attaching a leather leash to my sac.

This time my fear wasn't apparent at all. I had become so consumed by the experience that I was unable to worry. I was only drunk with the awareness that I was being chosen. The game of dressing up Franco in my leather jacket was nothing compared to this reality: I was being chosen. I wasn't going to direct the action. I was going to be taken into the backrooms, and I didn't have any idea what was going to happen to me. I sunk into the reality. I collapsed into the fact of it all. I was a slave of the arena, and I was being claimed.

The two men pushed and pulled me through the corridors. We didn't go far, only to one of the first cells inside the back of the arena. There weren't any comforting words for me—and I realized there wouldn't be in this place. I wasn't there to be comforted.

"Good one," one of the men said.

"Great ass," the other one agreed.

I flushed with pride. I did have a great ass—it was my most obvious attribute—yet, as much as I would study it in the mirror in my own privacy, I had never felt comfortable flaunting it. Now I didn't have to worry about that. These men were going to do that for me.

I finally had a chance to look at the two men. They were in their late thirties, I thought. They both had substantial bellies on them—firm, big, round

stomachs that were covered by worn flannel sh.
These guys weren't wasting any of their time workin₃
out on Nautilus machines. They weren't flabby,
though. I could sense the strength in their bodies as
they pressed against me.

One of them pulled on the leash on my balls and
dragged on it painfully, forcing me to follow him to
the corner of the cell. He took off the key to my
handcuffs and undid them. I was free for only the few
seconds it took him to connect my wrists to shackles
that were attached to the wall. He bent down and
captured my ankles in other restraints, leaving me
spread-eagled, stomach against the brick.

"Very nice ass," he said. He slapped my butt, hard.
The sting of his palm left a hot impression on my
skin. I didn't recoil from the pain. Instead I pushed
backwards, lecherously offering my butt for more.
He gave it to me. I barely caught the transition from
the hard bites of his hand to the sharper pain of his
friend's belt.

Before long, without their having to tell me what
to do, I was moving my ass for them. True, sometimes I was trying to avoid at least a few of the blows,
but other times I actually was trying to meet some of
the others. I would dance between wanting to escape
the kiss of the leather and trying to accept it.

I did well by them. Both of them seemed to think so.
The two men kept shouting encouragement—telling
me how good my ass looked, how quickly I moved,
how nicely the color was coming to my flesh. I wanted
them to be happy that way. I wanted it so badly, I didn't
even notice that I was crying. Tears were running down
my cheeks like small rivers.

They liked that dance of mine. One of them
reached down and released my ankles from their
bondage. They laughed, now I could have more free-

dom to move while the belt continued its caresses. I tried to be strong and keep my back to them, but any hope of escaping the belt became too strong a force. I began to twist around, first one way, then the other. I escaped nothing. The belt would avoid my ass, but I'd find its embrace pounding on the front of my thighs, my stomach, my hips.

My tears didn't mean a thing to the men, except a bit of entertainment. I bit my lips hard trying not to scream out. I could taste blood as it slipped down my throat. Finally I had to scream. I had to. The pain was too intense.

The belt stopped. My chest continued to heave and I kept on crying as the men undid my wrists. I fell to the floor, trying to protect myself for that one moment. They wouldn't have any of that. They grabbed my arms and pulled me back up, pressing their heavy bodies against me so that I was crushed between them and the brick wall.

Fingers wandered over my burning flesh. My skin felt as if it was on fire, as though the whipping were still going on. My whole body was receiving more stimulation than I could handle. Parts of my brain seemed to be shutting off from all of it. One finger began to fuck me. A mouth began to chew on one of my tits. They eased up the pressure again, and I immediately got back into their rhythm. I just started to flow with them all over again. I was crying, but I was still feeling as though I had been honored by this attention.

"I want the ass, man, I want that ass." One of the men stood back and looked at me. He had his cock out of his denim jeans and was playing with it. It looked like some kind of weapon, blunt and broad, thicker than I had ever thought a man's dick could be. It was uncut, and the stringy fluid was being

THE ARENA

trapped by his foreskin and making the dense knob glisten in the reddish light.

"Spread for my buddy, guy, come on, spread for him," the other one was saying. I wasn't quite sure what he wanted me to do, even though I knew I wanted to do it. He helped me out. He pushed down until my knees were bent, but not so far that I was on the floor. He guided my hands to my butt so I could spread the cheeks aside again. I was facing both of them. They wanted this fuck to be face-to-face. I was going to look into the eyes of my assailant, and this spectator. I knew they wanted me to be involved; those tears weren't a veil that could keep me from being part of it. I didn't even think when I stuck a finger up my ass and felt the wetness of my hole. I wanted them to see me doing that, I wanted them to see that I was still ready, even though I had begged them to stop only a few minutes earlier.

That was how they wanted me. That was the way I was going to get fucked. The first man moved toward me, ripping a condom package open with his teeth and then rolling the latex over his dick.

He ducked down a little bit as he came at me, just enough to let his hard dick hook up behind my legs. He hefted me up with his thighs, rubbing my back against the brick wall. I could feel his bulky cock press against my ass and then, with all the strength and weight he had behind it, the erect dick shoved its way up my ass. It was a spiked pain, an invasion as harsh as any I'd ever had. I cried out in a burst of agony.

He didn't care. He just started to slam me against the wall, using his powerful leg muscles to stretch me open and force me to take him. He got his arms around my waist and held me up a little higher, to give himself better access to me.

I thought my insides were going to fall out. I tried to fight him a little bit at one point, but his buddy just moved in and helped him splay me open. Somehow the three of us moved to the platform in the middle of the cell, and I was forced down on it.

His buddy got behind me and got hold of my ankles. He lifted them up over my head and then apart. I had no choice but try to fight him—it was an animal's bid for survival, not a rational man's decision—but I couldn't do much, given the way he was gripping me. My knees pressed down against my collarbone. The first man continued his invasion of my asshole. Now, with my legs forced up and apart, there wasn't any protection against him at all. There was nothing to keep him from enjoying himself in every way he wanted.

He finally came. I waited for my legs to be allowed to relax, but that wasn't their plan. They switched roles. My legs stayed up in the air, one cock painfully popped out of my butt, another one smoothly slipped into my well-stretched ass. The fucking started all over again.

The biggest surprise was that, when they were finished, when I had collapsed onto the floor, curled up to protect myself, I still felt chosen. I savored the rank odor of our sex as they peeled off their condoms and threw them aside. Their sweat and their come were perfumes in that room to me then, even though I couldn't breathe steadily yet. I had been chosen. I had been successful.

"Good piece, Duane," one of them said. "But you better take him and clean him up."

Duane took me to a strangely antiseptic locker room off to the side of the arena and led me into the large open shower area. I barely registered that he stripped

THE ARENA

his own clothes off until I could feel the warm metal of his cock piercing pressing against my naked hip. It felt reassuring, wonderfully sexual. Even though my skin was flaming, I liked the added excitement of his touch. He moved a bit, reaching behind me to turn the shower on. The rings on his tits pressed against my chest, and one of his earrings brushed against my cheek. There was metal and sex in this man—hardness—but especially sex.

My dick filled up quickly and pressed against the warmth of his belly. He smiled at me. Then the water came on. There were three showerheads in the open space; all of them began to pour a torrent onto our bodies.

Duane soaped his hands and began to lather me up. The suds spread across his own body. We moved against one another, slipping and sliding against one another's skin. I wanted him to do something about my cock. I had never known so much need to have an orgasm before.

Duane's face moved forward, and his lips found mine. Even as he ran his rough hands over my sensitive skin, I could only feel the heat of his growing dick as it met my own lust. I remembered what it had been like to stand on the platform with Franco and to tease one another's bodies for the other's enjoyment. The memory jolted me with an even more powerful sexual need.

I began to writhe against Duane. I wanted to move down, to take his cock in my mouth. I started to, but his hands stopped me as soon as he realized where I was headed. He wouldn't let me move. I realized that we shouldn't, that we should stand there and hope that some of the members of the arena would come in and see the two of us consumed with our own special heat.

There wasn't any warning when I shot. I usually have plenty of signs that it's going to happen, but this time I had become one with my dick and there wasn't any way my mind could register my cock as something separate. I could only *do*. I didn't have that kind of separation between brain and body when the muscular spasms shook me. The come just plunged out of me, shooting up between my belly and Duane's, losing itself in the flow of the shower.

The orgasm took over all my being. My legs shook, my belly clenched, my arms spasmed. I screamed out. I whimpered. I yelled. I cried.

Duane boosted me up. He held me while I slowly regained my strength, at least enough that I could stand on my own.

When I was able, I reached up and kissed him on the lips, softly, just a small gesture to tell him thanks.

That smile had never left his face.

"Now you're going to become one of my boys," he said. "I can tell you're going to be a good one. You're going to be a very good boy, aren't you?"

I didn't have any sense of fear the next time I went to the door of the arena. I was more than merely calm. I was doing what I needed to do. I was doing what was natural to me.

I had waited until Duane had called me, as he promised he would. He told me the day and hour that I was expected to present myself. It hadn't been much of a wait, just long enough to keep my anticipation at peak level.

Duane had told me that clothes weren't going to be important; in fact, the fewer I wore, the better. The faster I could strip, he'd said, the easier it would be. I knocked on the door wearing only my jeans and a polo shirt, shoes, and socks—no underwear.

I usually wore jockey shorts, tight briefs of one sort or another. I was used to my cock and balls being balled up in the gentle embrace of a cotton pouch. Having them hanging loose this way proved to be all the more sensual because of the change from the usual. I could feel my cock swinging half-hard as I stood there and waited for someone to answer. I probably would have been that excited in any event, but with the lack of anything really constricting, I was able to feel the sensation of my dick rubbing against the denim and my balls squeezing themselves against my thighs.

I didn't know the man who answered the door. He evidently knew me. He opened it wide and then let me into the vestibule. Only after he'd securely relocked the first door did he open the second and let me into the club.

I was struck by the stale odor of the place. Without the bodies in it, the musty aroma of old booze and the moldy smell of tobacco seemed so much less alive than the place I had been to before. The room was also strangely silent. I had been here only when music had been playing, I realized. The man at the door motioned for me to go in, farther into the club. When I did, I could see Duane waiting for me on the other side of the room.

He looked regal—that's the only word for it. He was naked, sitting on one of the platforms that lined the place. He had his feet up on the surface, his knees were apart so I could see just how aristocratic his piercings were. He had added something to them. Two small chains connected two sets of rings. One chain ran from a ring that cut through one tit to the ring that punctured the other. Then, at his crotch, another chain was attached to the ring in his cock-head. It went down to the ring inserted in his flesh where his balls and shaft met and then continued farther, to the ring that cut through him between his balls and his ass.

I walked over to Duane and waited for him to say something. "Wait until everyone is here." That was all he had to tell me. I stood there, my hands behind my back in my own version of what should be an appropriate stance.

Another man was already there; I was standing beside Chris, the blond youth that Jacques had picked out the first night I had come here. Of course, I remembered that someone had called him "an apprentice." That was precisely the term that Duane used when he explained what this next step would be for me.

Duane was, he'd said, the trainer of the arena. He was the one who was entrusted by the members to sort through the applicants who would serve them and then make sure that those men had what was necessary before they were used. He always waited until there were enough men involved to make it worth his while—until there was a class of novices to introduce to the arena. I had been waiting for him to put his new group together, and Chris and I were obviously part of it.

I heard some noise behind me. Someone else had entered the room. I fought my curiosity and didn't turn. I didn't get to see who he was until he was standing beside me, as obediently silent as I was. It was the black man, the second choice that Jacques had made in front of me. I had heard someone call him Alex.

I felt as if I was positioned between the extremes of masculine attractiveness. Chris's blondness wasn't just a question of hair color. He was wearing an athletic T-shirt, and it was possible to see the light-colored smoothness of his skin under the straps. His pectorals were curved sculptures of flesh. His blue eyes were darker than you might expect, but the feathery traces of his facial hair were as delicate as you could hope for.

The other man was handsome in a totally different way. Chris might have gracefully rounded muscles; this man's torso was hard and massive. His skin was as dark as Chris's was light—so dark, in fact, that parts of it appeared to have a purple hue. His face was strikingly handsome, showing the attractiveness of some African king's lineage.

We didn't speak. We waited. Duane nonchalantly handled his cock and balls, playing with his chains. I could feel my dick getting hard over his display and over the sight of his cock stiffening itself from his manipulations. He was toying with us, I suspected, just letting us see his magnificent cock and balls, knowing that we were probably going to taste them soon.

Duane had one of those long cocks that had a nice shaft to it and then was crowned by a mushroom-like knob that was much broader than the shank. Duane's balls hung low. I wondered what the weight of the chain felt like. It pulled down his skin where it was attached to his body, but not so much that his cock couldn't rise up when it was getting erect.

I wouldn't have thought about those things before all this began to happen to me. I would have seen a man's naked genitals only if he were involved in some lewd show in a men's room or in a sex bar. If I had been in bed with a trick or a lover, I would have had a good look, of course, but it would have been so private—and so controlled—that I don't think I could really have gotten into his dick. I was certainly doing that with Duane's. I could taste it, it was so real to me. I watched a minute pearl of liquid form at the piss-slit, and I was thirsty for it. Duane's cock was more real to me than any other I had thought of for years.

When the door was answered for the fourth time, it was apparent that all of us who were expected were finally gathered together. The newcomer wasn't familiar. He was, though, the most attractive of us all and, in some way, the one least likely to be standing here.

He wasn't very tall, about my own height. He had jet-black hair. His skin was unflawed, so smooth it made me want to reach out and touch it, just to know what it would actually feel like. The most amazing thing about him was his eyebrows. They were like small wings spreading out across his face. I'd seen older men with expansive eyebrows, but no one as young as this guy. And I realized he was young—probably the youngest of us all, no more than twenty-five. That was part of the attraction of his skin, its promise of youth and freshness.

He was wearing only a T-shirt and I could see a small tattoo on one of his biceps, a pink triangle. It excited me, as though that political statement was part of his entire sexual testimony. It was all part of him, I realized, and he was willing to declare it.

There was one thing that was particularly intimidating about him. He was the least frightened of us. Chris and Alex had the same discomfort about them that I felt in myself. As nonchalant as we were trying to appear, anyone could tell that we were uncomfortable here. We were excited; we were being swept up in something. This man seemed much less uncomfortable. He was a natural, I understood. He belonged. Then another thought whispered across my mind: I belonged here as well. This man was my brother. This man was my partner. He knew something that I was beginning to understand. He, above everyone else, was the person I needed to talk to. He could explain things to me. No, that wasn't quite right. He and I could share experiences together. We were after the same thing. He was further along in his discovery, but he was looking for the same goal.

"Take off your clothes." Duane said it very informally.

We all pulled our shirts off, kicked off our shoes, and then undid our pants and bent over to remove our socks. It was nothing, just a few guys stripping down, the way we would have done in a locker room.

I checked out the others when they got naked. Chris and Alex were what I had assumed: they were handsome, each in his own way. But the new guy—the one I automatically thought of as Irish—was stunning.

His body was a study for an exquisite piece of sculpture. Every part of him seemed perfectly formed and it flowed together with every other part to make a whole that was as close to perfect as a human torso could be.

"You gentlemen all have some experience of this place," Duane began. He jumped off the platform and let his chains clink as he stood up. He ran a hand over his bare belly; it was curiously exotic to see him do that. I was surprised that I even noted his action, after all he had been sitting there nude with his metal decorations for quite some time—I was learning that nakedness wasn't necessarily the most sexual way a man could act.

"You have agreed that you want to explore the arena and your place in it. We've agreed that you can do that.

"You were looked over before you walked in the

door the first time. There are always scouts for the arena out in the community looking for new recruits. The members of this place have a big appetite for new meat, and there aren't many men who can sustain the effort of being what we call the volunteers of the place.

"You probably realize that you were seduced by being brought here. No one told you then that you were a candidate for the arena. It was just something they wanted you to see. When you first came here you were even invited to use the ... facilities. There wasn't anything that was denied you. You got to experience the rush of picking out a man in the arena, of seeing the elaborate floor shows the members enjoy watching, all of it.

"You weren't told that you were aspirants for playing those roles yourselves because we already knew that it was possible. You had already been judged.

"Are any of you surprised by any of this?"

I wasn't, at least I couldn't say that any of it was a revelation. Jacques had implied as much to me before. Certainly Guido, Franco, and even Duane had never expressed any incredulity over what had gone on. Still, I found it frightening that I had been studied for so long. Knowing that I was a specimen to these men—something that had been studied and evaluated without my knowledge—was the most extreme submission I could imagine. The savage beating I'd gotten from the two men that last night at the arena was nothing compared to the offense of being analyzed by strangers I hadn't even known were looking at me. I wondered how many people were under that kind of observation. What would they feel like if they knew there were men who prowled through the backrooms and the baths, the bars and the parties, looking for someone to be snatched and brought to a place like this?

I kept my eyes on Duane and his magical nakedness, but I could sense that the other three men were squirming a bit. Maybe the scrutiny they'd been subjected to hadn't been quite so apparent to them until now. I wondered what I would have felt like if this had been the first time I'd heard that story. I could imagine that the others might think they'd been betrayed, and part of me felt that way, but perhaps they felt the other emotion I did, that they'd been found.

"It's pretty, Kevin." Duane was standing in front of me and was handling my hard dick. My thoughts had left it standing up perpendicular to my belly. The touch of his palm over the straining glans was a small ecstasy. He reached over to the strange man, the Irishman, and grabbed hold of his cock, too. It was as hard as mine. We stood there and let Duane touch us. "Yours is good and solid, too, Sean," Duane said. I felt as though some message was going between Sean and me, some communication was going from my dick to his, carried there through Duane's body. Sean liked this as much as I did; that's the message I was getting.

Duane let go of our cocks and moved back, leaving the two of us standing there. At least I knew his name now. Sean, as Irish as I'd expected. I looked down at his hard-on and saw a nice Celtic member, a flesh-and-pink staff that did the Emerald Isle proud. What I liked best was that Sean didn't seem the least self-conscious about it. He seemed to be showy, as if he enjoyed having Duane tell him that his erection was something that was appreciated.

"Since no one's speaking up, I'm going to assume that means you're all happy to be here."

Duane smiled at his own proclamation; he thought it was amusing.

"You have all been told the same thing. You are to go through your period of apprenticeship under my supervision. You're going to be taught your place in this world that we've constructed at the arena, and you're going to be taught to enjoy it.

"The whole point of the arena is to be a space where the stupid restrictions of society are swept away. The rules on which you men have based your lives don't exist anymore.

"The arena is a place where the subservience of a group of men to others is a great good. You might have thought that it was humiliating and horrible to think of yourselves as subjects, slaves to other men's desires. It might have been some kind of weakness in your mind to conceive of yourselves as objects that a master might enjoy playing with. Forget it. Forget it all. You're now in a place that exists only because you are obedient servants. You are the reason that the arena can exist. You should be proud of it, not ashamed.

"And you should be proud that this is no little playground for men who have a few games to play. The arena may be the other side of that mirror, but trust me; it's real.

"Your being here means you've agreed to the basic rules of the arena. One of them is that there are no rules, none in terms of what can be done to you. Oh, you won't be exposed to disease, and you won't be maimed or permanently marked without your agreement, but there is nothing that a member can't do to you when you—as a volunteer—are inside these walls.

"You have no privacy. You are allowed no restrictions. You have no rights. No one is going to treat you like a potential lover. No one cares if your feelings are hurt, no more than they care if your body is bruised.

THE ARENA

"Just because a stupid, repressive society thinks that sex has to be attached to romance, that's no reason for you to expect it to be true. Just because that same society thinks that you have an intrinsic right to privacy, that doesn't mean we're going to respect it. Just because some fool decided that men aren't sex objects, that doesn't mean we're going to buy into that stipulation.

"In fact, the one thing you're going to learn from your time in these lessons and your time as a volunteer in the arena is to appreciate and even esteem just what a beautiful sex object your body is. And we're going to let you use one another to learn that lesson right from the beginning."

Duane had been pacing back and forth in front of the line of us while he spoke. Now he stopped, right in front of me. "Kevin, just how handsome do you think these men are?"

I looked over the other three standing in a row. "Very."

"It's a shame you've been denied men as handsome as this in your life, isn't it?"

This was like a fraternity initiation. I flashed that, to carry this off, these other men must have gone through something just like it at another time in their lives. Besides Duane, there were five other men in the room in addition to the four of us apprentices. They weren't nude, they were all wearing those leather pouches, and some of them also had on armbands or wristlets or other metal or leather decorations. I wondered if men could put other men through an ordeal like this if they hadn't been through it themselves.

"I've always wanted men like this," I admitted.

"And you've wanted them to want you, too; isn't that so?"

"Yes." I didn't have to equivocate for a second. I knew it was true.

"What part of them do you like, Kevin?" Duane spoke in a way that assured me that he wasn't trying to trap me.

I looked at the three naked men and wondered if there wasn't any part of them that I didn't like. They were so different, but each one was definitely an archetype of the range of men I found attractive.

"You three!" Duane suddenly said to them. "You're being examined. A man is looking at you. Why are you just standing there stupidly? Why aren't you showing yourselves off? There might be something that Kevin would like that he can't see from this point of view. Why aren't you trying to give him what he wants? Don't you know that's why you're here?"

Before any of them could respond, Duane walked over to Sean. "This one, Kevin, what do you like about this one?" He took hold of Sean's shoulders and began to turn him around slowly so I could see him in profile and from the rear. I stopped him.

"His ass." It's true. That heroic Gaelic dick was certainly wonderful, and its glory was shown off by its still-hard state; but when Duane turned Sean around and I saw his butt, I knew that it was remarkable.

Sean had a sharp tan line. He'd worn briefs to the beach, and they'd left only his mounds uncolored by the sun. The difference in color made his ass stand out even more. It was a *gorgeous* ass. There were deep dimples in both sides. The two halves were rounded, so that they stuck out from the rest of his physique. Like the rest of his body, there was little hair; there wasn't a single blemish on his butt that I could see.

"If this were the rest of the world, you couldn't really look at Sean's ass, could you, Kevin?"

"No," I said softly.

"But this is the arena. Here you can certainly look at it. Would you like an even better view?"

"Yes."

Duane shoved Sean towards the platform where he himself had sat at the beginning of the night. Sean climbed up on it and took a position on his hands and knees. Duane thrust Sean's thighs apart, as far as they could spread.

"But you can't really appreciate this ass unless you have something to compare it to, can you, Kevin?" Duane didn't wait for an answer. He looked at the other two. "Get up here. Take this position. Show Kevin what you have."

Chris and Alex both moved quickly. There were the three of them—all three of their asses—sprawled out for my admiration.

"Don't hesitate, Kevin." Duane spoke more softly now; there wasn't that air of authority he'd had when he'd given the others their orders. "This is for you, this time. Go on, go on up to them and test them. See just what it is that you love about Sean's ass and make sure that's the one you think is so special. Are you really sure that it's better than the other two? Let's go, Kevin. Let's go look."

Duane guided me up to the edge of the platform. I realized that the smells of the arena were coming to life. Perhaps it had been dank with the odor of leftover vices—sex, drink, tobacco—but now the aroma of the three men and their spread asses was filling the space. My nostrils came alive with the stimulation. Duane had me stand directly in front of Sean. I was surprised—and more than a little pleased—to see that the cleft of his ass wasn't as smooth as the rest of his body. There was a surprisingly thick lining of dark brown hair that ran up the length of the crevice.

I had been so taken by his hard cock when he had been standing up before that I hadn't really savored how low his balls hung. Now I could see that they descended far down from his torso and swung easily in their supple sac. They were covered with a nice pelt of hair as well; again, one that was richer than I would have expected from the smoothness of the rest of his body. These details of body hair seemed all the more distinctive because of the contrast.

"It is beautiful, isn't it?" Duane asked, his voice becoming almost a whisper now. "But is it really more beautiful than Alex's?"

I let him move me over gently to look at the muscular expanse of the black man's ass. The comparison was difficult to make; the two men looked so different. Where Sean presented two white globes of flesh, Alex showed off an expanse of ebony skin. While Sean's private hair had been an unexpected pelt of smooth dark strands, Alex's was a thicket of tight black curls.

"Or Chris's?"

Duane had me stand in front of the blond boy. Even between his ass, his hair seemed to be an adolescent's. It was fuzzy, so light you could only make out some of it because of the way the light fell on it.

"I don't think you should trust your sight to make this decision, Kevin," Duane said now. "These men have such beautiful bodies, you should taste them, you should get in close enough to enjoy just what they have to offer."

Duane put a hand on the back of my neck and pushed down. "Lick them, Kevin, get a taste of them."

He guided my mouth so it rested just below Chris's

asshole. My nose was assaulted by the rich smell. My tongue ran over the soft skin right at the top of his scrotum. Chris even tasted young; he even tasted blond, clean.

I used my tongue to lift up his balls, and they fell into my mouth. My face was still buried in between his asscheeks. "Good," Duane was saying. "Get into them."

I did. I sucked on his testicles and savored the velvet flesh.

Duane wanted me to explore more. He still had his hand on the back of my neck. He maneuvered my face away from Chris and in between the larger spheres of Alex's ass. Chris's butt had felt firm, in a youthful way. Alex's was hard, masculine. There was nothing soft or giving about the ample muscles on his body. He tasted hard, too; an almost metallic flavor came from his skin. His balls were much bigger than Chris's. They were drawn up to his body more tightly as well, leaving his scrotum with a tautly wrinkled surface.

"Yes, another good one," Duane said.

He moved me again. Now I was lapping away at the line of pelt between Sean's butt. This flavor was different, once again, from the other two. He was more responsive as well. Chris and Alex had stayed in their positions and accepted my attentions, but they hadn't expressed any reaction to the intimate exploration I'd been making with my face and mouth. Sean wanted us all to know that something was happening and that he enjoyed it.

He moaned slightly at first, but that murmur grew in intensity as he and I both became more involved with the physical sensation of his display and my investigation.

"Very good," Duane said, slapping one of Sean's

asscheeks in encouragement. "You're both very good."

When Duane pulled me back, I was ready to fight him. Having my face buried in Sean's fragrant butt was one of the most inspiring moments of my life. I didn't want it to be taken away from me.

"But you don't want to just have this part of the fun, do you, Kevin?" Duane teased me. "Don't you want to know what the whole thing is like?"

He wasn't looking for an answer; he certainly didn't wait for one. It took me a moment to realize that he was positioning me so that I would get up on the platform myself, so I would be on my hands and knees just like the other three.

"This is a good way for you to get to know one another," Duane said as he pulled Chris down on to the floor. "You're going to be like a pack of dogs, you should get to know one another's odors. You shouldn't have any secrets from one another. You're going to be spending a lot of time together, and this is a great start."

I felt the warm wetness of Chris's breath against my own asshole. There was a moment of extreme defensiveness, a moment when I thought I wanted to close myself shut and keep anyone from getting to know me this closely. But this was the arena. This is what I'd come here for. I wanted men to know me. I wanted them all to enjoy me. I relaxed and I could feel Chris's face moving tighter between the two halves of my ass. I could feel my butt quiver a little bit, but I didn't worry about it. I thought it must have felt good to Chris, to have that trembling flesh massage his face.

We were going to live in the arena for two weeks. "Then we'll see what we can do with you," Duane

THE ARENA

explained. Before any other decisions could be made, though, we had to go through that period under his close supervision.

We knew that privacy was the last thing we were ever going to get at the arena. It was still a shock when we were led to our quarters. The men who resided in the arena all shared a single large room. They had no beds, but slept on pallets that lined the walls. There were no blankets; they weren't needed in the warm humidity.

There was no solitude for any other function, either. The toilets were all exposed, lined up with a couple of urinals in the same room as the shower, just off our sleeping area.

Clothes weren't even a thought. "You're always attainable," Duane explained. "There's no need for you to cover anything up."

We were available to anyone who wanted us. The men who worked at the arena were our masters; not just the attendants I'd seen in the front rooms when they'd been dressed in nothing but a slight leather pouch to cover their genitals, but also the ones who worked behind the scenes.

There was kitchen help to prepare food. There were delivery men who had to know about at least some of the secrets of the arena. There were men who came in during the early morning hours and cleaned. They were all to be served, and who would be better to serve them than the new class of initiates that Duane was teaching?

"If any one of you so much as hints at stalling when you think one of these men wants you, then you're out of here. Each one of you is nothing more than a couple of holes with some interesting attachments that some men might want to play with. Remember that. Forget your ideas of who should or might play with your body. *Anyone* can play with your body. The reason you're here right now is to teach you to be happy with that fact. You've been holding back your asses and your mouths and your pricks for too long and from too many men. You thought they were special, something you should save up for some exclusive moment. Well, that's over. You're sluts here, the most common piece of ass any of the rest of us is ever going to find. We're going to take you, so you might as well give it to us."

There had been something about the situation of the arena at night that had given the rooms something graceful. When someone took you from the arena, you were able to have fantasies—of being a warrior who was being used by his victorious captors, or of being a slave in the household of a sophisticated master. There was a sense of being, well, a luxury for the men who used you.

But the workmen of the arena were crass when they grabbed us for sex. They weren't all comfortable with all that went on, and they would often laugh nervously when they came across us naked. They were often coarse in the way they would make us come to them.

The first afternoon I was at the arena as an apprentice, three young men, barely out of adolescence, were working on the wiring of the main room. They laughed when they saw me. "Come and suck a big one!" one of them said. He grabbed his crotch and pulled it into a tight package. I was embarrassed at first, but then remembered that this was one of the reasons I was here. No matter how roughly put, he had the right to tell me do just that: to suck him off.

I moved over to him and his friends while they continued to laugh. The one who'd called me snorted while I fell on my knees in front of him.

"They said you gotta use a condom," one of the others said.

"So give me one," my master demanded. I could hear plastic being torn and then the sound of his zipper being opened. He was awkward about putting on the safe, but he finally did it. Then he pulled me by the hair and forced his dick down my throat.

The other two didn't speak, nor did they really join in. They did undo their pants eventually. They began to stroke their hard cocks silently, being turned on by watching the ritual going on in front of them. They moved in closer to me, their legs straddling my kneeling body as my head continued to pull and suck at their friend's dick.

I could feel the soft skin of their cocks as the heads began to rub against my hair. Every once in a while, a set of balls would brush against my neck. When my master came in his condom, the warm pulses of liquid pushing against the plastic, his guttural sounds seemed to evoke their own passion in his friends. In minutes they were moaning as well. My master wouldn't let his cock out of my mouth while his comrades were so close. He held me tight until the first man, then the second one sent waves of hot body liquids spurting over my shoulders. Then my master did take off his condom. He poured its slimy contents on me, letting the cooled fluid join his friends' loads. All that ooze ran down my chest and back.

Only then was I released. The trio was done. They quietly stuffed their cocks back into their pants, and I was amused to see that they seemed to be flustered by me now. I had seen something private that they weren't sure they wanted another man to observe. I felt my own little victory over their discomfort, stood up calmly, and proudly walked away from them.

John Preston

Sean was standing in a doorway on the other side of the room. I could see him leaning against the wall. His cock was partially swollen, and I knew it was because he had viewed the whole scene. I studied him as I walked closer, seeing how low his balls hung down, especially one of them that descended much farther than the other. Franco had said it was all right to touch when it would excite the members, but there were no members here. No matter how much I wanted Sean, I knew that my desire was going to have to wait. Of course, it was probable that my desires could never match his.

"It's really not a waste," he said to me when I got close enough. I wasn't sure what he meant at first. "Whatever helps you learn is a good thing. It'll make you stronger." He didn't explain any further, but stood up, away from the wall, and walked with me back into the other room.

The way those workmen treated us was vulgar, but their vulgarity was the point. Who were we, Duane was saying, to think that we deserved anything else? We were only the students—why should we expect to be used only by the nobles? Even more: look at what we had deprived ourselves of by not seeing that these possibilities for sexual use were all around us. Why had we been so foolish that we had held out our asses and our mouths from these men who were so appreciative?

Duane would have us sit in a group and talk about the men we'd met and the ones that we knew were coming back. Coarse confessions of what turned us on were the important thing; there was nothing subtle about who we were or what we did, nor should there be anything elusive about how we talked about it.

"Those painters are coming back today," Duane said once. "They thought you had a great butt, Chris. I think you better be prepared for some more attention from them."

There was no acceptable response to a statement like that except "That's good." Chris knew enough to make it.

"What are you going to do to get ready for them? They'll be here by ten."

A deep red blush spread across Chris's golden chest. "I better get myself cleaned out. Then greased up."

"Good. Do it deep. Maybe you can get Alex to help you. Alex, will you get Chris's hole ready for the painters? Make sure there's plenty of oil. I think all three of them are going to want to have a go at him."

We all walked into the toilet area. There were long metal tubes that could be easily attached to the showerheads. Duane, Sean, and I sat there and watched while Alex took one of the tubes and carefully attached it to the water supply. He studiously regulated the flow of liquid, making sure it would be strong enough to do the job, not too much to do any harm. Just as carefully, he adjusted the temperature of the water. He lubricated the metal head and gestured to Chris to come over to him.

The blond man obediently bent over and even pulled apart the halves of his ass for Alex. The metal dildo brought an expression of pain to Chris's face while it invaded his anus, but there was no other reaction. Alex let the water flow into Chris. I could actually see his stomach bloating. At precisely the right moment, Alex removed the nozzle, and the trapped fluid erupted out of Chris's rear end. No one commented. No one judged. Alex turned the hose onto the floor and flushed the filthy residue down the drains. Then he repeated his ceremony once again. Then again. He did it until the water that escaped Chris was pure and clean, proof that Chris's ass was ready for the men who were coming to use him.

Then Alex took a container of grease and began to apply it to Chris's blond bottom. The black man carefully separated the pink cheeks of Chris's ass and moved two fingers into the crease between them. The clean pink hole seemed to be astonishingly small, too small to take anything as large as Alex's hands. But it was so elastic when it was being manipulated this way. My cock rose up with excitement as I saw the grease disappear inside Chris. He was being prepared—he was getting himself ready, and his friend was helping him. I looked over at Sean and wondered when we would be able to share an experience like this one. I wanted it to happen. But we were in training, and our training told us that we were supposed to be looking for others' pleasure. There were the painters to think about, after all, and that was our focus.

My hard-on wasn't going to be ignored, though. After all the years of hiding what turned me on, I now found myself standing in front of a group of men with an erect dick pushing up, almost pointing at my navel. It was a strange sensation. Wouldn't you think that a man as sexually experienced as I would have known what it felt like to have an erection? But, in fact, a hard-on like that is usually held; it was usually caressed and protected by my own hands or someone else's. I hadn't really known what it felt like to have a stiff dick standing so exposed. The weight of it was incredible. It pulled on its roots, causing a slight ache in my belly. My balls were tightened up as well, lifting themselves up as though they'd like to hide in the cavity of my abdomen.

Everyone always talks about a hard dick as a weapon, a symbol of masculine power that could be used as a tool, even as a club. God knows I had enough men whack me on the face with their dicks when I was trying to suck them. The hard-on I had now wasn't the same, though. It was a great vulnerability. It pained me—physically and mentally. It felt overexposed. I thought it would hurt me.

And it was hungry. It was famished. It wanted to taste the touch of another man, to have the protection of an asshole. It wanted to be slicked up with spit. It wanted to be cradled in a palm. It was need, blind need, a need to connect with another person, not to feel this loneliness, this susceptibility.

The painters were immigrants—from Bulgaria, I think. None of them spoke the best English, but they didn't need to do that to let us know what they were after. They loved Chris for his blondness, as though it were a rare thing they'd been deprived of for all their lives.

They hurried through their work, eyeing the naked golden-skinned man whenever they could and chattering away when they did get a glimpse of his nude body. There must have been some agreement as to how much they had to do before they could take their break and assault Chris, because there was no other signal when they came down off their ladders and moved towards him.

I could see Chris tense at first, anyone would have when three such large men approached with such obvious gusto. They pulled off their overalls and stripped down quickly. They were speaking in their native tongue, laughing, joking with one another. The first one undressed started to play with Chris's tits. They quickly stood out from his chest in a way that was obviously irresistible to the Bulgarian. He leaned over and began to chew on them hard enough to force Chris to wince in pain.

The other two joined them quickly, their thick uncut cocks spearheading the way. The laughter increased as their fingers began to shove their way into Chris's asshole. The blond man understood his role; he spread his legs even farther to invite a deeper invasion. They obviously liked the response and the greasy layer of lubricant that Alex had left up Chris's asshole. The condoms came out quickly. It was a shame to see the sloppy uncircumcised cocks disappear under the latex coverings. Chris didn't let his disappointment show; he just continued to accept their interest, trying in every way he could to make their enjoyment more complete.

That's what Duane was teaching us to do: If someone played with your nipples, you were supposed to push your chest out to make it easier. If a man explored your ass, then you were supposed to take a pose that made it easier for him. If another man wanted to feel your balls—even if you knew he was going to use them for an easy form of torture—your only response was to thrust your pelvis forward to give him a better grip.

If there was a hesitation, then there was also a response from Duane. It was always a threat to have whoever was reluctant thrown out. "You don't have to be here," he would always say. "At least, I don't care if you're here. But if you want to stay here, then you're going to do it by my rules."

Duane's threats never involved violence. It would have been useless. After all, violence was something that we learned to live with every day. Savagery was nothing more than another way the men who came into the arena might want to enjoy us.

THE ARENA

Duane took all four of us through every cell in the place, and he put us into every possible situation we might ever find ourselves in. He had a diabolical way of finding out what we needed to experience. After we'd been given a preliminary tour, he asked us what had scared each of us the most. I admitted that the stocks that had turned me on so much when I had been in charge were the most frightening. I had loved putting Franco in their clutches, but I was terrified of being trapped in them myself.

Duane smiled and immediately took me to the big room. I was sweating while he put my arms and legs in the stocks. I could smell the sourness that my body was giving off. Being captured inside the device was as horrible as I had imagined. It wasn't just the bondage, but also the posture that I was left in; bent at the waist, my ass spread apart, my hands unable to protect me. Duane told the other three to feel what my capture felt like to them, to actually feel me in the stocks so they might have some sense of what their future masters were going to experience when they were in this same position.

Their hands moved across my body. I couldn't turn my head enough to see who was doing what, but someone was pinching my nipples, someone else was playing with my balls, someone else was running fingers along the crack of my ass. The entrapment made the sensations seem even more overwhelming. I was at their mercy; there was nothing I could do but yell, beg them to stop.

Even that wasn't going to be possible. I had never had one of those terrible ball-gags in my mouth before, the kind I had seen the first night I had been in the arena. Now Duane forced my jaw open and put one between my legs. I fought it a little at first, mainly because it was so unexpected, it was something I hadn't anticipated. But I gave in quickly. Duane applied the straps while the rest of them continued to handle my body. I couldn't have made any sound that made any sense. Even if anyone would have responded to whatever pleas I might make, it was going to be impossible to let them know there was something wrong.

The hands continued to explore me, to poke, prod, invade me. Whoever was playing with my nipples began to work at them harder, pulling them, twisting them. I couldn't help screaming at the pain. I thought the muffled sounds of my distress might mean something to whoever was working on me, but of course he didn't pay any attention. Nor did the vain attempts to contort my body let me escape his assault.

I remembered the desperate sounds the man with the gag had made that first night, how incomprehensible they had been. I wasn't there to tell someone that something was too much, that he had gone too far. I was there to endure. That was my fate. There was no use in fighting it.

The sharp smell of my body got stronger. I could feel sweat running down from my armpits, along my chest, onto my belly, some drops of it falling to the floor. The fingers became even more cruel. I screamed again, I thought louder, but the ball-gag kept the sounds all at one pitch, an animallike moan.

Tears began to flow down my face, and they, too, dropped onto the floor. I twisted every way I could, but there was no escaping the three pairs of hands that were continuing their offensive. The fingers in my ass went deeper, were joined by others. I was being spread apart. The ones that grasped my balls clutched them harder.

And always, continually, those on my chest dug

harder, hurt more, made me revolt more. But my rebellion was purposeless. I knew that. Then suddenly, I began to *feel* it. I was sobbing now, the tears cascading from my eyes and a line of drool threading out of the edges of my mouth. I began to feel how ridiculous it would be to rebel anymore. My chest began to relax. My breathing came more easily. The pain didn't go away—far from it. The wave of calm that was coming over my body seemed to provoke my attackers to try to make me experience the pain even more. But I had submitted.

When I did, I became my tits. I blocked out the sensations of my ass and my balls, I forgot my nakedness, I didn't fight against my defenselessness. I became my nipples. Those two pieces of flesh defined me. The pain didn't evaporate, but it became a part of me. It became warm. I focused so much on my tits that I could actually envision the fingers that were digging into them. I could sense the actual fingernails that were straining against them. The heat flowed from my nipples into the rest of my body.

I began to sense that there was someone there who understood how important those two small parts of me were. He was a master at his exploitation of my senses. He *knew* what it was like to have all of one's self be so central to one's being. He *understood*.

When I realized that, I also realized that it was Sean who was doing it. I knew that he was the one who understood how important this was to me. Duane had known I had a problem, and he knew the way to get me past it was to put me in the stocks; but only Sean could have understood what else had to be done to free me.

My tears became gentle. They were a rainfall now, not a storm. I began to move my ass about as much as I could, as much as I had made Franco do it when

I had put him in this apparatus. I was going to be like him; I knew it. Franco and Sean and I were all going to be alike.

The warmth continued to spread all over my body.

It's unfair to say that there was violence in all of this. I want to clarify that statement. Violence lay on the very periphery of everything we did and everything that happened to us, but there was no brutality. Our wills weren't being broken. We weren't being threatened. We had all chosen to be here, after all, and we were constantly reminded of that choice. If we were led up to the barriers we had allowed into our minds and we were forced to crash through them, we were still the ones who had to do the work. We were never thrown through our bourgeois barricades. We were only shown where they were. We weren't shoved past any boundaries; we were just allowed to see that they existed.

A cry here, a moan, a physical response to intense pressure or experience—yes, those happened. But we weren't being broken down. This was no boot camp where we were being forced to change into someone else's image of ourselves.

Far from it. Far, far from it. We were often treated as the luxurious playthings that we were. We were never exhausted, for instance. We were never driven to an extreme where sleep was impossible. In fact, Duane would often dismiss one or all of us to sleep when he thought that we had gone through enough to deserve it. We were not only clean, we were kept clean. We didn't have to wash ourselves. The attendants would come in and stand with us under the showers or put us in bathtubs and soak us. When we were done, they would massage us, oil our skin, shampoo our hair, shave our beards. We might be the holes for the workmen, but we were also the prized possessions of the enterprise. We were the new ones, the fresh ones, the ones that the members would soon be using.

That was the most important thing on our minds. After the first week, the members were made aware of us. It was torture of a new form, indignity of a new degree.

All four of us were led into the front room of the arena. We could see that there was a sign over a large wooden block that now dominated the room. It read: NEW MEAT. Each of us had a leather hood put on his head. Then our hands were held behind us and were attached to the wooden structure. Our ankles were secured with shackles that left our legs spread apart. We were left there. The hoods muffled the sounds around us. I could barely tell when music was finally turned on in the room. I could hardly sense when there were other bodies moving closer to us.

Since I was deprived of my senses, I was shocked every time someone came up to explore and evaluate me. There would be little or no warning before hands were moving across my belly or fingers were pushing into my asshole.

I had used to love the anonymity of the men with whom I had sex in the leather bars. I liked the cloak that the alcohol had usually given me when I stumbled blindly into their backrooms. I could deal with only my own fantasies; I never had to acknowledge that I was the fantasy for any of my partners. Now, without any element of choice left to me, without any ability to judge who my masters were or what they looked like, I was forced into a new realm, one where I was truly the object.

The night seemed to take forever. There was no relief, not for hours. I stood with my arms behind me, my scabbed nipples twisted and squeezed by strangers, my cock and balls caressed by men I couldn't even imagine.

When it was finally over, we were left with our hoods on and hands connected behind our backs while attendants took us from the front room and back to our sleeping quarters. That one night we were secured to our pallets with shackles. We were left in our darkness. We were left blind, our hearing impaired. It was still another night of passage for me. Once again I faced new demons as one part of me left my body and something else new came in. Because, while I began the night full of dread and fear, by the end of it I was calm, more than relaxed. I was succumbing to still another level of experience. I was entering the arena, but not an arena defined by the walls of this building. I was entering my own arena, one where a mask was welcome, where any master was desirable, where all experience was seductive.

The next morning, I was calm. Duane came into our sleeping quarters and removed our hoods. He undid our restraints. We stood up, rubbing our wrists and stretching our bodies. All four of us had smiles on our faces, I realized.

Duane led us into the showers, and we all washed ourselves and each other. I didn't hesitate to touch Sean's body now. Whatever I had been afraid of was gone.

He had remarkably white skin, skin so pale that it made the black hair of his body seem even darker. I rubbed soapsuds into his chest and felt the thickness of his pelt. His two nipples were as well—used and sore as mine, but he didn't move away when I moved a palm over each of them. His cock got hard, in fact, lifting up from the nest of his low-hanging balls and pushing its thick glans against my abdomen.

He was rubbing my upper arms while I did that, softly, gently. We were soon both covered with suds. Duane had to speak to us a couple times before we came out of our dream state and rinsed our bodies off under the warm shower.

There were attendants waiting for us with thick towels. They came up and began to rub us dry. It didn't bother any of us—certainly not me, certainly not Sean. I could see him watching me at one point, as though he wanted to observe even more of my body.

The days at the arena became easier. They were more tranquil, no matter how severe the sexual action was. I could sense that the other three initiates were sinking into the arena's world with me.

I had learned to accept something. My jaws would always ache from being stretched over so many cocks all day long. My ass was always going to have a burning sensation from the number of times that dildos and cocks and fingers and even fists went in it. My nipples were always going to be scabbed, no matter how often the attendants applied ointment to them. Those sensations were a part of my life now, as was the odor of pubic hair, the smell of men's balls, the aroma of their assholes, the perfume of their sweat. Those were my realities. Those were who I was becoming.

It became easier to accept all the attention I received. I was even better about the workmen, not even noticing if they were vulgar in their approaches. I knew only that they had cocks and I had places for those cocks to go. I smiled even when I was insulted by their immature behavior.

Most of all, I became closer to the other apprentices. One afternoon Chris and I were given over to being used by the kitchen crew. They came at us with the pungent odors of food preparation all over them. They were playful. They had decided to use the food they were fixing as sex toys. Chris and I were fucked by bloated eggplants. We sucked cucumbers. We had strawberries shoved up our asses and then were forced to eat them. Two men poured custard sauce over themselves and made us lick it out of their pubic hair and off their cocks and balls. We were paddled by spatulas; our tits were twisted in presses.

Sex took on the flavors of cooking. Grease hung in the air. The young men's laughter bounced off the enamel walls of the kitchen. In the end we were both fucked, both of us thrown across the big table in the center of the room. Without being told to, Chris and I reached for one another and kissed. His tongue was a warm smoothness in the midst of the rough treatment the rest of my body was getting.

The workers seemed to think that our affection was charming. They applauded it and then turned it into something to entertain themselves, forcing Chris and me to kiss more deeply, even while they slapped our bodies.

They were finally done. Chris and I didn't seem to be. There was something between us that hadn't existed before. His tongue had been so insistent when it had been meshing against my own. It had been so sweet-tasting, so much sweeter in ways that the fruit and dessert we'd been forced to eat never could have been.

We were exhausted when we were taken from the kitchen. I had long ago stopped trying to count the number of times that I was fucked or the number of cocks that were forced down my throat. I don't know how many men we had satisfied back there, how many men walked through our lives every day we were in our apprenticeship.

I was pleased when we were taken back to our sleeping quarters. Duane had a tub full of warm water waiting for us. He told us both to get in it.

It felt like a childish way to be with another man, as though we were both boys again. The tub was large, and we could almost fit in it sitting facing one another, but there didn't seem to be quite enough room for our legs. We laughed as we tried to find a way to accommodate them. Finally, I had my calves resting on the rim of the tub by Chris's head; his legs were pushing gently against my ass.

The soapy water seemed to finish off the impression that we were just a pair of kids playing with one another. We splashed and let the water run over the lip of the tub. I turned on the spigot to let more warm fluid into the tub to replace what we'd spilled out.

The playfulness was a change from the tension that sex usually carried with it in the arena. It seemed to relax Chris as well. I felt I could talk to him now, in this boylike intimacy.

"How did you get here?" There wasn't any need to explain that further. He knew what I meant; of course he did.

Chris leaned his head back and studied the ceiling for a minute. "The choice was death by boredom," he said. "Blond death by boredom."

"What does that mean?"

"It means that I was faced with the oblivion of what little soul I had," he said, lifting his head up to face me now. The friskiness was gone. He was quite serious.

"I grew up in a small city in the Midwest," he began. "I was a perfect child." His voice dripped with sarcasm. "I was blond and pretty and wholesome, and I did everything that I was supposed to do.

"I did well in school. I was on the gymnastic team. I went to church. I was polite to my elders. I was suffocating.

"That's all I really knew, that I was suffocating. I knew that I was so white-bread that there was no flavor to me. I was so vanilla, I was never going to have any flavor.

"All the while that I was smiling and succeeding and doing just what my family and my teachers wanted me to do, I was being tortured inside. I knew there had to be more to life. I knew there had to be *feelings*. I just didn't know what feelings were.

"I didn't have any idea what an adventure might be. Even when it was time to go to college—and I had good-enough grades to choose just about any place—I stayed at home and commuted to a Bible school in town. It wasn't that my parents were forcing me into anything, it was just that I couldn't imagine what anything different would look like.

"I did have some idea about the symbols that came with things different from what I knew about. That much I understood. "There was one set of symbols I responded to most powerfully, even if I didn't really understand them completely. There were men who hung around the bars in the downtown area who were full of passions. I could see it in the black leather clothes they wore, in the beards and piercings they displayed, in the way they were full of a physicality that I had never experienced myself.

"I think they would have stayed there, on the edge of my existence, if one of them didn't finally come forward and offer me some of what he had.

"His name was Wolf. He was the leader of a motorcycle gang. I used to go by the beer hall that was their headquarters and catch glimpses of them at nighttime, or on Sunday afternoon when they were having their weekly parties. I always tried to be careful about it. I didn't really think I wanted them or anyone else to know what I was up to. But Wolf read me. He must have recognized how often I had an excuse to be in that neighborhood, one where I obviously didn't belong.

"One afternoon I was walking by there and he came out of the beer hall. 'Hey, schoolboy, what you up to?' he asked. He was grinning, like he already knew the answer. I was shattered that he'd spoken to me, and more excited than I could imagine. I'd never been to anyplace where there was more than a Baptist punch served, and here was this guy with beer on his breath leering at me on the street. I had only chastely kissed one girl in the Methodist youth group, and here was a guy decked out in leather acting like he was trying to pick me up.

"I could hardly answer him. I just smiled. That was enough; that was all he needed. 'Come on, have a drink with a buddy, schoolboy.' He grabbed my arm and led me into the beer hall.

"The other men there hooted when they saw Wolf guiding me through the door. 'Got a new pup!' one of them yelled. Wolf laughed out loud. Then he put a hand on my ass—my ass that no one had touched since my mother had last changed my diapers. I thought I'd faint from the shock of that touch. It was all I could do to keep standing.

"Someone put a mug of beer in my hand and I drank it—the first drink of my life. I listened to the laughter, and I smelt the leather and the sweat on the big men. There was also a heavy air of motor oil from their bikes. Their hands were filthy, encrusted with grease, and there was dirt under their fingernails.

They had big paunches for bellies, most of them, and their hair was long and grimy.

"Wolf was a little different. He wasn't as heavy as the other men. His stomach was firm, almost flat. His beard was kept more trim. He wore black leather gloves, so I couldn't see if his hands were cleaner, but I suspected they were.

"We drank more beer. Wolf treated me like a long-lost little brother. It wasn't like any other relationship I ever had. It was physical, for one thing. He had a heavy arm slung across my shoulder all afternoon. We were buddies, just like he had called me, I was his buddy. We even went into the john together and took a piss standing side by side at a long urinal.

"I hadn't ever dared look at another man's cock when he pissed before. But Wolf didn't mind if I saw piss coming out of his dick. He seemed to be pleased when he looked over and saw me staring at his thing.

"It was a fat cock, a really fat cock. The most amazing thing about it was a ring that was pierced right through the head of it. It glistened with the wet of his urine, even after he shook his dick when he was finished. Wolf took his time putting his meat back in his pants. By the time he did, he and I could both see that my own was half-hard. I was just barely able to finish up, especially after I realized he was looking at mine with that smile on his face.

"I knew we were going to be real buddies then, a kind of buddy I'd never had before.

"When the afternoon was over and people began to leave the beer hall, I realized I was drunk, or felt drunk, or being drunk was an excuse not to go home. I told Wolf my parents would kill me; they didn't approve of drinking at all.

"'Well, then, you'll just have to come on over to

my place and sleep it off,' he said as though it was the most natural thing in the world.

"His place was a small house not far away. To get there, though, there was another new experience for me. I had walked from my house. Wolf expected me to ride on the back of his motorcycle to his.

"I had never been on a bike before, never. I had to ask him how to sit, where to put my feet, even how to hold on. He positioned me; then he lifted his leg up and straddled the bike himself. 'The holding on is easy,' he said, 'just grab your arms around me.'

"It was almost more than I could stand, but more was coming. He revved up the big engine. The intense vibrations of all that horsepower swept through my body. I panicked. It all gave me a hard-on, and I was sure that Wolf could feel it as his butt pressed against my crotch.

"I was so tense that I could hardly take in the ride through the streets of the city. The wind was the only thing that took my mind off my hard dick, that and the sense of rebellion and freedom that I felt.

"The ride ended much too quickly for me. It seemed like we were there in no time. Wolf turned off the engine and we both climbed off the metal horse. He didn't say a thing to me as I followed him up the walk to the door. He unlocked it and let me go in first.

"There was a stale odor to the place; I finally realized it was from his cigar smoke. It was spartan in every way. There were a couple of Harley-Davidson banners on the walls, a worn-out couch, a threadbare rug—that was it in the front. I followed him into the kitchen where there was a plastic dinette table and a couple of chairs. There were dishes stacked up in the sink. He didn't pay any attention to them, just went to the refrigerator and pulled out a couple of beers.

"The last thing I needed was more to drink, but I

took the cold bottle from him and followed his example when he took a deep drink out of it.

"'I always did want me a college boy,' Wolf said. He walked out of the kitchen and into the back. I followed him once more. It was his bedroom. There were a couple of mattresses stacked on the floor and a bureau with all its drawers opened and clothes hanging out of them. That was all.

"Wolf burped and put his beer on the floor by the mattresses. 'Gonna suck my cock, schoolboy?'

"I had never even *thought* about sucking a cock before. I could barely even picture what it would be like to do it. That wasn't important. What was important was that my stomach was churning, and not just from alcohol. What was important was that my skin was crawling from anticipation. This is what I'd been missing, this sense of danger and anticipation."

Chris stopped. I was anxious to hear more, but I could tell his story was taking him back to a different time, one that must have seemed very far away indeed for someone who was living in the arena.

Our bathwater had cooled. I let some of it out and then turned on the hot water. The new warmth spread quickly through the tub and seemed to relax both of us again. I picked up a sponge and lifted one of Chris's feet up out of the water, away from my ass, where it had been nesting.

I lathered up his foot, rubbing it with the sponge, more like a massage than any cleaning. He seemed to enjoy it. His eyes closed and he slipped deeper into the heating water. I ran my fingers between his toes and tickled him a bit. He laughed boyishly, recapturing my sense of our being young together. But Chris was with his memories; he was in a different boyhood. He began to tell his story again.

"I was too mesmerized to do anything. I just stood

there and watched him undress. His skin was surprisingly pale. I suppose I expected him to be dark because of all the leather, but he wasn't. He didn't have much more body hair than I did either. But he did have that fat cock.

"It was almost hard by the time he stripped his clothes off. It was nestled in a bush of thick dark hair, all the more shocking because there was so little on the other parts of his body.

"He began to stroke his dick while I stood there. 'Come on, schoolboy, suck my cock,' he said.

"I thought I had religious experiences before. I had given myself to Jesus. I had been saved. I had been washed in the blood of my Savior!" Chris was laughing at himself now. "But I have never had a transcendental experience like that one when I walked across the floor and dropped on my knees and began to suck Wolf's dick.

"It slipped right down my throat, like it had been there for years before. It was thick, but not that long, and so I didn't choke, I just had that sensation of being filled up by it. I had been so wrong. I hadn't known who my savior was until that moment when Wolf's dirty dick, stinking of old piss and sweaty leather, slipped down my throat. *That* was salvation. That was religion. That was something worth praying for.

"Wolf didn't seem to think it was anything all that special. Why wouldn't a little blond college boy want to suck on his thing? It made sense to him. He kept at it until he spurted a load of hot come down my throat, a load full of salt taste and thick ooze.

"I had found my adventure. It was going to be Wolf.

"Wolf didn't want to change anything about me. He liked my preppy clothes and my clean-cut appearance. He thought it was something to be proud of that I went to college. He even made sure I had plenty of time to study.

"But he didn't want me to live at home. He moved me into his house in another week, so I'd be around for him. Being around meant sex, at least three times a day—at the very least I had to get him off when he woke up in the morning, when I got out of classes in the afternoon and he drove me back to the house from campus, and at night, when he wanted to go to bed. Wolf said a man couldn't sleep right if he had a load kept in him at nighttime. He had to get it out of his system before he could be expected to spend a night in peace. Of course, that usually meant a fuck, not a blowjob. Wolf liked my blond ass; he said it was satin smooth, that it was the finest ass he'd ever had.

"Sex three times a day? It hardly ever happened that seldom. Wolf was always ready, and what he expected was me to be too.

"He was proud of me, and he liked to show me off to his club members. When he'd have a few beers—and that was pretty often—he'd want them to see what a good college boy he'd found for himself. One of his favorite things was to pull down my pants and show off my butt. 'Look at what's in my bed, you suckers. You think your pussies 're so good, look at this ass that's mine every night.'

"He'd slap me a few times to get my cheeks nice and pink for the rest of them. He enjoyed doing that. He enjoyed it a lot.

"If we were at someone's house and there was a bit more privacy, Wolf began to take another step. He not only wanted to show them the body he was getting at night, he wanted to show them how willing I was. The first time I sucked him off in front of other people was one of the most thrilling moments of my life. I'll never forget it. There was a whole group of bikers standing around this apartment when Wolf announced that I was going to have to do some work for him. He pushed me down on my knees and took out his dick and shoved it in my mouth.

"Someone called me a cocksucker, and the rest of them laughed and hooted. I didn't pay any attention to them. I just took that dick down my throat like it was the most natural thing in the world. That seemed to shut them up, when they understood that I wasn't just willing to do what Wolf told me, I was proud to do it.

They couldn't break that pride, either. One night, when there was a group of them drunk together and Wolf made me go down on him, the rest of the men who crowded around took out their cocks and aimed them at me while I was kneeling. They let loose a cascade of piss. They soaked my oxford-cloth shirt; they drenched my dress slacks; my loafers were heavy with wet when they were finished.

"I didn't stop what I was doing. I was sucking Wolf's cock, and no biker piss was going to make me want to do anything else. I earned some respect from those guys that night. They stopped giving me grief. I had been baptized in a way they understood. I had turned myself into a real in-your-face kind of guy. I might wear preppy clothes, but I'd take the best they had and throw it back at them. They knew that then.

"I used to wonder how long that life could go on. I never wanted it to end; that was for sure. But there were things built into the way that Wolf lived that made it all too difficult. Part of me wanted to become one of his biker friends, but he wouldn't let that happen. Like I said, he enjoyed the way I looked when he met me. But that wasn't the biggest problem, not by far.

"One thing was his drinking. Some nights he'd get carried away by it. He'd get me back to the bedroom and he'd tear off my clothes—I mean that literally, he would tear off my clothes. He would push me around so hard it was like a beating sometimes. If he had really a lot to drink, he couldn't always get his dick hard, and that would frustrate him. He'd scare me then; he'd get so mad that he couldn't get a hard-on.

"Not that it was enough to leave him. It was all part of the excitement. I never went home anymore. I never went back to the church where I had been such a good boy. I wasn't that person any more. I was a biker's suck-boy, and I liked it. I liked it a lot.

"I didn't even get freaked out when I realized that there was more than alcohol involved with Wolf. He did some hard drugs, too. When he was on them, and that got to be more common all the time, he was desperate for them. I never understood how Wolf made his living; I suppose there must have been some break-ins that he never involved me with. There had to be something illicit going on to support that house and his habits, but pretty soon there wasn't enough money.

"He didn't have to be that drunk one night to realize there was an easy way for him to pay for some more stuff when he was broke. He had this pretty blond college boy sitting there, and he'd already told everyone he knew what a pretty ass I had. Someone else would want a taste of it.

"I actually saw that part coming. I didn't try to avoid it. In fact, I looked forward to the first time Wolf would trade my body for a fix.

"It was with a dealer, a slimy guy Wolf knew from across town. I can't even remember his name. The only thing I asked was that we use condoms—I should have done that with Wolf, but I hadn't, and

I'm just lucky something didn't happen because of the lack of protection.

"But as soon as I saw this guy with his pockmarked face and his skinny limbs, I knew I wasn't going to take any chances. I'd come through for Wolf, but only if latex was used.

"No one seemed upset by that. I went into the bedroom with the man, and he put a rubber on as soon as his clothes were off. I sat on the piled-up mattresses and sucked him off. His body odor was so terrible, I was glad there was a condom on him just so I wouldn't have to taste him. I couldn't imagine actually having his naked dick down my throat without throwing up.

"That was easy. Wolf got a lot of dope with me with scenes like that. It was a clean trade. I don't know what I felt about it, except that continuing sense of excitement. I never knew what was going to happen any day, not until Wolf announced that someone was coming over, or decided that he was tired and just wanted a bit of my ass for himself that night.

"The next step was the dangerous one. If Wolf could get a bit of dope for my body from his low-life friends, there must be someone out there who'd like to pay even more for me. Wolf began to pimp for me. He asked around and discovered that there were some local businessmen who did, indeed, want to taste a college boy's butt. We started to go uptown with my dates, and Wolf wasn't just bartering any more, he began to charge real money.

"There was danger in it, but that danger was one of the things I wanted. It meant more thrills, more challenges, more of everything. I also started to get a sense of power out of it all.

"One of the first men Wolf sold me to was an elder at my old church, a guy who always read the

Gospel on Sunday and who stood as a pillar in the local conservative establishment.

"It turned out that he liked to suck ass more than anything else. He wasn't upset that I was someone he knew, he seemed to think it was even better that way, that his humiliation was more complete. He'd kneel behind me and he'd stick his tongue up my crack while he cried real tears and begged Jehovah for forgiveness. That turned out to be worth quite a bit of money for Wolf, and the guy became a regular.

"If it all hadn't been so thrilling and new to me, I probably would have taken up beer drinking and dope taking with Wolf. But I was fascinated by everything that was happening to me. I didn't want any of my senses blurred. I wanted to learn from it. I wanted to remember it all, every little bit of it.

"I just thought the customers Wolf was finding were a little sad; that was all. I thought they were unimaginative. Having a Bible beater licking my butt couldn't keep my interest for long. I was happier when Wolf was fucking me or making me suck his dick. There seemed to be more there to explore. I was willing to go through anything for his cock, especially when he'd take me for a ride on his bike.

"There was almost nothing I wouldn't do for Wolf after a long drive in the country on the Harley. The agitation of the vibrating motor was the most exhilarating thing I had ever experienced.

"But there was more to come.

"Word spreads fast in a small city when there's a new piece on the market, especially when that piece is attached to the biker world. Pretty soon there were some men who began to show up at the beer hall to have a look at me. They didn't start anything themselves, but they knew that Wolf would often drag down my pants and show me off to whoever was looking. They didn't seem to be intimidating, not like the bikers had been when I first used to spy on them. These were just regular men, the kind you'd find shopping at a mall, disguised so they seemed to be the kind of men who'd show up at a family barbecue.

"But a couple of them found out where we lived, and they started to come by the house and insist on talking to Wolf alone. He wouldn't tell me what they said, but he always seemed to be anxious to get them out.

"That is, he was until one night when he really wanted some dope and there wasn't any money in the house and he didn't think he could get enough just by trading me. 'You got to go to work tonight,' he said to me. I didn't say anything. I'd never complained when he'd peddled my ass before—why should I start now?

"Wolf took a card out of his wallet and made a phone call in the other room so I couldn't overhear him. Then he told me to get ready; we were going for a ride.

"We took the bike out into the country, miles from the city. I was holding onto him like always, loving the wind and the speed the way I always did.

"He finally pulled up to an old farm that was many miles from the city. He didn't go to the house, though. He drove around it to the barn behind. When he turned off the bike, Wolf didn't even look at me. 'This is going to be rough,' is all he said. 'I'll wait for you. I'll get the money when they're done.'

"I went up to the door of the barn and wondered what this could be all about. I didn't have a clue. I knocked and someone told me to come in.

"I could barely make anything out when I opened the door. The only light was coming from kerosene lamps that sent shadows racing across the walls as the breeze blew through the big old building. I stepped inside and closed the door behind me.

"That's when I saw them. There were two of them waiting for me. They were dressed the same way. They had on leather pants and boots, but no shirt or anything else over their chest. They both wore executioner's hoods, half-hoods that covered the top of their heads but not their mouths, and that had slits cut into the leather for their eyes.

"This, I knew, was going to be the most intense thing I had ever experienced. This was going to make my adventures with Wolf seem like nothing out of the ordinary.

"One of them told me to undress. I stripped off my clothes even as I was trying to make out more of the set up. There was a large cross in the center of the barn, shaped like an x. On each end of the beams that made it there were shackles. I had never even imagined such a thing, but I knew I was going to be secured to it. I knew they were going to put me in the grasp of those leather restraints.

"It only made me more excited. By the time I was nude, my dick was as hard as it ever had been. I reached down and grabbed hold of it. Even as long as I'd been with Wolf, I had never so flagrantly announced my sexuality to anyone before. Now I was telling these guys that I was ready. I was ready for their scene.

"They came towards me. They were gentle as they took my hand off my cock. Each one grabbed hold of an arm, and they led me to the cross. They attached my limbs so I was facing the wooden structure. My ass burned with anticipation. They weren't going to simply fuck me, I knew that. They weren't going to be as easygoing as Wolf and his friends, playing at some kind of domination game. This was going to be much more real than that.

"They began by attaching clamps to my tits. Then they tied leather bands around my cock and balls. When they were done weaving the leather around my crotch, each of my testicles was separated and pulled tight against my scrotum. My dick was hard, and the blood in it was trapped by more leather.

"They put a hood like their own over my head. I couldn't hear as well once the hood was in place, but mine had the same eye slits so I could see. They stood back then, as though they wanted to take a while to appreciate their handiwork.

"At first they used only a paddle on me. They were testing me to see how far I would go. I was jolted every time the leather hit my ass. It wasn't that painful in the beginning, at least, but the *idea* of being beaten was so exciting that I had to respond physically.

"They liked that. The way I was moving my butt around excited them. They used the leather more severely. I yelled, but it was from that excitement, it wasn't from hating the pain. They seemed to understand that.

"They took turns with that paddle. Then one of them got something else, something that stung even as it hurt me even more. I twisted around to see what was going on, and saw a riding crop in one of their hands. They were beating me with something that was supposed to be used on a horse!

"My dick just seemed to get harder. Then the paddle stopped while the crop went on. They were going to move up another level; I understood that by then.

"The crop continued to bite into my butt, leaving long, thin lines of hot pain on my ass. I almost got used to it. The man who was working with the crop had a rhythm to the way he used it. I was meeting him stroke for stroke by then, pushing my ass out to meet the blows he was delivering.

"Just when I was getting into it, a whip broke across my back. The long lines of leather wrapped around my shoulders and ripped through my skin. I screamed out in agony. I had never felt such pain before. The way they'd been beating my ass was nothing compared to what was happening now. Nothing at all.

"The whip tore away from my body and then came crashing down on me again. And again. I sobbed. I cried. But I never asked them to stop.

"There was a short break in the action. The crop wasn't working on my ass anymore. I quickly figured out that they were just switching off. The second man was going to get a chance to use that whip on me. I was right. The leather came at me from a different direction this time. It came with all the power and all the same ability to create pain.

"I thought that they were going to take the skin right off my body. I began to freak, thinking that the excitement had gone too far, that Wolf had delivered me up into the hands of Satanists.

"My cries started to have a sound of insanity about them. 'Stop, please,' I said. 'I'll do anything if you'll just stop.'

"The whip did stop. I kept on crying, but I was able to begin to catch my breath. I had some hope that the craziness I was encountering was over.

"But they were sly ones. I learned more about that later. They had a taste for all of this that was seldom satisfied. They knew they wanted too much for most of the men in our small city. They were worried about their reputations; but, even more, they were worried about men who wouldn't let them have all that they wanted.

"They came up to me and they put their arms around me. They reassured me that everything was all right. They began to tell me not to worry about disappointing them. They would understand. That message finally got through to me and created its own derangement inside me. I was *disappointing* them?

"But they had given me so much, I thought. They had shown me such experiences and such feelings that I should repay them. That was exactly what they wanted me to think. I got myself under control, told them I was fine, told them they could go on again.

"They kept that up for hours. Whipping me till I would go to the very edge of my strength, and then comforting me with their strong arms and their firm voices. They seduced me over and over again. They seduced me into letting them do just what they wanted to do.

"When they finally tired of their game, they took me down from the cross. But they didn't undo the clamps on my tits or untie the leather around my cock and balls. They took me over to a table and threw me on it face down. I heard the familiar sound of zippers being undone.

"One of them stood in front of me and forced his cock into my mouth just as the other one began to fuck me. My whole body was sore from the bondage and the whipping, but the sudden sensation of being skewered by this pair of cocks overwhelmed all of that. I forget everything else. All I could handle was those two cocks.

"I had to focus on that because I never wanted to forget what the feeling was like. It was a fullness that I had never known before. The two men used me without any more concern for what I thought of them and what they were doing. They had been kind and manipulative when they needed me to tolerate their whips and paddles, but now that was over. They had driven themselves to a peak and they weren't going to hesitate to fulfill the appetites that had been built up by the beatings.

"I had a new religious experience, one where pain was transformed, where I became beautiful, where my new masters were able to take me across a river into a land that had never been charted before.

"When they came—and they came together, at the same time, shouting while their loads were ejected into me—I felt a new panic. They were finished! They were done. What would ever happen to me if they were over with it?

"One of the men reached under my body and took hold of my cock. The other one removed the clamps on my tits. While the first one jerked me off, the second one played with my bruised nipples. They didn't remove their cocks right away. I was able to continue to suck on the salty slab of dick that was in my mouth. I could still feel the heavy presence of the other one in my ass.

"It took them only a short while to get me to push out my come. I shot all over their table while they laughed at me and the way I was still so aroused by everything that happened.

"They stood me up and finally undid the leather straps around my cock and balls. They helped me climb back into my clothes. They didn't say a word to me—they just rubbed my body appreciatively, as though it were some thing that had done its job well, not as though I was a person.

"They took me to the door and waved for Wolf to come and get me. He seemed to go pale when he saw me. He took some money from one of them and then half-carried me back to the bike. I could hardly hold on while he roared through the countryside and back into the city.

"He did carry me from the bike to the house when we got home. He laid me out on the bed and took off my clothes. 'You'll never have to do that again,' he insisted. 'I'm so sorry,' he apologized.

"I didn't say anything. I just fell asleep, I fell into dreams of masters in black leather and strong, handsome animals that delivered their pleasure.

"Wolf's promise was hollow, of course. A druggie like him has to have his fix, and he'd do anything to get it when the need arose. About a month later, he made another phone call. I was delivered to the barn again. They were waiting for me just as they had been before.

"Only one thing had changed—me. I had changed completely. When I went into the barn, I told them they should give Wolf some money now, to get rid of him, let him go back to the city and do whatever he wanted to do that night.

"Wolf had made a major mistake, you see. He'd given me access to something that was even more exciting than he was. He had shown me that there was another step to take, another level to go to. These men were it. They were my new guides. Wolf had served his purpose, and it was time for me to move beyond him.

"The men hesitated for only a short time. Then they went outside. I waited until they came back in and one of them told me, 'It's taken care of.'

"I looked at them and I told them, 'It's done.' They seemed to understand what I meant. They led me back to the cross that was once again in the middle of the room, and they lifted up my arms to attached them to the restraints. When I felt the leather wrap around my wrists that first time, I knew I had crossed another river. I also knew I could never swim back across it.

"I stayed with them for a few months. They taught me what they knew. Then they told me there was a place here in the city where I could go even further, where I could learn even more. I could come and be a part of the arena.

"They brought me here the first night, and I knew that I belonged. They made the arrangements. They were kind to me. After all, I had done well by them. There hadn't been many men who would let them fulfill their fantasies to the extent I had. They told me I deserved this award, the honor of working in the arena.

"And that," Chris said with a smile, "is how I got to be here." He got up out of the bathwater and stepped out of the tub. He stood there nude.

"Do I still look like a country boy to you? Can you find any innocence in me?"

The only thing that was surprising was that I could, in fact, still see the innocence in Chris. I understood the frankness of his desires. He had found the perfect place for them, I realized. Here, in the arena, he could do more than just have them lived out. Here, in a space as protected as this one, he would be safe.

Even as I looked at the stripes of red on his back and wondered how different they were from the ones he'd gotten in that barn those first nights, I knew that Chris was very happy. He had found something here. I only hoped that I was going to be able to find it as clearly as he did.

If I had been physically most frightened of the stocks,

it was the members' room that upset my mind the most. It seemed to be the thing that disturbed all the others as well. Duane knew that.

"Of course you're scared of it. Think! Spending some time undergoing a physical test is one thing; you know it'll end. But actually becoming a servant—understanding what it means to be a slave, discovering that you want to be subservient to other men—that's the hard part.

"The members' room doesn't have physical restraints. That's what makes it such a challenge. It's why you're worried about it, and it's why you should learn to make it your favorite place in the whole arena. You can't make-believe that something is being forced on you. You don't have the luxury of being able to deny your own part in what's happening. What is happening to you in the members' room is what you *want* to experience, but you just haven't faced up to that yet.

"You have to understand this part of it all, this is one of the most essential things that goes on here: When you're in bondage, you're making-believe that the men who are using you wouldn't be able to do it if you weren't tied up.

"Being in bondage is a slave's indulgence. It's something the masters let you have because it makes it easier for them to use you. That's all.

"You have to get over the dependence on bondage. You have to understand that, if you really want to go into this all the way, then you have to learn to submit without the external props that handcuffs and leather restraints represent.

"You have to get to the place where you'd be willing and able to take a whipping without any restraints on you. You have to move to the place where you could kneel and kiss any man's feet without any threat. That's your potential. That's what being here means to you. Don't avoid it. Move to it. Go to it. Become who you want to be."

The four of us were naked, as always. We had just been washed, and our skin had a gleam of oil on it. We represented a spectrum of attractiveness, from Chris's golden looks to Alex's black handsomeness. We were all marked by bruises, but we carried them with a certain pride.

"Come on, this is going to be important to you, and we're not going to make it any easier." Duane stood back and nodded to some of the attendants who were nearby. They came over and wrapped pieces of silk clothing around our hips. The cloth was startlingly sensual as it draped itself over my cock and balls and hung over my ass. It was tied to me in a way that left an expanse of one hip exposed. The material was secured so that it swept down from my waist, just clinging to my abdomen. It was so short that it didn't really conceal my balls. The bottom of my scrotum was without covering.

Each of us wore a different color. Alex's mahogany skin was set off by yellow fabric. Chris's blond complexion was complimented by a scrap of red silk. Sean's dark hair was emphasized by royal blue. They had sheathed me in forest green.

The small piece of silk made me feel even more sexual than I already had. The simple touch of it was erotic. It also had a strange effect in making me feel even more naked than I had been all the previous days when I'd gone around the arena without any clothing at all. The small bit of fabric accentuated what might be covered. The way it fell over my cock and my ass made me even more aware of those parts of my body, even though they had been particularly well used while I had been in the arena.

THE ARENA

When we were dressed, we were taken into the members' room. I could feel fear inside me as we walked through the door and into the quiet, heavily carpeted area. Up to this point we had been used only by the workmen of the place. This was obviously going to be a new ordeal.

I could recognize some of the members of the arena from my first nights here. They were lounging on the huge pillows that made up most of the furnishings of the place. There were only four of the men, but they were obviously waiting for us.

I couldn't look Guido in the face when I realized he was one of them. He had been the one who had taken me out of my games and led me to the arena the first time; of course he knew that I belonged here. But I still had that sense that he had caught me in something. I was surprised that I still had this residue of shame left in me. I vowed I'd get rid of it.

One of the men was older than the others, probably in his fifties. He had silver hair and was wearing only a pair of leather pants. I could see that the hair on his chest was the same gray color. He seemed to appreciate us even more than the rest. "A fine group," he said.

"You saw them the other night," Guido answered with a smile. I felt as though he were saying that just for my benefit, to let me know that he had been there the night I had been on display in the front room.

"Yes," the older man continued, "but the inanimate body, no matter how beautiful, doesn't show the full scope of a personality. A statue—even a living one—isn't the same as a body in motion. A statue doesn't have the grace or the beauty, no matter how perfectly executed. Look at these men with their little silk sarongs! Can't you already see them as something more than what you observed that night?"

No one spoke. I looked at Guido and saw a smirk on his face. No, I realized at that moment, he couldn't see any more than he had. That was all he'd wanted to see. I remembered back to the silent companion who'd been trained so well, the man with the padlock pierced through his foreskin. That was all someone like Guido wanted. He could find it here in the arena. I realized, too, and not for the first time, that he might even find it with me. He could claim me from the podium as easily as any other man could. I would go with him in to the back rooms of the arena and he could take what he wanted from me—my mouth, my ass, anything else. I wouldn't fight him. I was supposed to be in the arena, even if it meant submitting to a man like this.

But another man, perhaps one like this silver-haired man who was speaking, could find even more in me than someone like Guido ever would. He was a man who knew secrets, who could make someone feel as though he were really a special find.

"Well, enjoy yourself, Matthew," Guido said as he stood up. "If this is what you want, if you really aren't satisfied with finding these men naked and tied to the block, then go for it. Go and get whatever else you want."

Of course, that was it. Guido was the mirror image of the slave who had to be bound in order to serve. He was the master whose imagination never went beyond the physical act. He could have found his pleasure from any willing hole. He wouldn't understand what we went through, those of us who were so determined to be his servants. That was why he didn't attract me. And that was precisely why Matthew did. Matthew was someone who would appreciate the intricate dance that we would do together. No matter how difficult it might be for me to perform my part in it, he would understand that I was at least reaching to fulfill my role.

After Guido left, Matthew looked directly at me. "I think you should learn to read." I didn't understand. "Go and get a book from the case, why don't you. Why don't you find something to amuse us?" The other two members were obviously willing to follow his lead.

I went over to the bookshelves. I wasn't really familiar with all the titles. I had read only a few of them. The cover of one—*The Claiming of Sleeping Beauty*—seemed especially handsome. I took it down.

I went back to where Matthew was reclining on the pillows. "Just open it to any page and start reading," he said. "It's a good choice. Ms. Rice has been an inspiration to many of us in many different ways."

I opened the book and began:

Go to the chest in the corner," he said to Prince Alexi, "and bring me the ring that is in it."

Prince Alexi went on his hands and knees to obey. But obviously the Prince wasn't satisfied. He snapped his finger, and Squire Felix at once drove Prince Alexi with his paddle. He drove him to the chest and continued to torment him with the paddle while he opened the chest and with his teeth removed a large leather ring and brought it back to the Prince.

"Put it on," said the Prince.

Prince Alexi was holding the leather ring not by the leather itself but by some small piece of gold attached to it. And still holding it this way in his teeth, he slipped the ring over the Prince's penis, but he did not release it.

"Enough," Matthew said. "What a beautiful image, don't you think?"

I was surprised that he was asking me my opinion, but I told him that I agreed. I had to admit that. My own cock was erect and lifting up the little slip of silk that was supposed to cover it.

"Then we should see just what it would look like. The author has created such a brilliant scene, it would be a shame not to be able to see just what she wanted us to imagine.

"Duane, bring us a cockring, something that would approximate what was in the book. Then put it over there, on the ledge under that window.

"You," Matthew said to Alex, "look like the person of a prince. You shall be him. And this"—he gestured to me—"will be Alexi. I need a squire. Which one shall that be? You"—Matthew pointed to Sean—"are a man who looks like he knows what to do with a paddle. Don't you?"

"I've had some experience," was all that Sean would admit.

"Yes, and on both ends of the handle, I'm sure," Matthew joked back, happy with his humor.

Duane came back into the room holding a leather cockring. He went across the room to put it on the sill where Matthew had indicated. He had anticipated Matthew's wishes and had brought back a thick leather paddle as well.

"Perfect," Matthew said. The other two men were still sitting on their own pillows watching this scenario develop. I could see from the growing bulges at their crotches that they were very pleased with developments.

Duane handed Sean the paddle and then stepped back again.

"Squire! Why is Alexi still on his feet?" Matthew demanded. "Why isn't he on his hands and knees? That's what was written. You should make it happen. Now!"

Sean reached over, grabbed my neck, and pushed it down onto the floor until my face was buried in the plush carpet and my ass held up in the air. The small piece of silk was hardly covering anything now. It hung open to expose my balls and my hardening cock, and it spread apart across my ass, leaving it bare.

"Yes, that's it!" Matthew said. "Now paddle him while he goes to the ledge and takes the ring off."

I felt the sharp sting of leather fall on my ass. I started to move, but I obviously wasn't fast enough for Sean. He kept up a tattoo of blows against my butt while I scampered across the room. Even when I got there and took the leather cockring in my mouth, Sean continued to beat me.

I felt a strange betrayal by this. It was one thing to put up with the attentions of the members, but it was something else to have a comrade be so very happy about having a chance to whip me. Sean was obviously pleased with the opportunity he was getting. He displayed a great deal of enthusiasm as he followed me back. Sean didn't stop until I got to Alex and was panting at the black man's feet, the leather ring carefully held in my mouth.

"Ah, you've polished his butt well," Matthew told Sean with obvious appreciation. "It looks like a well-ripened apple now, with such fine red color."

It must have been. My rear was burning from the paddling. Sean had done it as hard and as quickly as any of the trainers had done. I found myself slipping into appreciation, glad he was going to be so good at what he did, if he had to do it at all.

"You," he said to Alex, "you are now the prince. Alexi is at your feet and you are going to make him work for your pleasure. The book says that he puts the ring around your cock without using his hands.

Make him do that."

Alex turned so his thickening purple-black cock and balls were right in my face. I leaned up and was able to slip the ring onto the dark-red knob of his glans. His dick was already half-hard from expectation. He was as bad as Sean; he was enjoying all this just as much. Alex stood there with his arms crossed over his chest, looking like a prince from one of Anne Rice's novels. His cock was swelling with the victory of watching me as I struggled to pull the ring down past the glans.

"It must go all the way to the root of his cock," Matthew insisted. "He must take it all the way down the stem."

I pulled the leather cockring along the span of Alex's dick until my chin rubbed against his beefy testicles and my face was scrubbed by his kinky pubic hair.

"Yes!" Matthew said. "That's it. And now, in the book, the prince walks around the room and the slave is forced to follow him. Go on! Squire! Paddle him to ensure he does his part."

The leather slammed down on my ass again just at the moment that Alex began to turn. I had to move quickly on my hands and knees to make sure that I didn't lose my grip on the ring. If Sean was already using this paddle so effectively, what would he do if I failed and let go of Alex's crotch?

The black man's thick pubic hair continued to scour my cheeks and my chin as I struggled to keep up with him. I was obsessed with the task. I wasn't going to be separated from his cock, no matter what. My shoulders hit against Alex's massive thighs. The silk he still wore drifted against my face. My hands would sometimes hit against his feet or calves while I moved as quickly as I could to stay with him. The paddle kept assaulting me. The heat spread all over my butt as Sean continued to work away at it.

Alex was hard by now. The ring gripped hold of the base of his swollen cock, and it was difficult to retain my bite. Once it slipped away from my teeth. Alex purposely twisted around so I had to jump quickly to get it back between my teeth. Sean seemed displeased that I wasn't giving him some pleasure he wanted. He not only didn't stop the paddling, he began to use the thing on other parts of my body.

I had to spread my legs far apart to assume some of the positions that Alex's movements forced me into. When I did, Sean used the paddle mercilessly on my inner thighs. The sensitive part of my body rebelled at the sudden and unexpected pain. I nearly cried out, but realized that would mean my mouth would open and the ring would escape me again. I couldn't let that happen.

Sean wasn't deterred by the small defeat when I was able to cling to the ring and, through it, to Alex's mammoth erection. Sean began to paddle the outside of my hips, where the bone was closer to the surface and there was much greater pain because of the lack of fleshy protection. He even managed to get in some hits on the soles of my feet and on my calves.

I was intent not to let Alex get away from me, though. And I succeeded. Matthew eventually called an end to the scenario. "Excellent! Excellent! Look at the glow on his body, the way it looks so seasoned and edible.

"We have to continue this," Matthew insisted. "Find another book." I stood up, my mouth sore, my body covered with sweat, and stared at him. He wanted *me* to continue in this role? "Another of the Beauty books," he insisted. "You're all so good at this, we should stay with success, don't you think?"

There wasn't any room to discuss the matter; there was no question in what he was saying. In his patrician manner, Matthew was giving an order just as firm and unyielding as anything that Guido or Jacques would have commanded.

I went back to the shelf. It hurt my ass and my thighs just to walk that short distance. I pulled down a copy of *Beauty's Punishment.* Matthew told me to open it at random once again. I found a chapter about the escapades of Prince Nicholas. He was sold in a common village, auctioned off to a man who took him home where he and his sister fitted Prince Nicholas with phalluses from which plumes came, a fantasy tail for the young man who was about to be used as a beast of burden. Every description in the chapter went right to my center. I understood every hesitation the prince had. My cock was left rigid with erection when I was finished with the chapter.

"You have an affinity for the author's words," Matthew said with a grin. "That shows a great deal of potential, indeed.

"Duane, what do we have that could be equivalent to these contraptions that the book describes? Surely you can find something."

Of course he could, and off he went to do it. My cock wouldn't subside. I stood there in front of the members and the other initiates with my thick dick standing straight out, raising the silk rag up away from my body, the blood trapped in my glans as securely as I had ever been entangled in bondage. The existence of the silk continued to make me feel more shamefully naked than anything else I'd known in my time at the arena.

Duane brought back a selection of dildos. They seemed so much less elegant than the phalluses described in the book, but they were obviously going to be sufficient to act out Matthew's fantasies.

"You"—he pointed to Sean—"shall do some reading now. Take the book and find the section where the phalluses are being put into Prince Nicholas. You"—he said to Alex—"shall continue your good work as this man's master. You," he told me, "are to continue to be the slave.

"Now, pick up one of those dildos and insert it in this one's ass," he told Alex. "You, read a passage the describes what the slave is going through while his master has his way," he told Sean.

Alex pushed me over, bending my body at the waist. He pulled my legs apart, and I could feel a welcome coolness from the air blowing on my hole. The chill of that small part of my body was a contrast to the burning sensation that covered my ass.

Sean read:

> "The smaller of the two phalluses was lifted from the desk and slipped sharply and firmly into me. I shuddered."

I did shudder just at that moment when Alex put the head of the dildo against my hole and began to shove it into me. It had been covered with grease, but I was barely able to stop myself from fighting against the invasion. I could feel the exaggerated head of the rubber device being forced past my sphincter. Then my muscles clamped shut on the shaft.

> "Push out your hips, yes, and open to me. Yes, that's much better. Don't tell me you were never measured or mounted on a phallus at the castle."

I didn't even consciously decide to act out the words; the movements came to me naturally. I moved my hips backwards, trying now to welcome the very intrusion that I had so recently rebelled against. I swiveled my hips to make the dildo's passage easier, helping it to slide farther inside me, pressing against my prostate with a unique urgency that forced a long line of ooze to escape out of the slit of my cock and hang from my glans, suspended like a ribbon of slime from my body.

Sean continued to read from *Beauty's Punishment:*

> I wanted to cry out, "I cannot," but I felt it worked slowly back and forth, stretching me, and finally sliding in so that my anus felt enormous, throbbing around this immense object, which seemed three times what I had seen with my own eyes ...

"Keep his eyes open," Matthew shouted. "He's closed his eyes to what's going on. That won't do. Open his eyes and make him look at us."

Sean grabbed me by the hair and jerked my face so I had to stare directly at the members who sat on their pillows watching me. One of them had his cock out and was calmly masturbating while he watched the dildo moving in and out of my ass. I flushed, both from the exertion of accepting the artificial cock and from the embarrassment of seeing these strange men watch me take it all.

The author's words were my own experience. The examination by the members didn't alter the sensations that I was going through. My asshole felt immense with the dildo firmly implanted in me. It seemed the center of the world—not just my own world, either, because everyone in the room was watching while the phallus was being shoved farther and farther into my body.

"Excellent," Matthew said, almost in a whisper now. "Excellent. Take it out, slowly. We've done this scene very well. We should move on. I'm sure there's more to the author's fantasies that we should explore."

Alex withdrew the immense dildo from me, forcing a final spasm to shudder through my body when the head escaped from the clutches of my sphincter. I stood up and looked at him. He was smiling, but he also seemed to be disappointed. I understood that he wasn't happy that this act had ended so soon.

"You read well," Matthew told Sean. "Find another passage that can give your friend a new set of experiences."

Sean went to the shelf and brought back a third book, *Beauty's Release*. Was there going to be a release from this display? Everything I'd thought about the members' room was proven, everything that Duane had said was coming true. There was something easier about being held in the stocks, no matter how much they had scared me. It was much more difficult to stand here, the scrap of silk plastered against my skin with sweat, and have to follow through on the orders of a member who insisted on compliance, but didn't use any of the reinforcements of bondage to get his way.

Sean had found another passage for Matthew's entertainment. It was the story of another prince, this one named Laurent. He was being held captive in a sultan's stronghold. He was taken to something called the Punishment Cross, where he was strapped to it and whipped. He began to read again:

> "Yes," I thought, "do it. Do it harder. Whip me soundly for what I've done. Let the blaze of pain grow brighter, hotter." But it was not this coherent, what I thought. It was like a song in my head, made up of the rhythms—the strap, my cries, the creak of the wood."

"Yes!" Matthew said, interrupting Sean. "That's one of the best scenes of all. We don't have a Punishment Cross here," he said, turning to me, "but certainly you and your handsome dark prince can act this one out for me. You can stand just where you are, lift your arms up in the air, make believe you are tied to the post. You will be whipped and you will understand that you want to have more of it, that you want him to do it and to do it even harder.

"Take a whip from Duane," Matthew insisted, "and we'll have another enactment. You," he said to Sean, "can be his whipping post. The two of you stand together, face-to-face, and lift your arms up in the air. Grip one another. Keep our slave in position for his master's punishment."

Sean put down the book and turned to face me. He took hold of both my hands and lifted them up in the air, high above our heads. In the background, I could hear Duane handing something to Alex.

"Keep him still," Matthew insisted. "Make him feel his whipping just as Prince Laurent had done."

Sean's chest and mine were pressed together. I could feel his hard scabbed nipples scratch across my skin. His cock wasn't as hard as mine, but it was pushing up against my scrotum. He leaned towards me even farther, and I was surprised that he wanted to kiss me.

Then the lash fell on my back for the first time. I pushed harder against Sean, who resisted. He was going to do just what Matthew had ordered him to do; he was going to be my whipping post. The leather came down again, harder this time, and lashed across my shoulders. Sean gripped hold of my hands and held them in place even as his tongue moved against my lips and opened them up.

The contrast between the gentleness of Sean's kiss

and the fierceness of Alex's whipping sent my head spinning. These two things shouldn't exist together. They shouldn't be able to be together. But they were.

Sean's mouth was insistent with its embrace; his tongue was wet with its own passion as it moved inside my mouth and explored. I was moaning from both the pain and from the tenderness. My mind tried to isolate them, but then I realized they were inseparable. These were the two things that would come from the arena; the sweetness of a tender kiss and the harsh pain of a master's whip.

Our kiss communicated an appreciation Sean had for what I was going through. He wasn't comforting me, that would put the wrong impression on what was going on between us. He was *appreciating* it. I understood that Sean could have been in my place and he would have understood what the feelings were, not just the pain of the whipping, but the feeling of submission that came from it. It was so much more tractable to have a whip on my back than any amount of effect that could have been had if my butt were being beaten. There was a abdication of something involved in allowing this to go on, and there was even more than that in Sean's being part of the whole thing. He could have been me, but he didn't make any move to make the experience less real, less painful. He wasn't trying to take away from any of the experience I was going through. He was trying to make me have that experience all the more intensely. There was no pity from him, but there might have been envy, or at least there was recognition that he would be in a place like this soon enough.

Alex moved the target up and down my body, sending especially harsh waves of pain through me when the lash wrapped around my thighs and the end of it caught my balls with a sudden sting that forced my mouth open. I was trying to scream, but Sean was keeping the sounds inside me. He took that moment as an opportunity to move his tongue even more deeply inside me. His hands were holding mine so tightly that my fingers felt cold from the pressure.

Tears were inevitable. When they started to cascade from my eyes, Sean began to lick them. His tongue roamed over the whole of my face, sucking up the hot liquid that escaped from me. The feel of his tongue sent me reeling backwards, into some time and place even more primeval than this one.

Without thinking, I began to lick him back. I tasted the salt of his skin and wetted the hair on his head. We were in a small orgy of our own flavors and smells. The impact of the lash as it continued to assault me became less important, became something I could accept. After all, it was a part of this other experience I was having, the sensation of Sean's chest hair rubbing against me and his tongue washing me clean of pain and hurt.

"Excellent," Matthew said. "You've done your jobs well."

Everything stopped then. The whip wasn't attacking me. Sean let his grip loosen on my hands and let my arms come down to my side. The kisses ceased. Our tongues finished their searching.

I could barely stand. I was exhausted from the exertion and from the emotions of it all. All of my back burnt with hurt from the whip. My ass was stinging from the dildo that had been used to fuck me. The small piece of silk finally fell off my body and I was left standing there totally nude, and totally exposed, because, through all of this, my cock hadn't retreated. I was still hard.

"Look what a good job you've done," Matthew said. He unzipped his leather pants and reached inside to bring out his hard cock and a pair of large balls, all covered with silver hair. "You've done just what you were supposed to. You've made me interested and excited.

"Come over here," he said to me. "Let me give you your reward." While I stepped towards him he reached and took out one of the condoms that were kept in baskets all over the room. He quickly unwrapped it and then unrolled the latex over his stiff cock.

"Sit on it, fuck yourself with a real dick. That's what you really deserve."

I straddled him and then squatted down so the protected erection could find its goal. My ass was already stretched loose from the dildo, and I was able to let Matthew's cock slide into the already greased hole.

"Yes," he said softly. "Now fuck yourself. Give yourself the fucking you really want. I'm just going to lie here and let you show me how much you want this dick up your ass. Show me how much you love being in the arena."

I squeezed down on his hard-on and was rewarded with a sharp hiss of pleasure. I didn't let up while I lifted my body a bit higher, riding Matthew's erection, then sliding back down over it until my ass was firmly against his pubic hair and I could feel their silvery roughness against the tender flesh that had been beaten so recently.

Matthew's hands slid along the sides of my body. He just grazed me with his fingertips. My ass was full again, as full with his flesh as it had been with the rubber dildo. I was also having the same split experience as Matthew touched me. He did it so delicately and with such appreciation. I suddenly realized how much younger I was then he—I hadn't even realized it before—and I thought how much he must enjoy this touch of a fresh body. Sean, of course, was even younger. I remember what he had felt like even as he held my arms up during my whipping. I recalled how smooth his skin had felt to me. I realized that I was giving Matthew that same pleasure, and I was very pleased with the idea.

I continued fucking myself on Matthew's erection. I began to sense more completion. I was giving him pleasure. I had done my job well, just as he had said. I had performed for him, and that had made him need me and my willing, sore asshole for his gratification.

I forced my sphincter to open and close over Matthew's cock. I threw my head back from the sheer delight of it all. I slide myself up and down his shaft. I was full of him. His dick was becoming all of me. I could barely feel his fingers as they continued their journey over my chest, my belly, my legs. The sensation of his cock inside me was all that I could really pay attention to. I had created this erection with my sexuality, and now I was being repaid by the having it deep inside me.

Matthew came with a startling cry. His hands dug into my biceps, and his head rolled violently against his pillow. He lifted up his pelvis and carried me up with him, taking my knees off the carpet with a furious thrust.

I waited for him to finish pumping his come into the condom. I stayed there, carefully straddling his belly and holding my weight off him with my knees and my hands, until his breathing was regular once again. His hands relaxed and began to caress me once more. "Very good," he said with a smile. "What a very good fuck you are."

Then I let him slide me off of his deflating cock. I

didn't wait for an order, but reached down and took off the condom and lifted it carefully to hold in the precious cargo of Matthew's creamy white spunk.

Matthew pulled his pants back up and repositioned himself on the pillows. "Duane, have someone fetch me a glass of wine. I need some refreshment after all that." Duane gestured for someone to go to the kitchen to fill the request.

Matthew looked over at his two friends. They had grabbed Sean and were using him, one fucking his ass, the other his face. "It looks like this man is well taken care of, but not my prince." He turned to Alex. "You've done superbly. You should be rewarded." Matthew smiled at my still hard erection, "This one still has some spirit in him, and more as well. Why don't you take advantage of it? Take him over to the corner and use him any way you'd like. For this little bit of time, black prince, you are released from your bondage. You can become the story you just acted out. I sense that in you, you'd like to have a go at this fine young man, wouldn't you?"

Alex smiled, "Yes, sir."

"Then do it. Your training will start again soon, and Duane will have you back in your place before you know it. But right now, be the prince I saw in you. Take your slave over there and use him well. You deserve it."

Alex was gentle. He put an arm around my waist and used it to guide me away from Matthew and the others. The members' lounge was a large room. When we got to a far corner, there was plenty of privacy. We could be seen by the rest of them, but no one could overhear us. There was no one to interfere with Alex and whatever he wanted to do to me.

He sprawled over a pile of pillows, took off his silk cloth, put his arms behind his neck, and laughed.

"This is just what I wanted," he said. I didn't understand, but I didn't question him either. "This is just the way it should be."

The smile left his face. "That nice pink mouth of yours would feel real good on my tits, Kevin. Why don't you kneel down here and let me feel just how soft your lips can be."

I followed his command and sucked in one of his nipples. They had been large and flat when we'd begun, but they were scabbed as badly as mine now, from all the use they'd been given. I could imagine how wonderful delicate attention would feel.

I was still drained from our psychodrama and my body was still in pain, but I discovered that it was easy for me to suck on Alex's body with as much concern as ever could be expected. My black master had requested something from me and as tired as I was, I wouldn't deny him.

He brought down one of his hands and rubbed it through my hair. "What a good boy you are, Kevin," he said softly. "I've watched you. You're one of the best. There's so much you could do."

He eventually moved my mouth from one side of his chest onto the other tit. My tongue continued licking and softly sucking on him. I could feel the result as his big cock rose up hard again and began to press against my belly.

He pressed down so I was forced against his erection. I could feel the big knob of his glans as it sweated a thick liquid that smeared itself all over my own midsection. He took one of my hands and led it to his shaft. I gently cupped the bulky hard on and ran my fingertips over the surface of the knob.

"Yes," he said in a low voice. "Yes."

I didn't speed up. I just kept on sucking his tits and holding his cock. I could feel his dick begin to jerk

THE ARENA

and realized that I must be close to getting him off. I wondered for a moment if he really wanted that to happen. He answered my unspoken question by finally taking my hand away from his crotch. He took my head and guided it down, away from his nipple. He forced my face into his pubic hair. I felt its scratchy denseness as he rubbed my head against him. I realized he wanted me to suck on his balls.

They were of an amazing purple-black color, even darker than the rest of his skin. They were covered with the curly hair that I had just felt on his abdomen. I lapped at them, taking first one, then the other in my mouth, never able to fit both of them between my lips, they were so large.

Alex took his hands away once he realized that I understood what he wanted me to do and that he didn't have to direct me anymore. I was obedient and didn't even have to think about it. I wanted to be between his heavily muscled legs. I wanted to feel the power of his thighs as they pressed against my chest.

I looked up at him, barely able to see his face over the mass of his chest. His arms were behind his head again and he was staring at me with great intensity. He was studying me. And he was appreciating what he was studying. It crossed my mind that Alex had a strange attitude for someone who was an apprentice in this place, someone who I had seen standing on the arena waiting to be chosen, a position that I didn't doubt he would be in again, and soon, and probably often.

My mouth hurt from all the licking I was doing and from the sucking. I had been stretching it for some time trying to accommodate Alex's big balls in my mouth. Yet there wasn't any hint that he was tired. I gave into the discomfort and resigned myself to performing this ritual for much longer.

Some of his wiry hairs came off his body, and I could feel them between my teeth. I loved how tightly curled they were, how much stronger they felt than that pubic hair I'd known on white men. I liked the strong odor that was coming from his asshole as well. It had a pungent quality to it that seemed stronger than the other men's.

I especially loved the feel of Alex's skin. Even though he had a very muscular frame, the touch of him was soft and smooth. There were only small areas of his body that were covered with the kinky hair that I found so attractive. The rest of him was uniform in its satiny texture.

Finally Alex lifted me up off his balls and had me climb over his reclining body. I wasn't sure what he wanted this time until he reached up and took one of my sore nipples into his mouth. He might have wanted me to be careful and tender while I had his in my own mouth, but he had no intention of being that way with me. His teeth scraped against the raw surface of my tit and then took the bit of flesh and pressed against it.

I couldn't help crying out. It was a soft whimper that escaped from between my lips and wouldn't be denied. My nipples had suffered so much from the men at the arena that I didn't know how much more I could take, if I could take anything. I remembered the way that Sean had manipulated them while I had been in the stocks. I remembered the way that I had broken through some barrier when the torture had become too intense for me to survive. I'd need something like that to get through this torture as well.

Alex even seemed to realize that; he appeared to know how difficult it was for me to stay there, on my hands and knees, with his mouth chewing at my chest. That didn't bother him in the least; in fact, it seemed to goad him on. He moved back and forth between my tits, chewing one, then the other. He would take me a step further into pain with each stage of his torment.

I was crying again. I hadn't cried for years before I had come to the arena; now I was shedding tears many times a day. There was no reason to try to maintain any kind of facade about the suffering I was being put through. Why should I hold back tears?

Besides, I'd learned something. I'd learned that most of the masters enjoyed our tears. It added a level of authenticity to the action that they appreciated. Why should I stop myself from crying if it was something that my masters so obviously enjoyed? Wasn't I there to be enjoyed?

Alex rolled me off him and onto my back. I could only be thankful for the relief I got when his teeth left me in peace. I didn't have time to realize that he obviously wasn't finished.

"Lift up your legs, put your calves in the crook of your arms. Spread your legs apart for me."

I followed his directions and splayed myself open for him. The position lifted my hole up and took away the protection my asscheeks provided. I was open to him, totally. He looked down at my hole with fascination. Obviously it wasn't true, but it seemed as though he'd never really looked at a man's anus before. He smiled while he stroked his heavy cock. He reached over and took a condom and spread it over the expanse of his dark skin.

I was full of grease from the dildos and from Matthew's fucking. I was totally prepared for Alex when he positioned his cock at my hole and began to shove in. "Keep your legs up," he warned me when I started to tense my muscles against him.

I held myself open for him while he drove inside me. He reared up away from me, lifting his chest in the air, holding his body off the ground with his toes. Only his cock was touching me. It was sheathed in my belly with a single long push that sent pulses of excitement pushing through me. I hadn't been this open before in my life. After the dildos and Matthew's cock, here was Alex's even bigger dick shoved totally inside me. This was as exposed as I could ever be.

I couldn't stop my head from rolling back and forth on the pillow as he began to thrust in and out of my ass. He wasn't going to be willing to just be there the way Matthew had been. Alex was going to *take* me with this fucking. He would pull back so that the knob of his glans almost but not quite escaped from my sphincter. Then he would shove himself back inside me in one single motion. He repeated this over and over again until I was whining for fear that he was going to leave me without finishing his fuck. I wanted his dick inside me like I hadn't wanted any other in years. This continual fucking I'd been going through was more than pleasurable, this was attainment of a plane of physical understanding that I had never known before. Once again I was becoming part of my body. I was becoming my asshole. It was taking over my mind just the way my nipples had when I was in the stocks.

How much more learning like this could I take? Would I go through all my body parts one by one and experience this level of awareness with each one of them? I was frightened when I first had that thought, but then I became excited by it. I was overwhelmed with gratitude to Alex for all he'd shown me that afternoon. Yes, it had been Matthew who instigated it all. He was the master who had demanded that it all take place, but Alex was the one who had accomplished the goal.

I wouldn't put my legs down; he'd forbidden that. I couldn't use my arms to embrace him, no matter how much I wanted to. I could lift my head up and try to kiss him though. He moved backwards against the move. His smile deepened as he continued to pound away at my ass. Then he must have changed his mind. The enjoyment of watching my face go through endless contortions while his cock plowed away at me was overcome by some desire to give me that little gesture I'd attempted to ask for.

He leaned down and kissed me. His broad lips seemed to encompass my own without any effort. He tasted sweet. It didn't feel the same as it had when Sean was kissing me earlier. This was a conqueror's demonstration. Even with his lips on mine, Alex was taking me. I was his claimed object, and he let me know that.

There wasn't any warning when his body suddenly stiffened. I could feel his cock pulsing as it pumped come into the condom and pressed in waves against my asshole. Alex bit me then—he bit my lips, as though he needed to underscore just how totally he'd taken me.

He collapsed his heavy weight on my body. His chest heaved as he fought to regain control of his breathing after his orgasm. My legs were cramping as I struggled to maintain the position he'd dictated. Finally he moved out of me, leaving me once more with that sensation of being emptied as my ass was again void of filling.

Alex rolled over onto his back and gathered me into his arms so my head rested on his pectorals. I ran my tongue over the near nipple. He sighed, content after his orgasm and happy to have my mouth back on his chest.

I pulled back after a while. He wasn't holding me in place, he'd simply been accepting my offering. We stayed there together quietly, enjoying the warmth of each other's bodies and the chance to rest.

"What did you mean when you said this is just what you wanted?" I finally asked him.

He smiled again. "I didn't think I'd have a chance to use a pretty white boy like you for quite a while," Alex answered. "I figured that the training was going to keep me on the bottom for a long time.

"Then Matthew not only let me work on you, he gave me you as a reward. Just what I wanted. That's what I said, that's what I meant."

"But you're here for the training. It seems like you wouldn't want that part of it."

"That's why I *am* here," Alex answered. "This isn't who I intend to be. This is just what I'm doing to get where I want to go."

"I don't understand."

"I started out as a mean fucker, a real mean one. It didn't take me long out of high school to understand that there were plenty of men of all colors who wanted to find a tough black guy who could take charge. I have a good dick; you have to admit that." Alex laughed as he played with his cock. "This is what a lot of guys dream about and, if I can offer them their dreams, they're willing to give me lots in return.

"I was working my way through college, having all the sex I wanted, when I finally met a guy who showed me that I didn't know hell about what I was doing. He hung out in the same leather bar I did; we were both regulars. I would strut around and pick up my tricks, and this guy would be watching me and I could tell that he thought I was nothing, that I was weak.

"I didn't know what to make of him. What difference did it make what he thought of me, anyway? I just ignored him.

"There was a guy in the bar named Danny. He was one of the sweetest things there, just a fine-looking young man with an ass that could send you straight into orbit when he was using it, and he very seldom didn't put it to work. Everyone liked Danny; everyone wanted him. I certainly did. I took him home a few times, and it was some of the best sex that I ever had.

"But I realized something was wrong as the nights passed. Danny would go home with me, but only if this other guy wouldn't ask or if he wasn't there. If there was even a possibility that the man wanted Danny, then he stayed and waited it out, just to see if there was any hope.

"I wasn't a bad catch, remember. I wasn't someone that the rest of the guys were avoiding. I was younger, more muscular, and better looking than that man was. But Danny obviously preferred him to me.

"That got to me. I couldn't understand it, because there hadn't been anything I'd seen or learned that could explain it to me. I just thought sex was something rough you did with someone who was attractive. If they weren't as good looking as me, then why bother?

"If they had been in love or something like that, maybe I could have understood, but that wasn't what was going on. The guy used Danny the way he'd pick up a trick, that was all. Danny wasn't looking for any relationship with him or with anyone else. Whatever the man had holding over Danny, it had to be something else.

"I thought I was being cool about all of this, but I wasn't cool enough to keep the man from knowing what was going on in my mind. One night he just walked over to me and asked if I wanted to go back to his place with him and Danny. It turned out he hadn't even asked Danny if he was willing. He knew Danny would be.

"I was sucked into it enough to say yes. We took Danny and we went to his house. It was nothing special, just a little house off in a subdivision. But when by the time we got there Danny was quivering with excitement. I had never made the boy feel that way; I was sure about that. But this man had that power over him.

"The man was pleasant, but he didn't make any moves on me. When we got inside, he just told Danny to get undressed and then had both of us follow him into the basement. Danny had been there, and he knew the drill. As soon as we got downstairs he got on his hands and knees and started to lick the man's boots.

"I just stood there in amazement. There was equipment of every type there. The man had almost everything I've seen in the arena set up in his own house. There were stocks, racks, restraints attached to the walls. It popped my eyes open, I can tell you that. Just being that close to all that stuff that I'd only seen in magazine pictures was exciting.

"I'd done some of that shit with guys. They'd be so taken up with their passion that they'd beg me for something special, like putting my leather jacket back on after we were undressed so they could feel it while I fucked them, or even licking my boots the way Danny was doing it.

"But no one had really done it the way that Danny was doing it. The man was playing with him. It was like you and that cockring today. He'd move around so that Danny would have to scurry all over the floor to keep his tongue on the man's boots. He'd kick at him, even.

"Danny didn't give up, and neither did his cock. When guys were doing that stuff with me, they'd always be playing with their meat, jerking themselves off while they were going at it. But Danny let his cock alone, like he knew better, like he'd been trained just the way they've been training us. His dick was as hard as I ever saw it, but he just kept his attention on the man.

"The man was playing with me a little bit, opening my shirt, fingering my tits, feeling up my ass. But he was really giving Danny all the attention he wanted.

"Pretty soon the man was ready to move on. He took Danny and laid his body out on this rack he had. He attached Danny's legs and arms to the table and then started to work on him. He played with Danny's tits, then his cock, then his balls.

"Danny stayed hard through all of this. The man finally got a small whip, something I'd never seen, and stood over Danny. He lifted up Danny's cock and began to beat the head of it with the leather. I nearly shot at the sight of it. The little whip must have caused a big pain because Danny was writhing all over the table, trying to escape his punishment.

"The man became merciless. He used that whip on Danny's balls. The screams that came out of his mouth were amazing. It was also amazing how hard that made my dick.

"I'd stripped down and was working away at my meat while the man went after Danny some more. He took a whole bag of clothespins and began to line them up along the insides of Danny's thighs and along his balls. He attached another whole line of them across Danny's chest. Then, when they were all set, he began to move his hands over the tops of the clothespins so they caused waves of pain to go through Danny's body. The screams got louder; my cock got harder.

"I could have watched the man all night. He was working it perfectly. He knew just what to do, when, and how. He eventually let Danny out of his restraints. He had Danny get on his knees and suck me off while he played with my tits and my balls. He told Danny it would be all right to shoot if he wanted to. All three of us unloaded at the same time.

"It was one of the most powerful things that had ever happened to me. I knew then that this was what I really wanted and what I really needed. I had to have more of it.

"The next time I saw Danny in the bar, I took him home with me. I knew what he was capable of. I understood what he could do. I wanted it all to happen with me as his master, not this other old guy.

"Danny was willing. There was nothing he would have liked better than another top to dominate him regularly. We went at it, but it was a disaster. It didn't work, not at all. I hurt Danny when I didn't want to. I moved too quickly, and he'd withdraw. Instead of the erotic screams I heard when he and I had been with the man, I just got real cries of unexpected pain.

"Danny was turned off to every move I made. He got up and got dressed as soon as he could and, when he left my apartment, that was the last time he'd ever come in it again.

"I was a failure, and I knew it. But I also knew there was a goal I wanted to achieve. I wanted to be like that man. I went to him when I saw him in the bar, and I explained as well as I could what had happened, how interested I was in what he did, and how much I wanted to learn from him.

"He told me he was from what he called the 'old

school.' So far as he was concerned, if I wanted to learn what to do, then I had have it done to me first. If I wanted to be a master, he said, then I should start as a slave.

"I was goddamned if that was going to happen. I argued with him and told him I was strictly on top. It was *my* dick that was going to get sucked, and *I* was the one who was going to give the orders. He just smiled at me and shrugged and said that, if that was my attitude, there wasn't anything he could do to help me.

"I was pissed. He didn't know as much as he thought he did, I decided. I could carry this act off myself. I had the appetite then. I began to change what I was hunting for. Now it had to be someone who gave off a distinct message that he was ready for something rough. It wasn't enough to be a big black dick for another man. I was looking for something in return.

"I found some opportunities, but they never worked. It was like that scene with Danny every time. I had the passion, but I didn't have the moves. I had the desire, but I didn't know how to carry it off.

"I went back to the man, but he was obstinate now. My unwillingness to listen to him the other time made him think I didn't have the right attitude.

"I couldn't believe it! I was giving in. I was admitting he might have been right, and I was even willing to let him show me his moves on my own body, but he turned me away.

"I could have stayed mad, but I didn't. I didn't because he was making me desperate. I was so naïve, I didn't even see it happening. Every time I saw him in the bar, I asked him again to show me what he knew. He'd just turn me off. The most he'd do was take my phone number and say he'd think about calling me someday. Maybe there'd be a time when he could use me.

"I gave up on him until a couple weeks later, when my phone rang. He had some people over who had an interesting proposition to make, he explained. If I was serious, maybe I should come over to his house and meet them.

"I drove right over there. There were three other men besides him. I didn't know any of them except one who was a professor at my college—he knows you, the guy named Jacques who teaches economics?"

Yes, I admitted, Jacques certainly knew me.

"They explained that they were running this place, the arena, and they had openings in a training class. I was so relieved that the man had finally responded to me that I barely took it all in. Then I realized exactly what they were saying. I would have to become one of the slaves in this place. I would have to start at the very bottom and work my way to the top.

"I couldn't believe that someplace like the arena even existed. I couldn't believe there would be a place where these things were allowed to go on. If I wanted to check it out, they told me to come with the man to visit one night.

"We came the very next night. He stripped me down and took me on a tour that ended up with me on the platform of the arena. Jacques claimed me. I was scared as I could be. I was terrified. I had been taken too far. I had become so obsessed with that man and what he knew that I ended up with my balls in a leash being taken into the back by this professor I had only seen across campus.

"He was good—you must know that—he was as good as the man was. I wasn't as good a partner as Danny might have been; I was awkward, and it embarrassed me that I didn't understand just what he wanted when. But I did understand that he was like the man; he had something to teach me.

"My pride didn't want me to go through this training, but I did know that I wasn't going to end up where I wanted to be without something like it. That night, when we were driving home, I admitted all that to the man. I told him, all right, I'll do it. I'll go through this hell if that's what I need to do to become like you.

"He was very pleased. He told me it's what he wanted. When I came out, he promised me, we could even live together. We could hunt men together and use them in his basement.

"'I won't be your slave,' I told him. 'I'm not going to do that.'

"'I don't want you to be,' he promised me. He only wanted me to become his peer. His friend. We wouldn't try to top one another, and we wouldn't compete with one another. We could just become pals. We could do all that if I went through the training for the arena and volunteered for at least a year afterwards."

A year? I was surprised by that.

"I have to come in here at least a couple times a week for a full year before the man will believe that I know what's really going on.

"I agreed. That's how I ended up here. He was right, of course. I'm still learning. I learn more every day. I hate a lot of it. I hate standing on that platform and having men come and pick me out. I hate having to have to take care of the workmen. I hate the torture that some of the members put me through. But I figure there are going to be more men like Matthew from now on, men who are going to give me experiences and even let me take care of one of the other slaves here."

Alex slapped my sore butt. "Just like I took care of you, Kevin. This is all just a long trip I'm taking. I have to go through a valley to get to the peaks I want to conquer, and that means that sometimes I have to be the one who get the lash and sucks the cock. I have to do it so I can teach my own boys in the future just the right way to act.

"I might have made it easier on myself if I had given in to the man a lot earlier. Maybe he could have taught me what I needed to know. But I held out on him—that's one lesson right there—and so he's making me go through the whole program before he lets me up off the floor.

"I just hope I get some more good ass like yours while I make this trip," Alex laughed. "You certainly are making it more pleasurable for me."

While he was laughing, I could see all of that in him. I could see that he was going to be other men's master in the future. His ebony body was handsome and strong, and there wasn't any doubt in the way he presented himself. That was who Alex wanted to become, and why shouldn't he?

I knew that I would submit to him when he wanted me, if he wanted me. I could imagine that dick of his becoming the center of my life while it plowed up my ass or dove down my throat. There were many men who would want a master like Alex, and he would get them once he understood just what he should do with them when they were in his grasp. He was certainly in the right place to learn.

There was no graduation ceremony when we were done at the arena. That night we were cleaned up as usual. But when we came out of the shower area, we weren't led to our sleeping pallets. Instead, we were taken to lockers where our street clothes were kept.

The Arena

We were each given the key. This would be our locker forever. Whenever we chose to come back to the arena, this is where we would strip down before we went to stand on the podium.

It was strange to be standing in that small area putting on clothes with Sean, Alex, and Chris. My jeans felt confining. My shirt made me feel strangely burdened. I thought my feet didn't belong in my shoes.

We all went outside. It was early in the evening. There were men arriving by taxi and car and making their way through the front door. I couldn't tell which ones were members and which were slaves, but I knew they were passing through doorways that I'd enter again. It was inescapable. There was no way I could live without coming back to this place.

We all stood around awkwardly and made our good-byes. I couldn't imagine the words I should use to talk to these men who had seen everything, who now knew so many of my secrets. I had spent two weeks with them and had been fucked by them, had sucked them off, had chewed on their nipples and kissed their asses. It was too artificial to be talking on the street as though we were just pals who had a few drinks together.

We exchanged names and addresses and phone numbers. While this hadn't been a true initiation, I certainly did feel as though I knew these men and that our lives would cross again.

I say it wasn't a true initiation because it hadn't ended. A real initiation would have had a sense of completion about it. You went through a hazing or other rituals, and you became a member of the team or the club. There was a finality to that kind of thing that didn't exist for any of us now.

We were standing on a street under a lamp and

writing our names on small scraps of paper, and we were going to go home to the lives we had led before this had all taken place. We were not finished. We had begun, but we hadn't completed whatever it was that we were going to have to learn about.

I went to my apartment. The place felt cold and unlivable. I had become used to the warm temperatures of the arena and now I discovered myself putting the thermostat on high so I could continue to live the same way—nude and ready, though I didn't know what I was going to be ready for.

I slept soundly in my own bed, happy for its familiarity. It helped a bit to get over the disruption of having left the arena. I woke the next morning and got dressed just long enough to go to the store to get groceries so I could eat.

I stayed in the apartment alone for a few days. I was always naked. I must have masturbated five times every day. An image of a naked Alex wielding a lash or of Matthew with his demanding cock insisting that I sit on it would come into my mind, and I'd become erect instantly. There was no reason not to jerk off now. I was alone, and I wasn't under Duane's tutorial anymore. I indulged myself and did it often.

I thought this would all pass, that the memories of the place would finally dim and that I could go on with my life as I had been living it before Jacques had first taken me to the arena. But, even though I started to go out more and shopped for new clothes and began to read the newspapers again, it was an idle hope that life could return to what I had considered normal. Masturbating only left me feeling lonely. It just made me all the more aware that I wasn't with other men, that I was alone in a private space and that I wanted that privacy taken away from me. The isolation was eating at me. I had found a bit of what

Chris had called his soul in those two weeks at the arena. If I didn't do something, I might lose it.

Sean was the one who finally broke my monastic seclusion. He rang my doorbell unexpectedly about a week after we'd left the arena. He seemed unsure of himself when I answered the door and invited him in. He was dressed in tight jeans with a white T-shirt and a black leather jacket. It was the first time since the arena that I had smelled leather on a man's body, and I was devastated by the mingled odors.

He came in and I made a pot of coffee. We sat at the kitchen table and talked as though we had never been through anything particularly noteworthy together. We could keep up that facade only for a short time.

"Do you miss it?" Sean finally asked me.

I nodded. "I can't deny it."

He smiled. The wide expanse of his eyebrows seemed especially handsome to me. I loved the way their dark hair contrasted with his white skin, just as I had noticed it in the arena.

"I miss the whole thing. I can't stand all of this." Sean pulled at his jacket. "I want——"

"We'll take off our clothes," I said. It felt as genuine as anything else I could imagine. I had only pulled on my own pants and shirt because he'd rung the doorbell. Nudity was what we had become used to; it was a tradition that seemed worth maintaining.

Sean didn't hesitate. He stood up and stripped off his clothes. My own went on the floor besides his. He did shock me then when he put his arms around me and kissed me. I remembered the last time he kissed me, when he had been acting as my whipping post, holding me in position for Alex and his cruel lash.

My nipples had barely healed. They were instantly excited by the contact with Sean's warm flesh. I answered his kiss and found myself further surprised by the passion that I felt for him. Our cocks were engorging with our blood and were pressing against one another. The center of our bodies felt more heated than the rest of us.

My hands moved down over Sean's back. I wondered once more at the feel of his young flesh. I was happy that Matthew had been able to do this with me, feel the freshness of youth at his disposal. The memory made my cock jerk with excitement. I felt Sean's ass and was specifically surprised to realize I had never touched it before. Somehow there had never been an assignment in the arena when I had reason to feel his butt.

Now that spongy but firm flesh was in my palms. Sean had a remarkable ass; it was really one of the best things about his body. Even as his strong chest pushed against mine and his cock was rising to full erection, the touch of his butt was the most exciting thing about him.

I pulled back from him. "Wait. I have something." I led him into my bedroom and pulled open a bureau drawer. When I had been shopping, I had found silk boxer shorts in a store. I'd bought some to help keep my memories alive. I handed him a pair and then stepped into one myself.

The silk fabric took me back to the members' lounge. It seemed to transport Sean as well. His hard dick escaped through the fly and stood outside it, making us both laugh. He didn't move to cover it up though.

We went back to our embrace, rubbing our bodies together through the silk and feeling once again like slaves to the harem keepers of the arena. I could remember sights and smells of those two weeks even more clearly. The memories were precious to me. I

THE ARENA

was grateful to Sean when I realized he was doing the impossible; he was reminding me of that place in a way that was even more vivid than I had recalled.

We moved to the bed and rolled onto it. Our legs intertwined and pressed our hard cocks and soft balls even more tightly together.

Through it all, for every kiss we exchanged, through every part of our body we exposed, we never touched one another's cocks. Part of us was back in that place where it would have been forbidden. As much as I wanted Sean and as much as I wanted his ass to be wrapped around my cock, there was no master there demanding it, and therefore it couldn't be done.

Sean had learned other tricks, though. We weren't going to go without any pleasure at all. He moved his chest so that his nipples touched mine. He did it slowly, carefully, so the very tips of our just healed tits brushed against one another. The sensual response was so intense that I thought I could come just from that.

The silk shorts slid over one another. Our cocks slipped against the fabric. We kissed again, and Sean began to grind his hips against mine. I was finally back in the place. Now I had all the feelings return to me. We were two slaves of the arena once more, dressed shamefully in the slight bits of silk and performing for the members in their lounge.

As soon as that image came into my mind, I could feel my orgasm welling up in my belly. The hot liquid wouldn't wait for anything. It moved through my body and burst out of my cock, sending spasms through my whole being. The hot fluid hadn't cooled before Sean's body began its own convulsions. The come flowed out of him and soaked through my shorts, cementing the silk fabric to my body.

We laughed a bit after that and then went into the shower. Even there we seemed to follow the prohibitions of the arena. We washed each other, but never touched one another's cock. I massaged his wonderful ass, but I didn't put a finger into his hole. He rubbed my nipples with a washcloth, but didn't make any attempt to feel any part of my body lower than that.

We were still enslaved. But it felt good. It felt right. We dried off, and then I poured us glasses of wine. We sat on the floor of my living room with the stereo playing some mellow jazz. Sean took one of his legs and placed it over one of mine. Our thighs were pressing against one another with a pleasant pressure. The music drifted through the room.

"When will you go back?" he finally asked.

When. He didn't ask me *if.* He didn't have to do that.

"I'm not sure. Soon. I want to …"

"I do, too," he said finally. "Together?"

I nodded. "Fine. I'd like that. When?"

"Tonight."

It all seemed so easy once Sean was with me. I hadn't been able to go back alone, but with him as a partner I found myself actually wanting to return. The idea of doing it that night created its own excitement. Why wait? Why not now? I wouldn't be alone. I had spent enough time by myself in my apartment. It was time that I left it, especially if I could do it with Sean's companionship.

Those thoughts all created a false sense of security. I was happy to spend the rest of the night with Sean. We were comrades while he cleaned ourselves out for the members—carefully douching in my apartment, first him, then me. We both joked about our preparations.

THE ARENA

"Who do you hope will be there?" he asked me while we were dressing again.

"I don't hope for anyone," I answered honestly. "That would defeat the whole purpose. I just hope to be there. I want to be part of it. To attach it to a specific person would take something away. I don't want a date, I want the experience."

He didn't reply. We took a cab down to the waterfront and got out. We walked to the door, and Duane answered our knock. "About when I expected you," he said with a smile.

He took us to the locker room and stood and watched while we stripped. It felt great to be back in the warmth of the arena and to have appreciative eyes staring at me again.

Duane didn't say anything when we were naked. He simply put on the leather strap around each of our scrotums and then handcuffed us. Then he put the keys on chains and put them around each of our necks.

"Welcome back, boys," he said, then slapped each of us on the ass and took us into the arena.

We were early. There were only two other men standing on the platform. I didn't recognize them. Nor did I know who the two men were who stood looking them over. They gave Sean and me a quick glance, but had obviously made up their minds about their night. They took the other two and leashed them and took them off into the back rooms.

Sean and I were left alone. I felt suddenly that this had been a major mistake. I wasn't sure that I wanted to dive all the way back into this scene so quickly. The arena should allow at least some kind of transition, I thought. They should make this easier for us to do. But then I realized that would destroy the whole purpose of the arena. It was not here to make it easy for us. If we had really needed help in getting up here, we would never have been chosen. If we had really needed limits on the degree of experience we were willing to go through, we would never have made it through the training.

Sean seemed much more comfortable with everything than I was. He moved closer to me and began to rub his cock against my hip. *If it turns the members on,* Franco had told me. I leaned into his warm cock and enjoyed the way it coasted against my. My cock began to get hard.

"I want to watch when they come and take you away," Sean whispered into my ear. "I want to watch them when they tie you to the rack and begin to put clamps on your tits."

I got fully erect as soon as he began to talk to me. He was as seductive as anyone could be as he described the scenes he wanted to witness. The surprise was how much I wanted to show him just those things. I wanted him to see. I wanted to perform for him just as I had performed for Matthew. Scenes from the *Beauty* books came to life in my imagination, and I thought I'd shoot just thinking about them.

"Good pair."

We had been so involved in our fantasies that we hadn't even noticed when two members walked into the room. They were dressed in business clothes. There wasn't anything about them that suggested they were part of a sexual underworld, but I knew instantly that they were going to be marvelously dangerous.

Sean and I stood back from one another and displayed our erect cocks and the way we were so willing to be back here.

"Both of them?" one man asked the other.

"Yes."

They took leashes from the attendant, and each one took hold of our balls. They weren't at all patient when they pulled on the leads and took us down the hallway.

Anxiety took over. What if they were going to take us to the back and put me in the stocks? I had encountered my fear of that particular bondage, but part of it was still with me. Part of me still held a special dread about it.

But they weren't interested in that. I was foolish enough to be relieved when they took us into one of the other cells. They didn't move to undo our restraints. They were more interested in taking off their clothes.

They had many surprises in store for us, but the first one was the discovery of what they were wearing underneath their suits. The first man was dark haired with a trim mustache. When he stripped off his T-shirt, he revealed a full body harness. Leather straps crisscrossed his chest. They were joined together by metal rings. From one of them, over his belly, another strap went down to his crotch. When he stepped out of his pants, I could see that it was attached to a cockring. He absentmindedly played with his half-hard cock while the other man finished undressing.

This second man wore nothing but a jockstrap underneath his suit. His nipples were pierced; both of them had thick gold rings through them. The second man had a full chest of hair. It was a lavish pelt. His cock was hard and strained against the enclosure of his jock. But he left it on. He wasn't ready to take it out yet.

"Let's get them going," he said to his friend.

I was laid out on the rack in the center of the room. They quickly and expertly attached my wrists and ankles to the restraints at the corners. When they were done, they stepped back, and the darker-haired man said to Sean, "Eat his tits."

Sean came to the head of the table. "You, too," the man said to me. "Get to work on his tits, too."

Sean leaned forward and put one of his nipples in my mouth just as he sucked one of mine in his. I heard a loud slap that jolted Sean. Someone was beating his ass. "You're not doing it hard enough. If you were, I'd hear something from you."

We understood. I felt the pressure as Sean's teeth dug into my just-recovered flesh. I answered with a bite of my own. We each moaned as the pressure increased. There was another slap and Sean jumped again. "More."

We both bit down harder. I felt as though our mouths and our nipples were becoming so attached to one another that some line was being blurred between us. We were becoming one sexual being for these two masters.

"That's more like it," someone said when I bit even harder on Sean and he groaned out loud. "More of that."

There was a slap again, and Sean gnawed at me with even more zeal. I began to squirm from the intense pain. "Good, good," a voice said. Then hands were taking Sean's chest away from my mouth and manipulating our bodies so we each took in the other tit. It all began again. There were more slaps as Sean was encouraged to work harder on me.

The action was having an effect on both of us. It wasn't just that we both had stiff erections. We were both sweating, and the sharp smell of fear was in our odors.

When the two men began to move us around again, I thought they might be finished with this episode, but they were only beginning. We were back to the beginning, chewing on the first tits again.

The slaps against Sean's ass began to increase in frequency. I felt someone undoing my ankle restraints. My legs were lifted up, and suddenly there was a *whack* as leather pounded against my ass as well.

The blow was a shock, and I shuddered from the sudden pain. The master began to flog me with the same tempo that his friend used on Sean. We were being beaten together. Both of our bodies jumped with each blow. The beating was all the more difficult to accept since neither of us could see our tormentors. We couldn't anticipate when the leather was going to land on us and bring back the once-familiar sensation of our skin burning from the attack.

Our heads were moved back and forth across our chests. Just when the pain and pleasure was too great on one nipple, my mouth would be transported to another. All the while the leather continued to slap across our asses. The loud blows reverberated through the cell.

Suddenly they were finished. The leather stopped attacking. Sean was pulled off my chest. The masters seemed pleased with themselves. The master with the body harness took Sean's hair and pulled his head back, forcing him to strain. We could all see the veins in his neck bursting from the tension.

"These are worth showing off," the master said.

My shackles were quickly undone. The red-haired master went to a bag in the corner and brought it over to the table. Sean's hands were released and we were both forced down onto our hands and knees. The masters began to attach clamps to us, on our nipples and our balls. The clamps had small bells on them. Whenever we moved, the metal would make a soft tinkling, a new layer of humiliation.

The men put leather collars around our necks and attached leashes to them. The they took up their paddles and began to beat our asses.

"Come on! This way!" They led us crawling into the corridor. The bells sounded a weird melody as we were forced to move quickly by the constant assault of the paddles. My ass was burning; the clamps were eating into my chest and my scrotum. But the arena had taken hold of me. I didn't worry about the pain or the degradation. Instead I felt a tremendous pride that Sean and I were doing so well that our new masters wanted to show us off. And I felt an intimacy with Sean that I realized I always wanted.

He was in front of me. Every time he moved forward, his balls were forced between his hairy thighs. I could see the line of fur between the cracks of his ass. The little metal bells were hanging from his scrotum, and they rang with every motion.

The whacks of leather on my ass didn't take away any of the fascination I felt over the way that Sean looked. The paddle being used on him was leaving side swatches of red, pink, and purple across his butt. I remembered what his fleshy ass had felt like, that spongy firmness, and I knew now that it would be even more wonderful, warmer, more open.

We were led past the platform where the slaves of the arena were standing waiting for their masters to claim them. The men who had been brought in since we'd left the stage looked down at us. In some eyes I saw disbelief at what they might have to go through themselves, but in others I saw pure envy. Those were eyes that belonged to men who only hoped that they could find masters as competent as ours.

We went into the front room. There was a slight buzz of conversation in the room, but our bells seemed to drown it out. The eyes of the arena were

THE ARENA

on us, on Sean and myself, as our masters continued to use their paddles to direct us around the room.

Sean and I both cried out; the beating was creating so much pain that we had no choice. The masters led us to the very center of the room. They rolled me over on my back and took the clamps off my nipples. There were still bells ringing from my scrotum, but now I had a sudden sense of relief from the sharp pain on my chest.

Once again Sean was directed to take a stance over me so we could each take our nipples in one another's mouths. His mouth actually felt as though it was sympathetic when it took my nipple between his lips.

They weren't done with beating him. The loud slaps of leather on flesh started up again. Each blow made Sean jerk with anguish. My hands were free now. I could try to give him some of the same comfort that his mouth was giving me. I ran my palms over his body, feeling the softness of his younger skin. He seemed to react, as though that touch alone was what he had been waiting for.

When the paddles stopped this time, the masters again rolled us over so I was now going to be on my hands and knees over Sean's body. I braced myself, convinced that I was going to be the one who got the beating now. Instead the red-haired master knelt down beside me. He milked my cock, "Been waiting a while to do something about this, haven't you?" he teased me.

He had a condom in his hand. He unrolled it over my desperate cock. While he did, his partner was greasing up Sean's ass. The red-haired master guided my hard dick into the furry hole of Sean's ass. After all this, I was finally going to get to fuck him.

I felt my cock move against his sphincter. It gave a

little fight to keep away my invasion, but the masters were pushing me, as though I needed them to encourage me. The head of my cock broke through the muscular barrier, and I could feel the shaft of my cock being grasped by Sean's body. I pushed until I was all the way in, until my belly was up against the pliable mass of his butt.

The paddles did start again then, and they were beating my ass, but I hardly paid any attention to the new stings that were eating away at me. All I cared about was Sean's ass and the way it felt while I began to fuck him. I moved against him without any uncertainty. I wanted to feel all of my dick inside him. I thrust my hips in him and then back away from him.

The masters stopped beating us. They stood in front of me. The red-haired master pulled me by the hair and shoved my face into the pouch of his jockstrap. I could feel his erection through the elastic fabric. There was also the taste of stale urine and the musky odor of his sweat.

The long tube of his partner's erection pushed against my face. My hair was pulled back, and I was forced to suck in the whole length of the other master, the one with the body harness. He began to pump in my mouth, gagging me, even as I continued to fuck Sean.

The body beneath me was squirming from the fucking I was giving it. The master with the jockstrap finally pulled his own cock out and forced me to suck on it. The two men moved me back and forth against their two hard dicks, actually trying to fit them both inside me at one point. The taste of them and the feel of the leather and the jockstrap was filling a part of me, but the rest of me was in Sean's ass, continuing to savor the unexpected and almost-forbidden fuck of my fellow slave.

THE ARENA

That was what we were—fellow slaves. We were two men who were being used in front of an audience of masters and their slaves. We were naked; our bodies were bruised; our cocks were hard. This is where we wanted to be. This is who I had wanted to become.

I had withheld my orgasm for as long as possible. The last thing I wanted was to give up the pleasure of having my hard dick up Sean's hole. The only thing I wanted more was to have the two masters' cocks down my throat. But there was no way to hold this level of intensity. There had to be some resolution.

The red-haired master came first, jerking his cock and then firing off his orgasm in puddles of warm come over my back. His partner came shortly afterwards. I was licking his low hanging balls, my teeth hitting up against the metal of his cockring. The bells on my and Sean's bodies were ringing more loudly and more quickly now. We were all moving towards the end.

I came with seizures that shook my whole being. I thought I'd never stop pumping my ooze into Sean, and I thought his sphincter would never end its embraces. I could tell that he was shooting at the same moment, leaving his own come on the floor, squashed by his belly as I pushed him down harder and harder.

The masters didn't give us any time to recover. The leashes were pulled up again. The clamps went back on my wounded nipples. We were paraded around the room on our hands and knees, the paddle stinging against our asses once more. There were appreciative comments made by the masters at the tables as we went by them.

I loved hearing what they were saying. But most of all I loved doing this with Sean. Our hips would touch one another, or our arms would brush against one another, and I was overwhelmed that we were doing this together. We had come so far, so far from our beginning, and here we were, the center of attention at the arena.

"What precisely do you want to know?"

Sean and I were having lunch the next day in a restaurant near my apartment. We'd slept late, getting over the exertions our never-named masters had demanded of us. We were both covered with scrapes and bruises, but we both felt alive when we had gotten up finally and showered.

We had made love, but in our own fashion, once again not touching the other's cock or ass. My having fucked him had only been part of the scene. Without the master there, there was no way I could have his ass again. I understood that and found it to be one of the most exciting things about this life we had embarked on. I was going to play a game with my own mind, I understood, waiting for the next master who would force me to fuck Sean. Until I found that man, then my comrade's ass was off-limits to me. It was a special perversity. Everything I'd done had been to make myself more open to every sexual activity; yet here I was, finding one place where something was denied to me, something I wanted probably more than all the rest. It seemed as though there had to be something proscribed in order for my imagination to work. I had to have a forbidden desire as my goal.

"I just wanted to know why you ended up here."

Sean winced as he moved in a way that evidently caused some of his bruises to hurt. I knew all too well how easy it was for him to feel pain in his ass, sitting with our sore butts on hard chairs.

"I started out just as a regular guy, in the bars, at the dance halls, that kind of thing," he began. "All I could think of was how much I wasn't able to have. I felt cheated. The damned virus had taken away all the fun to gay life.

"The older guys would talk about the way that things used to be and the places they used to go. I was pissed that I couldn't have the same things. Safe sex this, safe sex that, it all seemed like such a crime.

"I'd spent my whole adolescence getting ready to come out and *do it,* but now I couldn't do it at all, it seemed.

"I finally got so frustrated that I went to some safe-sex workshops that one of the AIDS groups was holding. It was just a few men who got together and tried to convince one another that they could still have fun; that's what I assumed.

"We'd tell stories and watch videos. There were two men who led the group every week. It became a joke that I kept on coming back, that I never seemed to get enough from just one session.

"Since I was a regular, the guys would use me for 'demonstrations.' At first, we just did role-playing to show how you could negotiate sex acts with a partner. But the leaders got more ballsy as time went on. I was always willing to do what they wanted.

"One night they really got into it and they pulled down my pants and jerked my cock hard so they could use it to give a demonstration on how to put on a condom. I was embarrassed as hell, but I was also turned on by having these men handle me that way in public.

"The lessons started to sink in. I could have a decent time, I decided, and I decided to have it with those two guys. I went to each one of them separately one week and asked for sex. They were both more than willing. After all, they'd seen enough to like to make me their demonstration, hadn't they?

"They were both rough, but not very. They weren't heavy into S&M, they just wanted to play some rough games. They each got the message that I liked it. I did. These were men who had been around when there had been sex bars in New York and San Francisco and other places where dreams came true. They were great lovers; they had moves and sophistication that no one I was meeting could even match. I respected them for their experience and for the way they could carry it all off.

"At next meeting, they both discovered that I'd been with the other. They laughed and began to call me a slut and other names. I just went with it, just laughed along with them. They were from a generation that used words like that as though they were compliments, and I knew that. I was a slut—a slut like them, a slut like their whole generation of friends.

"They got rougher with me in the group, and afterwards they both made dates with me. I started to meet their friends. I'd listen to all the stories of how life used to be and of how outrageous it was. I started to tell them how deprived I was. I wanted to do all that.

"I started to get calls from those men I was meeting. It seemed that each one was progressively heavier than the previous one. I began to see that I was being passed up a line of men, a whole hierarchy of men who were all working to get me someplace I didn't even know about.

"I loved that. I loved that there were men who were still willing to teach a young man. I threw myself into the lessons they offered.

"Eventually, some of them started to talk about the arena. They would say only that there was a place that was more intense than even the things they had known in the old days. As soon as I heard it even hinted about, I knew I had to find it. That became my purpose—to find someone who could get me here.

"And I did. It's been the most wonderful thing that ever happened to me. I'm in the arena. These are things that are as wild as any story I ever heard. This is an existence that would blow away the mind of Middle America if they even knew about it. I can be the sexual outlaw that the older gay men were and still live to tell about it.

"I can meet men like you and decide on whole other ways to live."

He seemed to think that was too much of a confession. Just as I held out one prize from myself—the luxury of fucking Sean—he still had to hold back one part of himself. There was so little privacy between us that it seemed curious to have him shut up on me. It had been only last night that I had been staring at his ass while he crawled through the arena with bells attached to his scrotum and welts building on his ass. But of course we still needed some moments of retreat. There had to be something that we held back, certainly if it had anything to do with our relationship with one another.

What was it going to be? Was this my younger brother? My lover? But how could we do that, if we were both so desperate to be slaves in the arena?

I met Jacques for lunch a few months later. We hadn't had that many chances to talk since he had first taken me to the arena. He had suggested the same restaurant as the last time, and I agreed. It seemed a nostalgic choice, but there was nothing wrong with nostalgia, I decided, not when I was going to visit with an old friend and mentor.

"You caused quite a stir last night," he said as soon as I had sat down.

"I didn't know you were there."

"I wasn't. But I heard all about it."

"It was Sean's idea. He felt we were becoming a little too complacent about our roles. He decided we should do something to show how much we enjoyed what we were doing."

We had shaved our entire bodies from the neck down. We had gone to the arena and stood on the platform together with our nude skin. Our cocks had looked enormous without their bushes. Our balls had hung low. We were very popular with the masters; that was certain. We had been chosen often by men who had taken us, together and separately, into the back rooms of the arena.

"What will be next?" Jacques smiled.

I wasn't going to disappoint him. "I've decided that we should be pierced. I've always liked the way it was done to Duane, with both ears and both nipples pierced. We're going to go on a vacation to San Francisco next month, and we'll get it done there, by a man we've found out about who does it professionally."

"It will look very handsome."

"Thank you."

Marcel still worked there, and he was our waiter. I thought that was a nice touch. I had seen him in the arena a couple of times since that first night. I had never had a chance to talk to him, though. Whenever he did show up, it was to perform in his metal gyroscope again, a favorite for the members.

Jacques placed an order for drinks and then looked over the menu. As always, he had the only copy. I was used to it by now. In fact, it didn't bother me in the least. Giving up control of a lunch request was the least of my problems.

"What are you going to do with this Sean?" Jacques said finally when he put the menu down.

"I'm not at all sure. It's obvious we enjoy living together. We've made our lives totally sexual. We go to the arena as often as we can, as often as our bodies will allow us to. We've joined a gym together. We're making travel plans. But it does seem that we're both so adamant about being slaves—at least for this part of our lives—that our relationship has to be formed that way."

"You do have sex with one another often, then?"

"Oh, yes." I laughed out loud. "We have sex so often I think my cock is going to fall off sometimes. We're committed to it. We're committed to using and being used."

"So admirable."

Marcel brought our drinks. I took advantage of the break in the conversation to turn it to another subject, one that had been on my mind. "Why don't you ever choose us, Jacques? When I've seen you at the arena and I've been standing on the podium, you've never picked me out."

"Why does that surprise you?"

"I thought … I supposed that the reason you had done all of this, had gotten me into the place, was for yourself. It seemed only logical that you would want to take advantage of the situation you've created."

"Kevin, you have never understood. If I had wanted you, then I would have courted you more directly. But that has never been the point. I have always been a teacher, dear boy. I have always gotten my greatest satisfaction from watching my students learn their lessons and achieve their greatest potential. You were not achieving well enough. You had such bourgeois attitudes about so many things. Before you could surrender to your desires, you had to make your fortune. Before you could be introduced to someplace like the arena, you had to feel you were in some kind of control of other situations. It was really distressing.

"Finally I thought you were ready for an experience for the sake of the sheer experience of it. And you were. My pleasure is in seeing you on the platform of the arena and watching men who deserve you leading you away.

"Not that I intend to always be so separate from you. I intend to have you, and quite often. Haven't you received a phone call from Duane about working a dinner party in a week?"

"Yes. I've never done that—worked as a servant at one of the dinners—but you'd told me about it. Sean hasn't either. We're a little nervous about all of it. But how——"

"I'm to be the host, Kevin. I chose you and Sean to be the waiters. I'm sure you'll do a very fine job. And, if you don't, you will once again learn just what a strict disciplinarian I can be in the classroom."

Jacques thought he was very smart, and he amused himself with his little threat. Though I didn't know if it was that minor. A part of my ass clenched at the thought of what would happen to me if I were to misbehave at a party of his.

Just then, Marcel came over and gave Jacques a piece of paper. Jacques read it and became more serious. "Interesting." He looked at me. "Do you remember the room where you went with Marcel the last time we were here?"

"Yes."

"Go there. Take off all your clothes and wait."

"There? Why? I——"

"There is a man who is interested in using you.

THE ARENA

He's seen you at the arena. You should be honored that you made such a good impression."

"But Jacques——"

"You aren't playing little bar games anymore, Kevin. You are a part of the arena. There is a man here who wants to use you. Go to the room and wait for him."

My main response was to be stunned to have found another obstruction in my imagination. I felt somehow violated by this intrusion of sex into our meeting. But, after all, who had I wanted to become? That was the real question. I had wanted adventure and excitement, and I had wanted a new level of sexual understanding and challenge. Here was a test.

I stood up and went to the back room. I shut the door behind myself and took off my clothes. I stood naked and waited, my hands behind my back, my head bowed down obediently, my legs spread apart in preparation.

I didn't look up when the man came in. He walked around me and felt parts of my body. My shaved crotch and belly obviously appealed to him.

He eventually stood behind me. I heard the familiar sound of a condom being opened. A hand on my neck pushed me over. I felt the hard anonymous cock press against my hole.

I had given in so easily! I had just followed the order and walked into a room where a strange man was going to fuck me! I felt the cock press against me and then spear into me. I let out a gasp of pain and pleasure while I was skewered on the length of hard dick.

This was just right, I realized. This was what I had wanted. The man's hand came around and grabbed hold of my cock. He began to masturbate me. I was so grateful! He didn't have to do that; he didn't have to worry about my pleasure. I was one of the slaves of the arena, after all. I was there for him.

I was filled with gratitude for what Jacques had shown me. I could have missed out on this experience if it hadn't been for my teacher's perseverance. I began to meet each of the stranger's thrusts with my own hips. This was the way I should be. This was the place I should be in. This was what was going to make me happy.

I thought of all the men who never even imagine the arena, who have no experiences like this, when they can find a hard cock to fill them up in the middle of the day, or night, or morning. I was being given the gift of this master's cock and I shouldn't ever have hesitated about giving something back for it.

The image filled my imagination and merged with the touch of the hand on my erection. He was taking me closer and closer. I finally came, shooting a hot stream of come onto the floor. The orgasm made my muscles clamp down on his dick, and soon I could feel him coming as well. We were there, groaning, sweating, shooting together, part of something even larger that was the arena.

He came quickly. I stood up after his cock was out of me. He put a hand on my chin and lifted my head up. "Very good."

"Thank you, sir." I meant it.

He walked out and I pulled my clothes back on. So it was back to lunch with Jacques, and perhaps we'd talk about the economy, or would the conversation be about his upcoming dinner party? I just knew that I would enjoy it, whichever way it went.

I opened the door and was surprised to see Marcel standing there, leaning against the wall with his arms crossed over his chest. I wondered if he expected to come into the room with me. Was he part of the assignment as well?

"I just wanted to tell you: Welcome," he said. Then he smiled and embraced me. We walked back into the restaurant together.

People are talking about:

The Masquerade Erotic Book Society Newsletter

◆◆◆◆◆◆◆◆◆◆◆◆◆◆◆◆◆◆◆◆◆◆

FICTION, ESSAYS, REVIEWS, PHOTOGRAPHY, INTERVIEWS, EXPOSÉS, AND MUCH MORE!

◆◆◆◆◆◆◆◆◆◆◆◆◆◆◆◆◆◆◆◆◆◆

"I received the new issue of the newsletter; it looks better and better."
—*Michael Perkins*

"I must say that yours is a nice little magazine, literate and intelligent."
—*HH, Great Britain*

"Fun articles on writing porn and about the peep shows, great for those of us who will probably never step onto a strip stage or behind the glass of a booth, but love to hear about it, wicked little voyeurs that we all are, hm? Yes indeed...."
—*MT, California*

"Many thanks for your newsletter with essays on various forms of eroticism. Especially enjoyed your new Masquerade collections of books dealing with gay sex."
—*GF, Maine*

"... a professional, insider's look at the world of erotica ..."
—*SCREW*

"I recently received a copy of *The Masquerade Erotic Book Society Newsletter*. I found it to be quite informative and interesting. The intelligent writing and choice of subject matter are refreshing and stimulating. You are to be congratulated for a publication that looks at different forms of eroticism without leering or smirking."
—*DP, Connecticut*

"Thanks for sending the books and the two latest issues of *The Masquerade Erotic Book Society Newsletter*. Provocative reading, I must say."
—*RH, Washington*

"Thanks for the latest copy of *The Masquerade Erotic Book Society Newsletter*. It is a real stunner."
—*CJS, New York*

Free GIFT

WHEN YOU SUBSCRIBE TO:

The Masquerade Erotic Book Society Newsletter

Receive two Badboy books of your choice.

Please send me **Two Badboy Books FREE!**

1. _____

2. _____

☐ I've enclosed my payment of $30.00 for a one-year subscription (six issues) to: **The Masquerade Erotic Book Society Newsletter.**

Name _____

Address _____

_____ Apt. # _____

City _____ State _____ Zip _____

Tel. ( ) _____

Payment: ☐ Check ☐ Money Order ☐ Visa ☐ MC

Card No. _____

Exp. Date _____

Please allow 4–6 weeks delivery. No C.O.D. orders. Please make all checks payable to Masquerade Books, 801 Second Avenue, N.Y., N.Y., 10017. Payable in U.S. currency only. Order by phone: 1-800-458-9640 or fax, 212 986-7355

JOHN PRESTON $4.95

THE FINE ART OF BEING A MALE HUSTLER   3091-1
Acclaimed author John Preston got hustlers to lay it all bare for some investigative probing into this infamous profession. All your questions are answered in this look at some of America's most misunderstood working men. Sure to become one of publishing's most infamous "how-to" volumes!

THE ARENA   3083-0
There is a place on the border of fantasy where every desire is fulfilled and temptation is to be indulged with abandon. Men go there to unleash beasts, to let demons roam free, to abolish all limits. In this place there is a story for each hunger, a mystery behind every lust. At the center of each tale are the men who serve there, who offer themselves for the consummation of any passion, whose own bottomless urges compel their endless subservience. This place is called the Arena, and it can only have been created by John Preston

TALES FROM THE DARK LORD   3053-9
"Here is a thirty-year-old man, college educated, employable, capable ... and he's my slave."
A new collection of twelve stunning works from the man *Lambda Book Report* called "the Dark Lord of gay erotica." The relentless ritual of lust and surrender is explored in all its manifestations, in this heartstopping triumph of authority and vision from the Dark Lord!

THE HEIR•THE KING.   3048-2
John Preston's ground-breaking novel *The Heir*, written in the lyric voice of the ancient myths, tells the story of a world where slaves and masters create a new sexual society. This stylish new edition of the *The Heir* also includes a completely original work called *The King*. This epic tale tells the story of a young soldier who discovers his monarch's most secret desires

MR. BENSON   3041-5
Mr. Benson is the compelling story of a young man's quest for the perfect master. Jamie is led down the path of erotic enlightenment by the magnificent Mr. Benson, learning to accept cruelty as love, anguish as affection, and this man as his master. A classic erotic novel from a time when there was no limit to what a man could dream of doing....

The Mission of Alex Kane

SWEET DREAMS   3062-8
It's the triumphant return of gay action hero, Alex Kane! This classic series has been revised and updated especially for Badboy, and includes loads of raw action. In *Sweet Dreams,* Alex travels to Boston where he takes on a street gang that stalks gay teenagers. Mighty Alex Kane wreaks a fierce and terrible vengeance on those who prey on gay people everywhere!

GOLDEN YEARS   3069-5
The second installment in the superhot adventures of gay hero Alex Kane. When evil threatens the plans of a group of older gay men, Kane's got the muscle to take it head on. Along the way, he wins the support—and very specialized attentions—of a cowboy plucked right out of the Old West. But Kane and the Cowboy have a surprise waiting for them....

DEADLY LIES   3076-8
Politics is a dirty business and the dirt becomes deadly when a political smear campaign targets gay men. Who better to clean things up than Alex Kane! With his lover and sidekick Danny Fortelli, Alex comes to protect the dreams, and lives, of gay men imperiled by lies and deceit. Together they generate the heat needed to burn away the political trash.

LARS EIGHNER $4.95

B.M.O.C. 3077-6
A crash course in Pubic Affairs! In this college town, known as "the Athens of the Southwest," studs of every stripe are up all night—studying, naturally. In *B.M.O.C.*, Lars Eighner includes the very best of his short stories, sure to appeal to the collegian in every man. Relive university life the way it was *supposed* to be, with a cast of handsome honor students majoring in Human Homosexuality.

BAYOU BOY 3084-9
Another collection of finely tuned stories from Lars Eighner. Witty and incisive, each tale explores the many ways men work up a sweat in the steamy Southwest. *Bayou Boy* also includes the "Houston Streets" stories—sexy, touching tales of growing up gay in a fast-changing world. Street smart and razor sharp, each scorching story is guaranteed to warm the coldest night!

ALL BADBOY BOOKS $4.95

SLAVES OF THE EMPIRE *Aaron Travis*
"*Slaves of the Empire* is a wonderful mythic tale. Set against the backdrop of the exotic and powerful Roman Empire, this wonderfully written novel explores the timeless questions of light and dark in male sexuality. Travis has shown himself expert in manipulating the most primal themes and images. The locale may be the ancient world, but these are the slaves and masters of our time...." —John Preston 3054-7

MUSCLE BOUND *Christopher Morgan*
In the tough, gritty world of the contemporary New York City bodybuilding scene, country boy Tommy joins forces with sexy, streetwise Will Rodriguez in an escalating battle of wits and biceps at the hottest gym in the West Village. A serious, seething account of power and surrender, in a place where young flesh is firm and hard, and those who can't cut it are bound and crushed at the hands of iron-pumping gods. 3028-8

THE SWITCH *Torsten Barring*
Sometimes a man needs a good whipping, and *The Switch & Other Stories* certainly makes a case! Laced with images of men "in too-tight Levi's, with the faces of angels ... and the bodies of devils," who are imprisoned and put up to be hung and whipped, Barring's stories deliver his darkest homoerotic fantasies in the hard-boiled, no-holds-barred language of 1940s detective fiction. 3061-X

REUNION IN FLORENCE *Sonny Ford*
Captured by Turks, Adrian and Tristan will do anything—and anyone—to save their heads. When Tristan's life is threatened by a Sultan's jealousy, Adrian begins his quest for the only man alive who can replace Tristan as the object of the Sultan's lust. Adrian's labor of love becomes a full-scale odyssey of the flesh—with wilder pleasures at every turn. 3070-9

MEN AT WORK *Edited by J.A. Guerra*
He's the most gorgeous man you have ever seen. You yearn for his touch at night in your empty bed; but you are a man—and he's your co-worker! A collection of eight sizzling stories of man-to-man on-the-job training by the hottest authors of gay erotica today. 3027-X

BADBOY FANTASIES *Edited by J.A. Guerra*
When love eludes them—lust will do! Thrill-seeking men caught up in vivid dreams and dark mysteries—these are the brief encounters you'll pant and gasp over in *BADBOY Fantasies*. Guaranteed to get you fantasizing about a beautiful BADBOY of your very own! 3049-0

SLOW BURN *Edited by J.A. Guerra*
Welcome to the Body Shoppe, where men's lives cross in the pursuit of muscle. From the authors who brought you BADBOY's *Men at Work* comes a new anthology of heated obsession and erotic indulgence: *Slow Burn*. Torsos get lean and hard, biceps and shoulders grow firm and thick, pecs widen and stomachs ripple in these sexy stories of the power and perils of physical perfection. **3042-3**

A SECRET LIFE *Anonymous*
Meet that remarkable young aristocrat, Master Charles Powerscourt: only eighteen, and *quite* innocent, until his arrival at Sir Percival's Royal Academy, where the daily lessons are supplemented with a crash course in pure, sweet sexual heat! Banned for decades, this exuberant account of gay seduction and initiation is too hot to keep secret any longer! **3053-9**

SINS OF THE CITIES OF THE PLAIN *Anonymous*
Indulge yourself in the scorching memoirs of young Englishman-about-town Jack Saul. From his earliest erotic moments with Jerry in the dark of his bedchamber, to his shocking dalliances with the lords and "ladies" of British high (and *very* gay) society, well-endowed Jack's positively *sinful* escapades grow wilder with every chapter! This Jack-of-all-trades is a sensual delight! **3016-4**

IMRE *Anonymous*
What dark secrets, what fiery passions lay hidden behind strikingly beautiful Lieutenant Imre's emerald eyes? An extraordinary lost classic of fantasy, obsession, gay erotic desire, and romance in a tiny Austro-Hungarian military town on the eve of WWI. Finally available in a handsome new edition, *Imre* is a potent and dynamic novel of longing and desire. A fable of forbidden urges from a time not unlike our own. **3019-9**

YOUTHFUL DAYS *Anonymous*
A hot account of gay love and sex that picks up on the adventures of the four amply-endowed lads last seen in *A Secret Life*, as they lustily explore all the possibilities of homosexual passion. Charlie Powerscourt and his friends cavort on the shores of Devon and in stately Castle Hebworth, then depart for the steamy back streets of Paris. Growing up has never been so hard! **3018-0**

TELENY *Anonymous*
Often attributed to Oscar Wilde, *Teleny* is a strange, compelling novel, set amidst the color and decadence of *fin-de-siècle* Parisian society. A young stud of independent means seeks only a succession of voluptuous and forbidden pleasures, but instead finds love and tragedy when he becomes embroiled in an underground cult devoted to fulfilling the darkest fantasies. **3020-2**

THE SCARLET PANSY *Anonymous*
The great American gay camp classic! This is the story of Randall Etrange, a man who simply would not set aside his sexual proclivities and erotic desires during his transcontinental quest for true love, choosing instead to live his life to the fullest. Sprawling, melodramatic, and wildly out of control, this novel features scene after scene of incredibly hot gay sex! **3021-0**

MIKE AND ME *Anonymous*
Mike joined the gym squad at Edison Community College to bulk up on muscle and enjoy the competition. Little did he know he'd be turning on every sexy muscle jock in southern Minnesota! Hard bodies collide in a series of workouts designed to generate a whole lot more than rips and cuts. Get ready to hit the showers with this delicious muscle-boy fantasy romp!

NON-FICTION

SORRY I ASKED *Dave Kinnick*
Unexpurgated interviews with gay porn's rank and file. How many haven't wondered what it's like to be in pictures? Dave Kinnick, longtime video reviewer for *Advocate Men*, gets personal with the men behind (and under) the "stars," and reveals the dirt and details of the porn business.
3090-3

THE SEXPERT *Edited by Pat Califia*
For many years now, the sophisticated gay man has known that he can turn to one authority for answers to virtually any question on the subject of man-to-man intimacy and sexual performance. Straight from the pages of *Advocate Men* comes The Sexpert! From penis size to toy care, bar behavior to AIDS awareness, The Sexpert responds to real concerns with uncanny wisdom and a razor wit.
3034-2

A Very Special Offer For a Limited Time Only!

Masquerade Books is proud to present a volume of unparalleled artistry in the field of erotica. *The Journal of Erotica, Volume One* is unquestionably the most stunning collection of erotic art, writing, and photography to be published in the last 30 years.

This sturdy, handsomely bound and embossed volume includes incisive, entertaining fiction and over 80 pages of provocative photography (including 43 full-color plates). From some of the earliest sexual images ever exposed on film (circa 1855), to the seductive, streetwise, and very contemporary work of Katarina Jebb, *The Journal of Erotica* is a feast for the eyes.

The Journal of Erotica will surely be regarded as the most unique and collectible publication since *Eros* burst on the scene in the 60s. No erotic library is complete without it; no afficianado will want to miss it.

The Journal of Erotica, Volume One lists at $25.00—but is available to you for $19.95 a copy (plus $2.50 shipping & handling). Only a limited number are available. Call toll-free: 1 800 458-9640, or fax your order: 212 986-7355.

MR. BENSON

JOHN PRESTON

$4.95 (CANADA $5.95) · BADBOY

THE HEIR

THE KING

TWO NOVELS by JOHN PRESTON

The master of gay erotic literature presents an incendiary collection of erotic stories that explore the full spectrum of gay sexuality.

Tales from the DARK LORD

$4.95 (CANADA $4.95) • BADBOY

John Preston

THE MASQUERADE LIBRARY

SECRETS OF THE CITY	03-3	$4.95
THE FURTHER ADVENTURES OF MADELEINE	04-1	$4.95
THE GILDED LILY	25-4	$4.95
PLEASURES AND FOLLIES	26-2	$4.95
STUDENTS OF PASSION	22-X	$4.95
THE NUNNERY TALES	20-3	$4.95
DEVA-DASI	29-7	$4.95
THE STORY OF MONIQUE	42-4	$4.95
THE ENGLISH GOVERNESS	43-2	$4.95
POOR DARLINGS	33-5	$4.95
LAVENDER ROSE	30-0	$4.95
KAMA HOURI	39-4	$4.95
THONGS	46-7	$4.95
THE PLEASURE THIEVES	36-X	$4.95
SACRED PASSIONS	21-1	$4.95
LUST OF THE COSSACKS	41-6	$4.95
THE JAZZ AGE	48-3	$4.95
MY LIFE AND LOVES (THE 'LOST' VOLUME)	52-1	$4.95
PASSION IN RIO	54-8	$4.95
RAWHIDE LUST	55-6	$4.95
LUSTY LESSONS	31-9	$4.95
FESTIVAL OF VENUS	37-8	$4.95
INTIMATE PLEASURES	38-6	$4.95
TURKISH DELIGHTS	40-8	$4.95
JADE EAST	60-2	$4.95
A WEEKEND VISIT	59-9	$4.95
RED DOG SALOON	68-8	$4.95
HAREM SONG	73-4	$4.95
KATY'S AWAKENING	74-2	$4.95
CELESTE	75-0	$4.95
ANGELA	76-9	$4.95
END OF INNOCENCE	77-7	$4.95
DEMON HEAT	79-3	$4.95
TUTORED IN LUST	78-5	$4.95
DOUBLE NOVEL	86-6	$6.95
LUST	82-3	$4.95
A MASQUERADE READER	84-X	$4.95
THE BOUDOIR	85-8	$4.95
SEDUCTIONS	83-1	$4.95
FRAGRANT ABUSES	88-2	$4.95
SCHOOL FOR SIN	89-0	$4.95
CANNIBAL FLOWER	72-6	$4.95
KIDNAP	90-4	$4.95
DEPRAVED ANGELS	92-0	$4.95
ADAM & EVE	93-9	$4.95
THE YELLOW ROOM	96-3	$4.95
AUTOBIOGRAPHY OF A FLEA III	94-7	$4.95
THE SWEETEST FRUIT	95-5	$4.95
THE ICE MAIDEN	3001-6	$4.95
WANDA	3002-4	$4.95
PROFESSIONAL CHARMER	3003-2	$4.95
WAYWARD	3004-0	$4.95
MASTERING MARY SUE	3005-9	$4.95
SLAVE ISLAND	3006-7	$4.95
WILD HEART	3007-5	$4.95
VICE PARK PLACE	3008-3	$4.95
WHITE THIGHS	3009-1	$4.95
THE INSTRUMENTS OF THE PASSION	3010-5	$4.95
THE PRISONER	3011-3	$4.95

Title	Code	Price
OBSESSIONS	3012-1	$4.95
MAN WITH A MAID: The Conclusion	3013-X	$4.95
CAPTIVE MAIDENS	3014-8	$4.95
THE CATALYST	3015-6	$4.95
SINS OF THE CITIES OF THE PLAIN	3016-4	$4.95
A SECRET LIFE	3017-2	$4.95
YOUTHFUL DAYS	3018-0	$4.95
IMRE	3019-9	$4.95
TELENY	3020-2	$4.95
THE SCARLET PANSY	3021-0	$4.95
THE RELUCTANT CAPTIVE	3022-9	$4.95
ALL THE WAY	3023-7	$4.95
CINDERELLA	3024-5	$4.95
THREE WOMEN	3025-3	$4.95
SLAVES OF CAMEROON	3026-1	$4.95
MEN AT WORK	3027-X	$4.95
MUSCLE BOUND	3028-8	$4.95
THE VELVET TONGUE	3029-6	$4.95
NAUGHTIER AT NIGHT	3030-X	$4.95
KUNG FU NUNS	3031-8	$4.95
SILK AND STEEL	3032-6	$4.95
THE DISCIPLINE OF ODETTE	3033-4	$4.95
THE SEXPERT	3034-2	$4.95
MIKE AND ME	3035-0	$4.95
PAULA	3036-9	$4.95
BLUE TANGO	3037-7	$4.95
THE APPLICANT	3038-5	$4.95
THE SECRET RECORD	3039-3	$4.95
PROVINCETOWN SUMMER	3040-7	$4.95
MR. BENSON	3041-5	$4.95
SLOW BURN	3042-3	$4.95
CRUMBLING FAÇADE	3043-1	$4.95
LOVE IN WARTIME	3044-X	$4.95
DREAM CRUISE	3045-8	$4.95
SABINE	3046-6	$4.95
DARLING • INNOCENCE	3047-4	$4.95
THE HEIR • THE KING	3048-2	$4.95
BADBOY FANTASIES	3049-0	$4.95
STASI SLUT	3050-4	$4.95
CAROUSEL	3051-2	$4.95
DUKE COSIMO	3052-0	$4.95
TALES FROM THE DARK LORD	3053-9	$4.95
SLAVES OF THE EMPIRE	3054-7	$4.95
MY DARLING DOMINATRIX	3055-5	$4.95
DISTANT LOVE	3056-3	$4.95
PASSAGE & OTHER STORIES	3057-1	$4.95
GARDEN OF DELIGHT	3058-X	$4.95
MASTER OF TIMBERLAND	3059-8	$4.95
TOURNIQUET	3060-1	$4.95
THE SWITCH	3061-X	$4.95
SWEET DREAMS	3062-8	$4.95
THE COMPLETE EROTIC READER	3063-6	$4.95
FOR SALE BY OWNER	3064-4	$4.95
MAN WITH A MAID	3065-2	$4.95
MISS HIGH HEELS	3066-0	$4.95
EVIL COMPANIONS	3067-9	$4.95
BAD HABITS	3068-7	$4.95
GOLDEN YEARS	3069-5	$4.95
REUNION IN FLORENCE	3070-9	$4.95
MAN WITH A MAID II	3071-7	$4.95
KATE PERCIVAL	3072-5	$4.95
HELOISE	3073-3	$4.95

ILLUSIONS	3074-1	$4.95
THE COMPLETE *PLAYGIRL* FANTASIES	3075-X	$4.95
DEADLY LIES	3076-8	$4.95
B.M.O.C.	3077-6	$4.95
ROSEMARY LANE	3078-4	$4.95
MEMBER OF THE CLUB	3079-2	$4.95
ECSTASY ON FIRE	3080-6	$4.95
SENSATIONS	3081-4	$4.95
LOVE AND SURRENDER	3082-2	$4.95
THE ARENA	3083-0	$4.95
BAYOU BOY	3084-9	$4.95
HELLFIRE	3085-7	$4.95
THE CARNAL DAYS OF HELEN SEFERIS	3086-5	$4.95
MAUDE CAMERON	3087-3	$4.95
WOMEN AT WORK	3088-1	$4.95
VENUS IN FURS	3089-X	$4.95
SORRY I ASKED	3090-3	$4.95
THE ART OF A HUSTLER	3091-1	$4.95

ORDERING IS EASY!

MC/VISA orders can be placed by calling our toll-free number

PHONE 800-458-9640 / FAX 212 986-7355

or mail the coupon below to:

Masquerade Books 801 Second Avenue New York, New York. 10017

BUY ANY FOUR BOOKS AND CHOOSE ONE ADDITIONAL BOOK AS YOUR FREE GIFT.

QTY.	TITLE	083-0	NO.	PRICE
		SUBTOTAL		
		POSTAGE & HANDLING		
		TOTAL		

Add $1.00 Postage and Handling for the first book and 50¢ for each additional book. Outside the U.S. add $2.00 for the first book, $1.00 for each additional book. New York state residents add 8-1/4% sales tax.

NAME _____

ADDRESS _____ APT. # _____

CITY _____ STATE _____ ZIP _____

TEL. ( ) _____

PAYMENT: ☐ CHECK   ☐ MONEY ORDER   ☐ VISA   ☐ MC

CARD NO. _____ EXP. DATE _____

PLEASE ALLOW 4-6 WEEKS DELIVERY. NO C.O.D. ORDERS. PLEASE MAKE ALL CHECKS PAYABLE TO MASQUERADE BOOKS. PAYABLE IN U.S. CURRENCY ONLY